FISHING FOR GOLD

Ron Foss

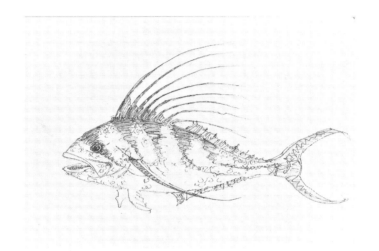

ISBN-13: 9781696037907

Cover design by: Art Painter
Library of Congress Control Number: 2018675309
Printed in the United States of America

CONTENTS

PROLOGUE

He could feel the beads of sweat forming on his brow and a trickle running down his neck, making him reach to flick it off - a crawling insect. He could feel the heat of his horse coming through the saddle. It was becoming uncomfortably warm. He was pushing himself and he knew it. Reflections of last night were troubling. He had shot into the dark with his revolver, through the door of his tent. Monkeys, he had thought, rummaging through his packs. But now he feared it may have been another human, perhaps one of the mountain Indians - the Bri-Bri. The river was rising and he knew he must cross soon while he still could. The heavy cloud formations in the upper mountains told him the river would only continue to rise.

He had come for gold and his saddle bags were heavy. He had traded with the Bri-Bri for hand tools - pliers, wire cutters, knives, and skin tanning tools. The magnifying glass that could start fire from the focused beam from the sun and the spyglass impressed the village elders most. For this they traded their gold.

To travel light was his craft - to reach the upper mountain tribes, meet, trade, and get out. Don't get greedy. Don't stay. Don't cause a disturbance.

He kept asking himself what had been rummaging through his camp. Good with a gun, he thought he heard the sound of the bullet hit. Flesh - an unmistakable sound. He had seen monkeys shot and, unless they were killed instantly, they put up a terrible noise, screeching as they scrambled to safety or bled to death. There had been no screeching. There was no dead monkey carcass come dawn.

He had to protect his gold.

His horse was fine and strong and well shod. His saddle and rig were all fine. His rifle was the new Winchester 1866 repeating rifle, his revolver a Colt. He had to keep going, make some time, cross that river and make his way down the mountain to the certainty and safety of civilization.

The huge oak and ash trees along the river provided some shade when he could make his way close to them. He turned his mount, Tico, down a draw to check out the crossing he had used to come up and the water was higher and faster, but there was no better crossing in sight. He didn't have time to search out another, if there was another. He spurred Tico down the draw, and Tico jolted the few paces forward to the rivers edge as a sharp sting bit the rider in the back of the neck. Reaching to knock off what was biting him, he felt two more stings in his neck and two more in his shoulder. Tico was skittering into the water. The rider pulled out one of the darts embedded in his neck. His adrenalin was spiking his awareness that he was being shot by...

The rider reached for his sidearm as he swung his head around to look up into the oak tree. In slow motion, he saw the movement of the Indians in the lofty branches of the trees. As he was swinging his body around to take a shot at his attackers, Tico plunged several strides deeper into the river. Tico was being hit too! Trying to manoeuvre to take aim, another dart hit him in the throat. Raising his Colt and lifting his line of vision up over his shoulder into the tree, the rider's world of vision spins once around, and again.

Vertigo.
A swell of nausea.
The world spinning.
Tico plunging forward.
All in a moment.

The father of the injured boy and another of his villagers are in the oak tree at the turn to the draw. Two more Indians are in an oak a couple trees back along the trail that the rider has already passed under. The father sees his horse-mounted target swinging back to take aim at them, but his arm never gets high enough to take aim. As the rider twists around, unstable in his saddle, the father of the boy sees the rider's eyes roll up into his head as he loses all bearing and balance and slides off his horse as though he has lost consciousness. He never pulled the trigger. He is taken by the current as the river takes control. His hat is swept along beside him. The horse carries on farther, pursuing its crossing to safety. The man makes no attempt to swim or to save himself.

He makes no motion.
The river has claimed him.
The river does not give up its dead.
With all that feeds in this river, it will not give up this body.

The boy's father and three companions, now all warriors, slip back and make their way down the tree. They start to jog through the undergrowth, heading upriver. There is no calling out or attempt to organize. Nothing is said. Like a well-trained tactical team, they disappear back into the forest without a sound.

In the village, the boy's father and his companions return unheralded. It is no different than any other day they return to the village. The boy's father goes directly to his hut. It is thatched construction, with several small sleeping rooms. His son is lying face down on a mat in the main area with his mother kneeling by and Grandmother attending to the boy, who is 13 or 14 years old. His buttocks are covered by a towel but partly exposed. There is a purple hole that is not bleeding. There are several bloodied swabs and towels of a sort near by along with a collection of small pottery containers. The grandmother is the village doctor. The secrets of botanical medicine bestowed by the gods and passed through generations lie within her. She is skilled. She has greatly slowed the bleeding through applying special herbs. She knows to remove the arrow, this arrow a bullet, before healing can start. This she has done. She has stopped the bleeding and leaves the wound open to heal in the air.

The bullet is sitting on a cloth in front of the boy. He is groggy from the sedative medicines Grandmother has given him. He gives a weak smile to his father and points to the bullet. Grandmother tells the father that the boy will be fine, that he will run again soon. The father acknowledges Grandmother and asks for time to be alone to speak with his son. She and the boy's mother quietly leave.

The father does not admonish the boy. He gestures for silence and retreats to his sleeping room. In a minute he returns with a leather bag tied tight with a leather thong at its top. He sits this bag in front of his son, beside the bullet on the cloth. He unties the thong and sets it aside. He reaches into the leather bag with both hands and lifts out a metal helmet. The boy's eyes widen with attention, but he does not move. The father sets the helmet in front of his son where he can see it clearly. It is a Spanish Conquistador's helmet.

Their language is simple, not overly descriptive.

"This was given to me by my grandfather. It was given to him by his grandfather. These men have come time and again for gold. We have had to kill to protect our lives from men who desire our gold. Do not trust these men. Do not be with them. They will come again."

The boy's reply is subdued but clear to his father. It is simply "I promise."

The father puts the helmet back into the leather bag and reties the leather thong. He stands and returns to his sleeping area.

Tico returns late one afternoon to the corral, in what later becomes the town of Gariche. Tico is a strong and fine horse, bred in Costa Rica. He has sought out his home where food and brushing down will come.

The few men of this settlement can see the remnants of broken darts in Tico's rump. The gold is in the saddlebags. The people regret the loss of their friend, Juan Morales. There are a couple of Indians who have given up their lives in the mountains to work here. They recognize the jewellery pieces amongst the gold from their days with their people. The jewellery has its own style. It is Bri-Bri, they say.

"This gold is from the Bri-Bri people. This is all very serious." They say very clearly, "You don't go up into the country of the Bri-Bri for gold."

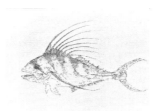

Tico making it back with the gold, the disappearance of Morales, the Indian stories of slaughtered Conquistadors and tales of other wayward adventurers build on solemn warnings, repeated again and again. "You don't go up into the country of the Bri-Bri for gold," all has its impact.

The Legend of the Bri-Bri grows as the years pass.

Corporal Eduardo Morales grew up with the Legend. It is still told to this day. And he knows the story of his great grandfather.

CHAPTER ONE

Samara is not a very big town. Most people who were ever there, or knew someone who was ever there, either saw my grandfather or his truck.

If this was Seattle, Bill would be unremarkable. But in a small town like Samara, he was noticeable. Americano. Bill, my grandfather, an American in this very Costa Rican village, looking like an elderly hippie - a grey ponytail complete with a palm-sized bald spot, beer belly, skinny legs, a cigarette hanging from his mouth, sometimes clean shaven, many moles and growths of one sort or another on his face and forehead. Not handsome and tending not to look happy in his blue jeans, t-shirt and running shoes, Bill stands 6'3" in this country of generally short people. He fit the profile of an American ex-patriot seen in South East Asia after the Vietnam War. This is Costa Rica. He speaks perfect Tico-Spanish.

His truck was more noticeable in many ways, in that you never saw many of them in North America never mind Costa Rica. It was a Mercedes Benz Unimog, civilian edition, white, with a wood-cased flat bed, a three-ton 4x4 that could drive through probably five feet of water, and as Bill so often boasted, could climb a palm tree.

How many times have I heard him say that! He could drive it up a palm tree.

In a town the size of Samara, we stood out as foreigners. And with this foreign truck, we just stood out more. Many of those I have gone to school with say my grandfather is C.I.A., probably because the truck looks so military. They never ask me if he is C.I.A., they just say so. So, after a while, what do you say?

We park Bill's truck in front of the chain-link fence at the building supply center. We are across the street from the bank, Banco Elca, which has a small lineup of locals and tourists out front. The guards only let a few in at a time, after checking their documents. The tourists and surfers are invariably in shorts and bright tops, the locals in jeans, slacks, or dresses. The locals handle the heat with indifference. The tourists seek out the shade. Two bank guards stand watching us in their dark blue uniforms, black boots, and black flack vests. Each holds a defender-style pump-action shotgun and sidearm. They look altogether over-armed and too warm, standing in the sunshine in this small town.

Costa Rica is supposedly a country of small crime - thievery, car break-ins, and muggings. That explains the chain-link fence with the razor wire top around the building supply center, but the bank and its armed guards? I've always wondered where people would run for cover if some big truck came all too fast around the corner, men in the back, bearing down on the guards too aggressively. A construction vehicle with a crew in the back is a very common sight here. I guess they know not to drive in too fast.

The bank guards have already checked us out as we step down from the cab and I follow Bill into the supply center. It seems dark, coming in from the bright sun. Bill stands at the counter where he hands a list to the clerk, who looks only a few years older than me. From a small corner office with a ceiling fan over the desk, Bill is spotted by the store manager. He stands and approaches.

"Senor Bill. How are you? That special order you gave to me. It has come in!" He is happy with this news.

Bill greets his approach with a salutatory nod and comes to life with this news.

"Good good! How much of it came in?"

"All of it I am sure. Let me check," and he is in to his office and back in seconds. He hands Bill a clipboard which has his original order list on top of the shipping invoices, and eagerly points out the check marks noting each was received.

"I checked it over myself. It is all here," he says assuredly.

A smile comes over Bill's face. "Good good. I didn't give it much hope that I would see any of it for another month or so. If/yet this year," he sarcastically adds.

The manager was obviously pleased.

"Senor Bill, our supplier is doing so much better since the construction work has started on the new hospital. They have been called on for more and more special supplies."

Bill kind of grunts, and the manager leads him by the arm behind the service counter and into a receiving area. I follow. It is darker here but the new Honda Motor and pressure washer stands bright on a pallet. Other boxes have been opened and valves, connectors, and clamps have all been counted against the order list. Bill pulls off some of the shrink wrap still holding things together and examines a larger box containing two hundred feet of high pressure hose.

Pulling out a few valves and fittings from an open box, Bill says, "And you say it all came in. No back orders?"

"It has all come in the best I know. I checked it myself. But I do not always know exactly what it is that you ordered - what it is supposed to look like," spoken with a look that seeks some recognition that he has done the best he can do.

"And this too," as he points out two pallets piled high with a rigid flexible pipe, strapped on and shrink wrapped.

Bill is gently nodding his head in approval.

"Well let's get it loaded up. Derrick," handing me the keys to the truck. "Bring the truck in the yard. Be careful backing up."

Turning, Bill directs the store manager, "Have your boys load this up, and I will run across to the bank. Have your bill ready and I will write you a check when I get back."

The store manager nods sharply as he turns and gives directions to one of his staff.

"And you might as well add the stuff on the list I just gave your guy at the counter."

Bill heads out from the counter area, out the door and across the street to the bank.

I back the truck through the gates into the compound, keeping a good eye on my mirrors to watch for clearances in the tightly packed yard.

I do not know the boys in the yard but they are chatting to one another about the truck and, before they direct their comments to me, I engage them in Spanish. Perfect Spanish. I was almost raised here. I've spent over half my life here - have gone to school here for the last eight years. We have all probably encountered one another before but as they are several years older than me, and at this age, we all change so quickly. I think the younger of the two is the older brother of Carlos Alferez, who is in my class.

I chat briefly with the two yard boys while the store manager supervises the loading of the truck. I look around at the few items on display out front as Bill settles up his bill in the office with the store manager. Hands are shaken and Bill comes out looking happy with things as the store manager is patting him on the back, assuring him of the best of service for the future.

In the truck, Bill is looking at me all smiles.

"Derrick, I didn't think this stuff would come in this soon. This gives us lots of options. I only ordered it two weeks ago!"

He carries on as I shrug to beg the question, and lights up a cigarette. He is all smiles and engaging me with his eyes.

"Give me a day or two to put everything together and we should head up into the high country and give it all a try."

"You sure you want to go so soon?" I ask. "Mom wants to take me into San Jose next week for a shopping trip."

Bill's eyes are still engaging, the smiles still all over his face. "Come on Derrick! You and Jess could go the next week."

"But why don't we just drive up the Ora River and give it a try for an hour to see how it wor-"

He is cutting me off as I say it.

"You don't let anybody see that equipment working! Never. It is one thing to see pieces here and there in a yard, but to see it together and working is a totally different thing. It'd blow their socks off."

I am nodding, taking this seriously. He flags his brow up and down as he forces a Cheshire cat's grin.

"And maybe we could pull up a good bunch of yellow stuff if we pick a good spot. Wouldn't you like that?"

Bill's face has taken on a glow. Nodding to himself he says, "Well I know I would like that. And that water pick I have been telling you about," Bill pauses then continues. "I'd love to try it out."

I am nodding and smiling. I find Bill most amusing at times like this, when he gets the glow.

It's the gold Bill is talking about.

"Give me a day or two," he says. And then with emphasis, "And let me talk to Jess."

As we turn into the compound across the dirt road from The Fennix Hotel, which is run by my grandfather and grandmother, Bill says, "And try and stick around for the next while. Don't go running off. I might be able to use your help in getting ready."

"Are we going to get Johnny to come?" I ask.

Bill gets serious now, and gives me the mildly disgusted look he gives when he talks about Johnny.

"We'll talk about it," is all he says.

"But I can go fishing?" I ask.

"See if you can find Johnny to give us a hand unloading. Then go. Get Johnny. If you can't find him, come back and help me."

Sometimes I know not to ask too much. Sometimes I know not to say too much. I head across the road to see if either Mom or Grandma has seen Johnny.

Johnny is my friend, but he works for us. He is Costa Rican. That puts him in the poorest of light as far as my grandfather is concerned.

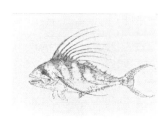

It hasn't happened yet, that Bill has talked to Mom or Grandma about our going - not that I have seen anyway. I never doubted his intention to go, but then there is the gauntlet of approvals to make it happen. Grandma is just swishing around the bottom of the sink to make sure she has gotten everything and giving me the look with a teasing smile.

"It is going to take two of you to keep up to me," she says.

"Hey! Drying just takes longer than running a wet dish rag over everything. And you know Bill likes his glasses dried to sparkle."

I line up my dishtowel at Gram like I am going to give her a flick in the butt with it. I give her a menacing look that pales in comparison the one I get back. It's all playful.

I turn from the sink, drying the last fry pan, Gram putting away odds and ends in cupboard spaces.

"Grandpa told me he wants to go, maybe up behind Carillo in the next couple days to try out his dredge. He says he needs you to go with him." Her eyes meet mine. "Your mom won't like it."

I try not to reveal too much by any expressions. Not too much surprise, not too big a smile.

"Has he talked to Mom yet?" I ask. "Do you know?"

"I don't know," she says with more than a hint of a smile, slowly shaking her head. "You two!"

"What I do know is that she won't be happy about it." Gram continues. "She won't be happy about it," repeating, and drawing out the "won't".

I give her a questioning what-can-I-do-about-it expression as I put away the fry pan, not saying anything.

"First, she won't like you to miss any time in school, and then she won't be happy with Grandpa making you part of his crazy schemes," slowly shaking her head again, with a forced smile.

"I'm okay in school Gram. Really." I insist.

My eyes meet hers, and the exchange is worth five minutes of talking.

My grandmother does not step aside easily. She can't, with Bill as her husband.

"Jessica is not up to this, this week. It's the end of the school year. She wants you to do well," trailing off.

"I'm okay in school Gram. Really. Mr. Santorini tells Mom he wants to see me do better, but I am way ahead of the class, and it's all review right now."

Grandma looks at me. What a look - radiation of concern, regard, love, unspoken protest, and unspoken questions. A face that reveals each detail, and I have to say, a face that looks close to perfection.

"Am I done Gram?"

"Go," she says, and I know by her expression that all of this will have to be revisited again.

I notice the Crosby, Stills, and Nash playing in the background as I am out the door. I get ten feet out, into the parking lot of our hotel and Johnny is leaning against Bill's Jeep.

"Hey! How's it going?" bids Johnny.

"Come on, let's go," I say as I walk by him.

We head across the yard to Bill's shop where the lights are on, shining out towards us. There's the sound of a hand grinder taking some metal down, and an air compressor comes on. A howler monkey growls at us from up in the tree in the middle of the parking area and we both veer off our straight line course automatically, knowing we have to. Howler monkeys are rude. They'll pee on you if you walk under them.

"It's not like Bill to be working after supper," says Johnny. "What's happening?"

"Hey you know, he got that new equipment this morning. It will be neat to see how some of this works. Bill calls it a water pick."

"What's a water pick do?" asks Johnny.

"It will clean out cracks and crevices when Bill is using his dredge. Bill says that with enough pressure it should clean out sediments from right under a rock, blowing the good stuff right up into the dredge. The dredge is big, but the water pick will fit in all kinds of small spaces."

Bill looks up just as he is snapping a brass fitting into a quick-release fitting on the pick-up head of the dredge. The coils of flex pipe that were on the pallets are unrolled, laid out like a long snake back and forth across the floor of the shop. The pressure hose for the water pick is clipped onto the flex pipe every eighteen inches or so with heavy zip ties. Bill snaps a four-foot piece of high pressure hose and wand on to the fitting he has just fabricated. He holds up the pick-up head for the dredge in his left hand and with his right he extends out his arm and waves around the wand, pressing the hand trigger on and off, showing us how this thing is going to work. His face is not smiling but smug, showing his satisfaction at what he has done. He looks up at us, one eye squinted, brow furled, as the smoke from his cigarette rises up into his eyes.

"Can't wait to try it," Bill says. Now he is smiling.

"Bill, how does this work?" asks Johnny.

Johnny is unsure of himself. I know he is wondering whether Bill is going to berate him or show him something he is proud of.

"Yeah Grandpa! Show us how it works," I add quickly, trying to give this some momentum.

"Okay.," Bill says, taking his cigarette and butting it in a big ashtray on the work bench.

"What you got to know is that when you are in a river, the bottom conditions keep changing. What you are looking for in terms of conditions is where gold would naturally be trapped. The rivers bottom is like a giant sluice box. The river has maybe been running this course for a thousand years or more. As it erodes through literally mountain sides, if there is gold in its geology it is washed down and trapped wherever the water slows down. Floods happen and the gold keeps getting disturbed and pushed along. But eventually it is right where the hell it is at, trapped in and under boulders or rock formations or pushed along in gravel bars. Gravel bars act like a huge gold pan, where the lighter material keeps getting washed away and the heavier stuff, like gold and emeralds, keep settling lower. Everything keeps moving. But in bedrock formations, like when you are into the mountains, wherever there is a crack in the formation, the fissure again acts like a sluice box and traps the gold. Unlike a gravel bar, it can't be pushed further in the next flood. There are places in a rivers bottom where the gold is held just like it is in the bank."

Bill picks up the dredge head again and goes through the motions of sucking up material from around his air compressor.

"Now you see, I can suck up all the material from around a boulder or a formation, but I can't get into the cracks and crevices. The best gold could be trapped there."

With the high pressure wand in his right hand he continues.

"With this at four thousand pounds of pressure, I can clean out all the cracks and fissures and blow the material up into the dredge. These are the spots that hold the best of the gold. This is the stuff that hasn't been disturbed in maybe a thousand years."

Bill walks over to the sluice trays he has built. He is getting wound up. I have seen it a hundred times.

"These are big sluice trays. Biggest I have ever seen, not being a commercial venture. And this is the biggest pump and dredge. I bet you I can pick up six-inch rocks with this thing."

"I am betting that, in good conditions, I can move a ton of material in just a couple minutes." Bill pauses and takes a deliberate cleansing breath. "But it is the pressure wand that I believe is going to give me my best colour."

Johnny is all smiles. Bill's excitement has stirred him up.

"This would be good to try. When are you going to try it Bill?" bids Johnny.

Bill turns to put a few things back in their place. I know Johnny is out on a limb. He is usually out on a limb when it comes to Bill.

"Are you still hoping to go out soon?" I throw in. "Have you talked to Mom yet?"

Bill pushes in several drawers in his tool chest, and pulls down the locking bar and puts the hefty padlock in place.

"Not yet. But I will"

Bill snaps up his head toward Johnny and says "You coming?" It wasn't asking him. It was more like telling him, with as much regard as that.

Johnny is still radiating some of the excitement of the past moments and his white teeth are bright in the fluorescent lights of the shop. Big smiles.

"Yeah Bill. I'll come. You just tell me when you are going."

"Do you know when you are going yet?" I ask.

"No, not yet. But soon. Real soon. I'll talk to your Mom to-night."

CHAPTER TWO

You hear the dredge - the water sucking up rocks and sediments and volumes of water. Rocks clatter up the flexible pipe like a huge vacuum cleaner. You hear your breathing. Breathing in through a regulator has a higher pitch than breathing out. Breathing in sounds something like sucking air through your teeth. Breathing out has a tumbling sound to it, as the breath tumbles its way to the surface. With a vacuum cleaner, you hear the air sucking through the attachments. With the dredge, the pitch is lower. It is water going through the attachments. It sounds like you are under water.

You are.

Bill is in his scuba gear, working his way up to a ledge in a pool of water ten feet deep at the base of a small rapid, and he can see the water spilling into the pool, sucking down air with it. The water is clear. The river is not flooding, probably running at half its usual capacity. The visibility is good and the colour of the water gives everything a green hue. The sunlight gives its special 3D effects as its light is refracted through the rippled surface of the flowing water. The dredge head kicks up wisps of sediments and sand that don't get sucked up the head. Bill isn't worrying about the stirred-up material as the flow of the water is carrying it away quickly enough to not ruin the visibility. It is mostly sand and coarser material.

Pulling away larger rocks exposes the sediments beneath them, which Bill focuses on. He knows that this is where the gold will be found if it is here. Mostly he is working the dredge head, holding it with both hands. The dredge head is exposing a clear rock surface. Bill bangs the dredge head on it and it feels solid. The rocks and sand are the size that the dredge picks up with ease and the surface of a rock ledge is exposing itself as it angles towards the head of the pool. He can work about a twenty-foot run if this ledge is what it looks like and if things work out. The ledge is clearing and Bill works eagerly and hopefully. The exposed surface is generally smooth with steps of sheared away surface, looking like shale that has broken away. This is a natural sluice box.

When Bill has cleaned away most of the material for about an eight-foot run, he pulls the water pick off its mount on the side of the dredge head. Bill gets his face close to the fissures he has exposed and uses the power wand to clean out the gravel and sand, blowing this material straight into the suction head. He blows out about a three-foot section along a near straight-line fissure, lets the water pick go, and fumbles around for his flashlight clipped to a vest he is wearing over his wetsuit. With the flashlight, as close as he can get it, he inspects how clean the water pick has cleaned out the fissure. The noise of the dredge is steady now as it is just taking in volumes of water. Bill's heart takes several strong beats as the adrenaline pumps in his excitement. With the light, Bill can see flakes of gold like golden crushed corn flakes still stuck in the fissure. They seem stuck to the irregular surface. They shine brightly in the intense light. Bill moves deliberately, positioning the dredge pick-up head to the first exposed edge of the fissure and focuses the water pick, using its hand trigger and its four thousand pounds of water pressure to blast at what Bill is sure is gold flake.

The flakes disappear. Bill knows they are being sucked up the dredge and trapped by the surface of the sluice box. His heart jumps again as he sees what he is sure are small dark gold pebbles that are exposed and dislodged and disappear up the dredge head. It takes another five minutes to strip out this exposed part of the fissure. Bill checks his gauges to see how much air he has left in his scuba tanks and sees he has twenty minutes to half an hour left. With his flashlight, he again inspects the fissure to see how well he has cleaned it out. He takes a small hand pick crevice tool that looks like a small meat hook and pulls at pebbles that seem wedged into the fissure that the water pick did not dislodge. Some are sucked up into the dredge and some fall into deeper openings in the fissure. Using the small head of the water pick, Bill tries to blast these pebbles up into the pick-up head. He can't see if it is working and checks again with his flashlight. They seem to be getting picked up.

Bill checks his air again, trying not to waste motion and effort. The less effort expended, the less air he breathes, and the longer he will be able to stay down. Use the equipment to do the work, he tells himself.

He is able to clear off another ten to twelve feet of the rock surface, and finds that the fissure fractures into several runs. For the moment, his excitement has settled and he works efficiently, deliberately, effectively. In twenty-five minutes, he has cleared off the rock surface with the dredge head and cleaned out the fissure and its crevice with the water pick. His technique is improving as he learns to manipulate the dredge head, the water pick, and his crevice tool. He only uses effort to move rocks that he needs to move. More than one boulder is bigger than he can move – not worth the expense of effort. The water pick effectively cleans out around it. He is checking his air every few minutes now. One more check and he peruses the area he has cleared. He pulls the slack out of the cable that runs up through guides to the pumps and sluice box on the

Zodiac anchored in place above him on the river. He gives it three sharp pulls, and within a few seconds the dredge head is being pulled to the surface from above.

Johnny and I are both on the Zodiac, running the sluice box. Johnny is standing guard with the rifle.

Bill scopes out the surrounding area, anticipating working this site more with fresh air tanks. Let's see what we are showing for gold, he tells himself and with his arm held above his head he breaks the surface of the water three feet from the Zodiac, holding on to one of the two anchor ropes he had set to hold the Zodiac in place. He gives Derrick the okay sign. Everything is good.

"How long was I down?" Bill asks, a little too loudly over the sound of the dredge motors and pumps.

I check my watch.

"An hour and ten minutes," I reply at the same volume.

"I can do better than that," Bill grumbles. "Too much wasted effort," He pauses then, "And too much smoking," he admits reluctantly.

"Derrick," directs Bill. "Just release the anchor lines and let the current pull us into shore."

Bill hangs on to the edge of the Zodiac, waiting for the shallow water to stand in before removing his weight belt and air tank. I release the starboard lines to the anchors Bill had set earlier on the far edge of the pool, and the portside line tied to a boulder on the edge of the bank stops us from being carried away. The three- to four-knot current pushes us over to the shallows where we are camped.

Bill pulls off his flippers as we are drifting over and places them in the Zodiac. When his feet hit bottom, he pushes us in until the Zodiac hits the gravel bottom.

Johnny is still standing watch over the water with the rifle.

"Did you see anything?" Bill asks Johnny.

Johnny is still holding the M-16 as he jumps to the shore, not getting his feet wet. He lays the rifle down and walks back into the water to help pull the Zodiac up.

"No Bill. Just one small snake feeding right along the bank. He never got close to you."

Johnny has been the lookout. These waters have a few dangerous creatures in them. Piranhas, crocodiles, water snakes - the worst being the mamba, which can kill a good-sized man with one bite. Very poisonous.

Then there is the land. Black pumas, wild boar, more snakes like the bushmaster, killer bees, scorpions, and mosquitoes. Bill always laughs when he hears me include the mosquitoes. Me? I am sure they could kill you!

"The visibility in the water was good," adds Johnny.

"Have you got the safety on on that thing?" Bill challenges.

"For certain Bill," Johnny insists.

Bill looks over the equipment, starting to dismantle the sluice trays.

"Sometimes the gravel was pouring onto the grizzly head so fast," I say. "It was hard for me to keep up. Then other times the water was just clear."

The grizzly head is where the dredge dumps what it is sucking up from the bottom. It is like a heavy grill of welded quarter-inch rods in the shape of a peaked roof. It is 2ft x 2ft on each side of the peak. The bars are spaced at 3/4-inches apart. Rocks that are bigger than 3/4 of an inch just slide down the rods lengthwise and wash off to the sides, down a stainless-steel tray over each side of the Zodiac. What washes through the grill, drops onto another stainless tray where the water washes this material through the sluice box.

"There are better systems to handle the volume of material we are getting," says Bill. "They're called trammel heads. Trammel heads have a rotating drum where everything washes through itself, but they are so big and bulky. There's no way to conceal them. They would broadcast what we are doing. They are used in commercial setups. I'll get you to show me what was happening."

Bill picks a pail out of the Zodiac and pours water in a spot on one of the sluice trays. A big smile comes across his face. He pulls up another bucket of water and starts pouring it slowly over the same spot.

"Come look at this."

As he pours the water in a single spot and the black sand is washed down the sluice tray, there is the gold – all within a ¾-inch area. Flakes that are shiny, laying on a darker gold-coloured sand.

"I think that is a nugget sitting there," Bill says pointing at a pea-sized stone.

Bill's face is wide with a smile. His eyes are radiating his delight.

"Johnny, get me a beer and my smokes would ya?"

Bill pulls up another pail and pours it slowly on a spot near the bottom of the sluice. Then another pail and pours it on a spot a little higher.

"Here, look at it," Bill says, showing me fine sparkles like stars in a night sky in the black sand. "We'll see how much fine gold we got after we slap out this blanket."

"Where are your cigarettes Bill?" hollers Johnny.

"Just get me a new pack out of the truck. And a lighter," Bill hollers back.

We undo the clips on one sluice tray and Johnny is back with Bill's cigarettes and a beer. Bill takes them and pops the top on the can of Imperial and drains half the can in his first long pull, then opens the package of cigarettes.

"Look," I say, pointing out the gold flecks to Johnny. "This could be good."

"How good do you think we did Bill?" I ask.

Bill exhales his cigarette and then bottoms up with his beer.

"Too soon to say." A good beer belch and, "But I am sure it will give us a decent return for a day's work. Help me carry this up," as we grab the sluice tray and set it up on flat ground on the bank. Johnny and I undo the clips on the second tray and carry it up beside the first.

Bill is out of his wet suit and pulling up a pair of shorts over his wet underwear. He slips into his runners and grabs his shirt off the front pole of the tent.

"Johnny, you and Derrick take the Zodiac into that backwater and cover it with the camouflage. Tie it up good. You never know when the river could come up."

As Johnny and I are walking the Zodiac down the edge of the bank, we are all of a sudden up to our waists in water.

"So where did that snake go that you spotted?" I ask.

Johnny smiles a silly grin.

"I hope not here!"

We gingerly step up from the pool and guide the zodiac into

the backwater and tie it to the mooring lines. The camouflage tarp is laying in a bundle on the bank from this morning. We sort it out and throw it over and tie it down. We walk back to the camp on the ground.

Bill has a large rectangular basin by the waters edge and is slapping out the blanket from the bottom of the sluice into a few inches of water he has in the basin.

"Get me another bucket of water," he directs Johnny.

"You see. The finer gold gets trapped in this blanket." The blanket is like a big piece of green scrubber pad you use to scrub a fry pan. Bill is holding it by its edges and using a slapping motion on the water in the basin a half dozen times, then rolling it up a few more inches to slap out the next little section.

"This stuff you never see in the sluice box," Bill adds. "Get me the other basin out of the back of the truck," he directs Johnny.

Bill has me hold the rolled-up material as he slaps out the last few feet.

"Hold it over the basin so you don't lose anything."

He takes the roll when he is finished and lays it in the basin that Johnny has brought.

"We can clean this out even better with a pressure washer when we get home. But we will use it again tomorrow so it doesn't have to be cleaned out perfectly."

I am glad that Bill is telling us what he is doing and what to watch out for. We are both eager to learn.

"Derrick. You and Johnny pick up that sluice tray. Keep it level and hold it over this basin. I'll wash out what's in it."

Bill has us tip up the top end as he pours a bucket of water to wash down the gravelly material into the basin. Then another.

"Put that on the back of the truck and cover it up out of sight," he directs us.

Bill spills most of the surface water out of the basin, not pouring out any sediments. He then gets us to repeat the procedure again for the second sluice tray.

It is hot now, probably one o'clock, and it takes two of us to carry the big rectangular basin up to the truck. It is heavy. Bill sits in a folding chair, leans back and lights up a cigarette. Johnny and I, both thirsty, take turns with the water cup. Johnny pours one over his head and lets it run down all over him.

"You can carry the water up from now on if that's what you are going to use it for," Bill berates.

The spiral gold panning machine Bill bought a month or so ago is gurgling away. Our campsite is nicely shaded now and there is a breeze running down the river valley. The leaves rustle from time to time as the breeze builds and settles. On a lazy day, I might have hoped to lay around more, but not today.

The gold panning machine takes a bit of tweaking to get it working at its best, but Bill has done all that. It is neat! A light-gauge electrical cable is hooked up to the truck batteries and it runs a small motor and water pump. The motor rotates a blue plastic pan clockwise, set at about a 45-degree angle.

The pan has a ridge moulded into it that spirals up towards its centre, where there is a one-inch hole that allows whatever has been able to climb up that far to fall into a holding pail hung on the back of the unit. There is a water bath that you can regulate that washes away the sediments and black sand. You can literally see the gold findings clear and climb up the pan and spill in to the catch bucket. It will process a pails worth of sluice sediments in half an hour. Bill hand-spoons them onto the gold panner, about a cup at a time.

Self-satisfied is too weak a term to describe Bill at this point.

Bill pulls the second beer off the six pack of Imperial and snaps back the top. He puts the four back into the edge of the water, not so deep that the water will wash them away.

"Look at this!" He is showing me gold sand creeping up to the centre of the wheel. It looks like sand and other bits, like a hand full of crumbs you would wipe off a table or sweep up from the floor.

Bill turns off the switch and the wheel stops turning. He leans over the back and lifts out a small cup-sized bucket that is collecting his gold findings.

"Look at this," he says again, more intensely. There is probably a handful in the bottom of the cup.

Bill's eyes widen as he stares at me. I am obviously not as impressed as he would like me to be.

"This is good!" This time with a couple quick little nods for emphasis, again, with the intensity.

"It doesn't look like much to me," I declare.

Bill's face puckers up in disbelief.

"It'll take you a long time to make a gold brick with that," I add.

Bill's face relaxes and draws into a smile.

"Well, you don't know what you are talking about," he says assuredly. And with a small shrug, "I guess you're just a dumb kid."

He picks up a beer can that he has cut the top off of, that is wedged into a patch of sand.

"I was going to show you these." Bill pauses and rattles the can around, then adds, "another time."

It sounds like he has a few rocks and pebbles inside. He pushes his tongue against his bottom lip, his mouth in a pinched smile, and shakes his head back and forth a couple times.

"This is good," Bill says to himself. He picks up his beer can that he has cut the top off of that is wedged into a ptch of sand, and takes a long pull. There is a pause for a few moments.

"Can we go fishing for a while and see if we can catch us dinner?" I ask.

"Yeah. Get lost." I guess he is tired of talking to me.

"Don't get yourselves killed," he adds a few moments later. "And be back soon enough to get supper done with before dark."

"Are you going upstream or downstream?" Bill asks as I'm heading up to get Johnny and our fishing gear.

I point upstream as I walk backwards a few steps, and turn and keep going. I hear the gold panner start up again.

The fire is burning and the sparks climb from the tops of the flames. Bill is in the folding chair, leaning back with a cigarette in one hand and a beer in the other.

"That was a good fish, hey Grandpa?"

"Yeah. That was a good day all around."

Johnny starts to put more wood on the fire and Bill tells him not to.

"Just let it go out. Better yet, pour a bucket of water on it and we'll head off to bed."

"So tomorrow we'll pack up and go?" I ask.

"No. We'll stay one more day. No one's bothering us and we can make do with the food we have. Since you caught that big fish," Bill adds mockingly.

It wasn't big, but it did feed the three of us a decent portion.

"I want to finish working that ledge as far as I can go. I have two tanks of air left, and if we get started early I should be done by noon. We won't have to pan out what we get. We'll put it in the pails and basins and I'll run it through when we get home. I'll get you up early."

Bill stands, a bit wobbly, and flicks his cigarette into the fire. He downs the last half of his beer, lets out a good belch, and then for our pleasure, rips a good beer fart for us.

"We'll get home for supper," Bill adds over our protests as he turns and heads up to his tent. "Cash it in before long, and keep the noise down."

Johnny and I sit for another minute staring in to the fire.

"Guess we better pick up," says Johnny. "Or the monkeys will clean us out."

CHAPTER THREE

Mom and Grandma are just finishing making a bed together. The vacuum cleaner is by the door of the suite, and the service cart is sitting just outside stacked with clean bed sheets, pillow cases, and towels. A laundry hamper is its own four-wheel cart, half full.

In Seattle, you'd call this a motel, but here in Costa Rica it is called a hotel.

It is on the beach with palm trees and ornamentals, planted twelve years ago when Bill and Grandma bought the place, providing a good stretch of shady sand that separates the ten-unit hotel from the beach. The ten units are in the shape of half an octagon and surround a thirty-foot pool, the units all single story, doors and windows facing the pool, all facing the ocean. There is a large patio area between the units and the pool, and there is a table and chairs in front of each unit. There is a bistro umbrella in the centre of each table.

It is hot during the summer season and only a couple of the units are rented out this week, unlike the winter months when everything is rented out to northern tourists. It is always hot here, though we get some heavy rains in the summer. Surfing groups come out anytime of year, but the surf schools run their own accommodations, mostly hostel style. It is part of the surfing cult Bill says.

Saul, my younger brother, is twelve years old and he is the only one in the pool today. He has a small dog running around the pool that he is trying to get to jump in to fetch a ball. It's not our dog, but it comes around all the time to play with Saul, and sometimes gets something to eat.

My mom, Saul, and I have lived with Grandma and Grandpa for the last eight years, since my father died. We moved down from Seattle when I was seven. At that time, we planned to stay for a year or so, but we are still here. Mom is Bill and Grandma's only child, and that makes Saul and I their only grandchildren. Mom talks a lot about getting our own place. Whenever there is an argument, it always sounds like we are going to get our own place right away, but it never happens. I know Mom doesn't make much helping out here, and Bill and Grandma have put most of the extra money they get into the hotel, and a few other toys.

Grandma goes back to Seattle to visit her parents every year or two. Bill doesn't go back. Only his father is still alive and he moved from the Seattle area to some small town in Montana with a lady friend. That happened before we moved here.

Johnny works for us doing maintenance and as a grounds-keeper. When things are busy from October to March or April, Grandma hires a lady to do the housekeeping, but at this time of year Mom and Grandma take care of things. In the busy months Johnny's dad, Ricardo, works night security. He has a revolver he likes to show us.

Mom runs the place whenever Bill and Grandma go away, be it for a few hours during a day, shopping trips to San Jose which take three, four or five days, or when they go down to Panama for a week at a time, sometimes more. Saul and I are in school. Mom stays here.

Saul is splashing water at the dog and the dog is barking at him.

"Leave some water in the pool," Mom yells at Saul.

Saul keeps at it and the dog barks more than ever, running tight patterns up to the edge of the pool and quick retreats to avoid the water Saul splashes at him.

Grandma pulls the door closed to the suite as Mom pulls the vacuum cleaner towards the centre of the suites to the open door of the storage room.

"Saul!" she yells, now as a reprimand.

Saul rotates around and splashes a sweeping spray of water at mom, getting her pretty good. Mom just stands there, staring down Saul. Saul rotates around and around, a couple turns splashing water in this and that direction. The dog gives a couple more barks but Saul settles down and jumps up part way onto a boogey board and swims around. The dog settles down, and Mom carries on to the storage room.

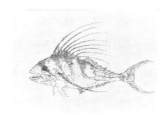

Grandma has come back with a tray of glasses and a pitcher of lemonade. She sets them on a table, winds up the umbrella for shade and sits down. Mom joins her, sitting across from her.

"I was just about ready to go in there after him Jess," says Grandma. "Seriously. He is not like Derrick, that one. Derrick always wanted to please."

"Saul is not Derrick, Mom," My mom cuts her mother off. Following the exasperated look, Mom continues.

"After Jim died, everything was so unsettled. Everything," she pauses. "Moving down here. You and Dad were as much parents to him as I was then."

Gram does what some moms do best. There is a softening that comes to her face. She listens.

"I don't think Saul even remembers his Dad. Derrick does," Mom continues. "He is good with Dad, and you know it. Some boys just need a strong father figure I guess."

A few moments pass.

"You make the best lemonade, Mom."

"Are you still wanting to take the boys shopping this week?" asks Grandma.

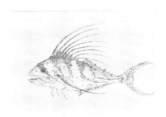

Saul is out of the pool and has been chasing the dog through the palm trees. There are no guests in the big wooden lounge chairs to disturb. The dog is chasing Saul more than Saul chasing the dog.

The dog is as hyper as Saul, and starts jumping up and snapping at Saul as he runs.

The beach here is white and flat, and runs for a mile each direction, generally north and south. It is hardly ever busy and it is not uncommon for there to be at least a quarter of a mile between you and the next person. There is a couple laying on beach towels under a beach umbrella up several hundred yards towards the town site. Their cooler and beach glasses are stuck in the sand. The ocean breeze is just starting to pick up. It must mean the tide is starting to come in.

Saul runs down the beach, away from anyone, and puts in some evasive moves to tease the dog. The dog gets more excited and jumps up at Saul and snaps at his waving hand. The dog just nips the end of Saul's finger and Saul makes another move and tears back up toward the palm trees at full speed. Saul sees the dog jump again at his hand and sees the blood flinging from the nick in his finger.

Saul takes a dive right into the sand. The sand is soft and is kicked up as Saul lands. He does not move. Saul's eyes have rolled up into his head and his hands flutter. He is unconscious as the dog lunges and fades back, barking. The dog settles down gradually as Saul is unresponsive.

The dog licks Saul's face as he regains consciousness. Saul lies there for a few seconds, bewildered, and rolls up onto his side. He looks at his finger and it is nothing. He wipes the blood that is drying onto his shorts and sits up in the sand with his knees pulled up to his chest. All of a sudden he feels exhausted.

The game is over. The fun is over.

Saul picks himself up and trudges back up to the swimming pool, brushing some of the sand off himself as he walks, with the dog trailing behind him.

Grandma and Mom are just putting their empty glasses onto the tray with the jug of lemonade.

Mom sees Saul as he comes up to her.

"Saul, do you want some lemonade?" she calls over to him.

Saul doesn't reply, but keeps coming. There is still sand stuck to his face and to where he has been sweating.

"What happened to you?" asks Mom, concerned.

"I fell," is all that Saul says.

"Well come over here and get that sand washed off," says Mom, as she leads him off towards the beach side of the pool where there is a stand-up shower for just this purpose. She turns on the water, washes the sand from his hair, and lets the water do the rest. The water is not at all cold. Water is never cold here.

Mom sees the dried blood on his finger and holds Saul's hand up in hers.

"What happened here?" She asks.

"He nipped me," Saul replies, nodding towards the dog.

"Well Saul," Mom lightly scolds. "You know not to get the dog so excited."

"He didn't mean it," replies Saul. "It was an accident."

We drive into Samara on the highway coming from the south. We turn left off the highway onto a dirt road and churn up a cloud of dust. We turn left again at the bottom of this road, which goes by a small store that has two arcade games sitting up from the sidewalk - the only stretch of sidewalk for blocks until you get closer to the town centre. We pull into our work yard as it is getting dark. Bill has me jump out and help him back up to the shop doors.

"Stay in my mirrors where I can see you. Drivers side," directs Bill.

Bill puts his hand on Johnny who was set to follow me out of the truck.

"Now I'm telling you to keep your mouth shut about working the dredge out there. You hear me?

"Sure Bill," Johnny agrees.

"It's nobody's business. And you don't want to raise anybody's interest." Bill brakes and reaches down to pull the park brake as Derrick signals to stop.

"And there may be a bonus in it for you if you do what I tell you," adds Bill.

"Sure Bill. What do I say we were doing?" asks Johnny, uncertain what this is about.

"First, don't say anything if you don't need to. And if you are asked, we were just out camping, fishing, exploring. Whatever. No big deal."

Johnny starts again out of the truck.

"Johnny!" Bill catches him with a direct look. "Okay?"

"Sure Bill," Johnny repeats and is glad to get out of the truck. He is glad to get away from Bill's attention.

As we are walking across the road to the house, Mom comes out on the front porch. She has heard us come in.

"I'll see you after supper Derrick," says Johnny as he heads down to the beach. It is the shortest route to his house.

"We'll unload everything in the morning." Bill calls after

Johnny, "Let's get at it early, before it gets too hot."

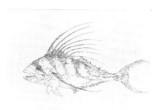

Mom gives me a hug and asks us how our weekend was.

Inside, the house smells good. Some cooking has been going on, and there is a platter with steaks all laid out on it, in seasonings and oil. There is more than a hint of raw garlic in the air of the kitchen. Saul is laying on the couch engrossed in some T.V. program. I give his runner a small kick as I go by, and he kicks back at me, and says nothing.

Bill comes up behind Grandma, who is working at the kitchen counter, and puts his arms around her and gives her a kiss on the neck.

"How was your weekend?" she asks.

"Good. Real good I think."

"How were the boys?" again, asks Grandma.

"I'd have to say more help than usual!" Bill gives me a wink. "Give me ten minutes to get cleaned up and I'll throw those steaks on."

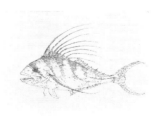

You can see we laid waste to dinner. Bill even opened a bottle of chilled white wine for Mom and Grandma, which he is now pouring the last of, sharing between their two glasses.

"Jess," says Bill. "I'll take you and the boys in to San Jose, well, let's say Wednesday, if you can wait a couple days. We'll stay with Mike and Myrna. You can do your shopping, and I've got a few things I want to take care of."

"That would be okay, wouldn't it?" Bill asks of Grandma, and adds, "I think I have some gold to sell."

"So how do you know you are getting gold?" Mom asks.

"Well, sometimes you can see it. Some of the flakes just shine like gold," says Bill. "A lot of it you can't see until you pan it out. But with that dredge I am sure I could come up with a gold brick in a week if we could just work a good spot."

"What's a gold brick worth Grandpa?" I ask.

Bill has that very pleased-with-himself look again, and he smiles broadly for a few moments, getting his figures lined up in his head.

"Gold is somewhere around $1600 and ounce, but that's a Troy Ounce. There are 31 grams in a Troy Ounce and 28 grams in what we usually think of as an ounce. It's about ten percent more. There are 16 ounces in a pound, but only twelve ounces in a Troy Pound. In a gold brick there are 400 Troy Ounces."

"Why is it done in Troy ounces instead of regular ounces?" I ask.

"Well Derrick, if I could remember, I'd tell you. Knew it once. It had something to do with how the Romans set standards for gold weight, having adopted the accepted Greek Standard of the time. Or something like that. It's what is referred to as an artifact - something that was left over from a previous time in history and gets carried forward."

"So what is a gold brick worth?" asks Mom innocently.

Bill pauses again. He stares at Mom for a few moments more.

"I think it's worth something like $650,000. And it's only this big," as he shapes his hands to the size of a brick. "And it weighs something like 27 pounds, as we know them."

Everyone's brows are lifted, and their eyes wide, except for Saul who gets up out of his chair and goes and plunks himself on the couch to watch T.V.

"So how much do you think you got this weekend?" asks Grandma.

Bill looks up like he is looking over top of eye glasses, licking a morsel off his finger he has wiped out of his dessert plate.

"I don't know yet. But give me a few hours and I'll tell you. I know the first day looked good."

Bill picks up the plate and wipes out the last of the apple pie, and licks his finger again.

"I didn't pan out what we got last night, nor this morning, to save time. It was good to get home for supper. Right Derrick?" Bill exhorts.

I'm smiling, and agree with a hearty, "Yup!"

"And that's why I'm telling you not to talk about this Derrick. Or any of you for that matter," Bill adds. "This stuff is worth a lot of money, and if the wrong people get wind of it, there could be trouble."

"What kind of trouble?" Mom asks.

"Well in this country, somebody is going to want to steal it from you. And if not that, then they will try to take it from you some other way. Reclaiming a National Treasure or some-thing," Bill says mockingly. "If nobody knows about it, then nobody's going to ask questions or get snoopy."

"Well Dad, is it legal?" Mom pauses and continues. "Are you turning my son into a criminal?"

Bill drops to the backrest of his chair and lets out a sigh.

"They probably want you to have a permit for it. I think you need a permit to dredge." Bill pauses a moment. "But then you would have all the trouble I've just explained. Best to be quiet about it, and not to be seen. Look, if we get down to Panama some day, you set up an agreement with a landowner who has a good piece of water running through it. Set up a profit-shar-ing arrangement. Everyone's a winner. No permits. Nothing." Then Bill adds. "It's nothing you're going to get thrown in jail for."

"Well I am glad you are going to try to keep my son out of jail!" Mom says mockingly in return.

Bill is annoyed with the treatment he is getting, feeling like he is in the hot seat. He gets up and says it was a good din-ner, picks up a pack of cigarettes and heads out the front door, probably over to the shop.

Mom and Gram are back and forth on the topic as I get up and stand by Saul for a minute watching what he is watching on T.V.

"I'm going to head over to Johnny's for a bit," I holler, and I am out the front door.

It is pitch black and I am laying in my bed staring at the roof. There are a bunch of howler monkeys in the trees next door making a racket. The wind has come up and a coconut is blown from one of the palm trees and crashes onto the roof. The front door opens and closes again and the two dead bolts are set. It's Bill. He has finished for the night.

Grandma marks her page and turns off her reading light as Bill crawls into bed. In the dark, she asks him, "So how much gold did you get?" The emphasis is on the word 'did'.

"$15,000 to $16,000 worth I figure," states Bill.

Grandma's surprise, amazement and exclamation comes in just one word.

"WHAT?!"

CHAPTER FOUR

Bill gears down the big four-wheel drive Mercedes as he pulls up behind a string of slow traffic heading up over the Terrazu Mountains, where the climb is steep, before we descend down to San Jose. We can't see far enough ahead to see what vehicle is holding everybody up, but we know what it will look like. It will be old, in disrepair, burning oil, noisy, rusty and overloaded. Costa Rica.

This is one of the premium coffee growing regions in Costa Rica - very hilly. Almost mountainous, but not quite. Bill says he doesn't like the area, that it reminds him too much of where he served in Vietnam.

Mom wasn't thrilled that we were taking the big Mercedes, but Saul and I think it's just fine. Though Saul is not taking in much of the trip as he has spent most his time playing a video, a tank combat game, somewhere down in his lap.

"You sit up high and you can see everything better. I like it," I say. "You can see more than just the car ahead of you."

"I like the air conditioning," adds Mom, the sarcasm like a splash of water in your face. There is no air conditioning. The windows are rolled down and that is the air conditioning. The breeze coming through is light, since we are travelling slow.

"But the air is cool up here, at this altitude," says Bill.

"Dad, can we stop at one of these coffee kiosks and take a break?" asks Mom. "Maybe one that looks like it has a decent bathroom."

"How about in 20 minutes or so? There's a spot coming up that has a decent restaurant and we can grab a bite to eat. It would be good not to end up at Mike and Myrna's like we haven't eaten for a week."

"I'm good for that long," replies Mom.

"Saul, what are you going to want to order, so it doesn't take all day when we get there?" asks Bill.

"Have they got fries?" Saul asks.

The service area has a gas bar with four pumps, and is busy. There is a single garage attached to the service station, and there is a car up on the hoist and the sound of an air impact wrench. Two different vehicles are on jack stands next to the garage - both pick ups, both Japanese, both waiting for parts. There are a couple of truck and trailer rigs parked parallel to the highway, facing up the grade. Then there is the assortment of pickup trucks of every make and model, loaded with sacks of vegetables and fruit, some vending to the traffic that is stopping. There are locals and travellers, tourists and truckers. The restaurant has a large deck area that wraps around the back, and the slight breeze feels good. Saul did get his fries and a hamburger and a Coke that he had refilled twice.

"If I can spend an hour in one of the sporting goods shops, I'll be happy," I say. "Mom, I really want to get a fishing rod if I can. That Frenchman landed that rooster fish last week with his fishing rod. There's no way you can do that with just a toss line. It must have been 40 pounds!"

"Well Jess? You're going to want to spend a couple of days' downtown? Or are you going to want to try one of the malls?" asks Bill.

"Maybe I'll try one of the malls for a day and see what we can get," says Mom. "There is way more selection downtown, and I think better prices. Mom gave me a pretty good list for groceries, which would be easier to shop for at a mall. So maybe I should do it the other way around, and go downtown tomorrow and the mall the next day, so everything is fresh."

"Well I am sure that Mike will loan you a car, but if not, just take a taxi," says Bill. "I'll bring it up when we get there. Maybe the next day we can go together to a mall or I can at least arrange to pick you up. There is that new one pretty close to Mike and Myrna's. What I would like to do is to be able to head back Friday morning, if that works for you. I'm hoping to be done by sometime Thursday morning."

Mom says, "It works for me."

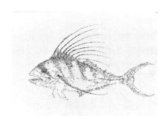

Driving the big Mercedes in the downtown area is a little work, but it is no bigger than most of the commercial delivery trucks. The traffic is always congested down here. Bill drives past the storefront he is looking for - Salem Brother's Fine Jewellery. It is in a new building, and obviously upscale. Bill wonders to himself if this is the type of place he is really looking for. Maybe it is too new, too well lit, too proper. There is full security out front of the entrance. Maybe some operation that looks a little darker would be better. Bill spots a sign in the window that simply says Gold Merchants.

Bill drives around the block looking for a parking lot. He doesn't want to be too close, and definitely not in view of the store and its staff. He doesn't want to be too far either, walking in one of the pickpocket capitals of the world with $15,000 worth of gold. He expands his search to a two-block radius and finds a parking lot next to a new construction site where there is an excavation, and concrete pilings with re-bar. Lots of re-bar. New earthquake construction standards.

Bill parks the truck after a quick conversation with the parking attendant. He takes up two parking spaces with the size of the Mercedes. He hands the attendant several bills from his wallet, and picks up his briefcase and starts toward the jewellery store.

Bill is wearing a pair of pressed Dockers and loafers. He has a custom-made belt that was the pride of some leather craftsman from some little marketplace. His ponytail is neat and hangs over the collar of his Oxford shirt. He is neat, presentable, and not too overdressed. His briefcase is black and nondescript.

Bill engages the eye of the security guard as he approaches the front entrance to the jewellery store. The security guard is in uniform - polished military-style boots, a full flack jacket, shoulder flashes, pump action shot gun, and an automatic sidearm. Expensive help, but not unusual for this kind of establishment in San Jose. Bill sets down his briefcase between himself and the security guard, and produces his driver's licence for I.D. The security guard uses a handheld radio to place a call, and a similarly dressed and equipped guard approaches the door from the inside, unlocks the front door, and welcomes Bill to enter.

Just inside the entrance is a walk-through metal detector. Just past that, an expensive wooden table with finely turned legs, a chair for the guard, and a metal detector paddle laying on top of the table. Bill is asked to put his briefcase on the table and then is asked to take 'the profile' while he is scanned with the hand paddle. There are the usual - car keys, pocket change, and belt buckle. He opens his briefcase on the table and sets out his two packages to the side and allows the inspection of his briefcase and contents. The security guard is very polite and explains each step of the security scan.

A very attractive woman with long dark hair, dressed in a black suit and white blouse buttoned to the neck, approaches. She waits politely as Bill collects himself and the security guard very formally introduces the clerk to Bill. She extends her hand to greet Bill with a beautiful smile, all perfectly engaging. Her makeup is perfect.

The place is well air conditioned.

The security guard quickly but clearly explains to the clerk that Bill is here to get an appraisal on some gold pieces he is considering selling, and the clerk extends her hand off to the side, pointing out a special counter that stands on its own in front of an opening through a wall. A young male clerk of similar stature and attire is working at cleaning jewellery pieces one by one, behind one of the many display cases that are ornate, well lit, and sparkling. He adds his greeting and acknowledges Bill as he escorts him across the floor to the counter, which has a finely finished wood sign that says 'Certified Jeweller' and another that says 'Certified Goldsmith.' Bill can see shelves, scales, electronic equipment, microscopes and other scopes through the opening. It looks like a small laboratory.

Approaching the counter, his escort taps on a gold-finished desk bell. In a moment a clean cut man, looking very Costa Rican, probably in his mid forties, appears. He is wearing fine slacks and shoes, and a fine short-sleeved white shirt. His black topless framed reading glasses are hanging from a black strap around his neck. They are resting on the black leather strap of a shoulder holster that is encasing a 9mm Glock automatic. The gracious clerk introduces Bill to the goldsmith.

Bill is greeted and asked to come around the counter to sit at a table. Every surface is clean and neat, like a clinic. He is given special trays to display what he has brought.

"Placer gold Mr. Platten," the goldsmith remarks as Bill pours out part of one Ziploc bag onto a tray. "Are you looking to sell? Or commission some custom jewellery?"

"I would like to sell," nods Bill. "Maybe some custom jewellery later."

"May I look at it?"

Bill slides the tray over and the goldsmith picks up a high intensity light and a metal tool, something like a pencil. He puts a jeweller's glass in his eye and peruses through pebbles, flakes, and particulate with the metal stylus and the light.

"Please. Your name again?" asks Bill politely. "Too many introductions as I came in, never mind the security procedures."

"Yes, certainly Mr. Platten. My name is Victor Salem. Please call me Victor," as Victor looks up and takes out his jeweller's glass. "It is very good quality gold. How much are you wanting to sell?"

"Well I have something like 290 grams of this," says Bill, pouring and tapping out the remainder of the first bag onto the first tray. Taking another tray, Bill pours his second Ziploc bag onto it - one large nugget and six pebble-sized nuggets, "And 74 grams of this. This one," Bill pointing to the large nugget "is 48 grams."

"Yes, very nice!" exclaims Victor.

Victor takes the metal stylus, high intensity light, and jeweller's glass, and examines the nuggets Bill has presented.

"Yes, very nice," Victor says again, removing his jeweller's glass and looking up directly at Bill.

"This one," tapping the 48-gram nugget "is certainly a jewellery class nugget." And, opening out his hands, Victor adds, "Are you sure you wouldn't like us to mount this one for you? It would make a beautiful pendant necklace. A beautiful piece. One of a kind." Victor smiles. It's a genuine smile. He loves his work.

Bill considers this option for a brief moment.

"I believe at this point I would like to sell it all. If you can take it," replies Bill.

Victor is still smiling, politely now.

"Yes, that we can do. But let me explain how we must deal with raw gold purchases. Have you sold gold before Mr. Platten?" Victor asks.

"Through others I have, but not on my own," replies Bill.

"Yes. Well then, you must know that the spot price for gold is for pure gold. 99.99% pure," Victor starts.

Bill nods. Victor continues.

"And gold such as this, placer gold, usually has a percentage of silver in with it, and other impurities. And, though this is clearly very fine gold, there will be some small percentage of impurity." Victor leans back in his chair, and opens out his hands as he is explaining. "If you have very large amounts of gold, it is best to sell it to a refiner, who, through the refining process will pay you for the full amount of pure gold, and also for the silver." Holding up his hands Victor adds, "Less five, and as much as eight percent for the refining costs."

Victor nods toward Bill with his eyebrows raised, looking for confirmation that Bill is understanding all that he has said so far.

"I'm with you," says Bill, gently nodding in agreement.

Victor continues.

"Now an amount like this is too small to batch through and get an accurate assay of its content. For small amounts, we typically pay eighty percent for the weight of the gold. This covers for the level of impurities, the cost of refining, and our handling costs. If the gold has visible impurities, then we discount from there." Victor pauses for just a moment. "Now here, we have an amount of gold where five, maybe ten percent of its value is starting to add up. So one option is that, for a fee of $400, we can do a chemical and spectrometer analysis that will give us a ninety-five percent to a Certified Assay." Victor sweeps his open hand across to the counter behind him which has an array of equipment. "We are licenced and have the equipment to do this. Then we can pay up to ninety percent on the value of the gold. Again, the remaining ten percent covers our handling and the cost of refining."

Victor waits for some response from Bill. Bill gives a slow nod to confirm he is following.

"The jewellery gold is different," Victor adds after a few moments.

"How so?" asks Bill.

"Well, again," Victor starts, "we have to establish the gold content of the individual nuggets. We will pay ninety-five percent of the assayed value, allowing for error and disagreement with other assays. We can only declare ninety-five percent certainty. But then we will provide detailed photographs of the pieces and post them on an international site that can be viewed by buyers and jewellers around the world. We will set an asking price that we feel will reflect its value as a piece for jewellery and buyers are free to bid against, or pay the asking price. There are, periodically, auctions where jewellery pieces are bid on by many buyers. What we will do then is take a commission of forty percent of the sale price above the value of the gold."

Victor is amused at the complexity of his own business and smiles apologetically. He loves his business and its complexities.

"Or," Victor adds, "we can make you an offer ourselves for the jewellery pieces, and if we agree on a price, then that is that."

There is a pause as Victor gives Bill time to consider the many options.

"Is there any part I can clarify for you Mr. Platten?" Victor asks.

Bill is wishing for a cigarette, but there is no ashtray visible. Usually a sure sign no one wants you smoking.

"Well," says Bill as he considers. "I can see it is worth my while to pay for the assay. And the nuggets, well you make me an offer for them. And how long will all this take?"

"Are you local?" asks Victor.

"No. I am from Samara Beach. Nicola peninsula," Bill adds. "Pacific side."

"Oh Samara! Yes, I am familiar with the area," says Victor. "I have friends with property close to there. Very nice area. Beautiful beaches. Samara Beach is beautiful."

"Yes." Bill smiles as he agrees. "We are staying here with friends, so I would like to conclude things as quickly as I can."

Victor considers for a few moments, looking pensive.

"Tomorrow at noon. How would that work?" he replies. "I will have a certified appraisal, one for the gold and one for the jewellery pieces. And I must add that the smaller nuggets do not have a high jewellery value, but some additional value nonetheless."

"Are we dealing cash?" asks Bill bluntly.

Victor draws out a "Yes, we can deal with cash. But that is a lot of cash Mr. Platten. Most certainly a cheque would be safer. We can have the cheque certified for you as an International Bank Draft if you like."

Bill considers for a moment and adds, "you are probably right. So all of this can be taken care of tomorrow?"

"Yes Mr. Platten. It will probably take another hour to do the banking transaction after you review our valuations."

Bill thought to himself that he was sure they would be doing business together so he might as well ask to have the Bank Draft ready for when he arrived. Then he thought, too much trust. Too much risk of them compromising their appraisal.

"I'll see you tomorrow at noon."

Bill, coming out of his meeting with Victor, only now notices the soft flute pipe music of the Andes. Zamfir-type music. And a spicy aroma. Aromatherapy.

Three ladies, maybe short of being seniors by a few years, are being waited on by the two clerks at a big display case. Bill hears the tone, cadence, and presentation of the sales professionals. Well trained. Well skilled. Victor does love his work. He employs only the best.

Bill thanks the security guard as he is let out the secured front doors and stands for a moment, looking both ways up and down the street and sidewalk as he goes through the automatic motions of lighting up a cigarette. He pulls in deeply, turns, and carries on.

The box of the big white Mercedes has four white poly water tanks, rectangular in shape, and six 55- gallon drums with clamp-down lids, also in white poly. There are 12-foot lengths of one-inch stainless tubing, a tube bender, and a box of odds and ends you might think a plumber would carry. The traffic in the city is heavy. It is always heavy. Twenty-four hours a day. The highway and infrastructure of San Jose is taxed to its limits of use. Everything is trying to keep up with the pace of economic growth, including the traffic. As a pedestrian, you take your life in your hands crossing a street. And don't step off a curb in this city. Traffic has the right of way, or at least presumes so, and you would easily get run over. There are angel-like halos painted on the road every here and there.

"Are those halos?" asks Saul.

We all snicker.

"Yeah they're halos all right," I reply. "It's to mark where someone has been killed in an accident, or got run over and killed."

Saul is sitting up as tall as he can, looking up and out over the front engine hood of the truck.

"There's another one," he says, and a moment later, "And another one."

"Yeah. Those are kids who didn't listen to their mothers," throws in Mom.

Bill laughs. I give my Mom a sideways look. I don't think it is funny. Saul is watching for more.

Bill slows down and turns up a ramp off the highway into a big new shopping centre. He pulls in to park past a double row of parked cars, and takes up two parking spaces wide and two deep.

Parked, Saul and I run up ahead toward the supermarket. Bill pulls out his wallet and hands his daughter two $50 bills.

"You should be able to get Derrick a good fishing rod for this," says Bill. "He deserves it for the help he's been up on the river. A school year present."

His daughter smiles. He is reminded of his wife when she was younger.

"No Dad. You do it," she says. "It's from you. And, if you would, take Saul with you and get him something just so he doesn't feel left out. You know."

"Then those are for you," says Bill.

With his wallet still out Bill pulls out the bank draft from the jewellers and hands it to Mom to look at. She studies it for a few seconds and lets out with a burst of laughter.

"Dad! That's fantastic!"

She spins in a circle with the cheque held out in front of her.

"You did that in one weekend? I don't believe it. $18,386!"

Mom spins in a circle again.

"Ssshhh!" says Bill with his index finger up in front of his lips in a full faced grin. There is an intensity to his eyes.

Bill takes the bank draft back and puts it in his wallet.

"The price of gold was a little higher than I thought. It was the jewellery valuation. I didn't know much about it, though I have heard you can get twice the price of gold for really good stuff."

Mom puts her arm around her fathers and does a little skip as they go through the doors of the mall. It is nicely air conditioned.

CHAPTER FIVE

Eduardo Morales is the police corporal in charge of the detachment at Samara. There is a sergeant north of here, in the larger town of Nicoya. The police station here in Samara is at the bottom of the main paved road that leads right down to the beach, on the right-hand side. It is a small, stucco-over-cement block building with a covered porch area for shade, a front office just through the door with a desk, an overhead fan, a bathroom, and a small interview room that shares the same wall as the bathroom. There is a partition wall inside that runs parallel to the beach, perpendicular from the main road. It is structural and sturdy. It has two metal doors that open outward and can be latched open or closed. These doors have a considerable lock system that includes a turnkey assembly that uses something like what you would imagine is the size of a jailer's key, and a 2x8-inch bar that can be lowered to mesh into a large steel bracket on the far side of the opening to barricade the two doors from opening, short of being hit by a truck. These two doors are latched open today to let in some light and let the breeze blow through the barred windows of the double cell-block inside. There is not a lot of light because of the small-sized windows, and not a lot of breeze. But for more light, and more breeze, keeping open all available doors and windows is good.

On the front porch are four chairs of sturdy wooden construction, built to withstand the stress of men leaning them back day in and day out, against the wall of the detachment office. The heavy corrugated galvanized steel roof overhead provides shade. It is half rusted from being so close to the beach and the salt air. On the beach side is a concrete pad, which is totally fenced over with chain-link fence. There is a door from the end of the cell block that opens in to this space, so that prisoners can exercise or get some sun. The corporal uses this area to kennel a visiting police dog, a German shepherd. The dog man is also a corporal, who travels from detachment to detachment in the region. Their home base is in Nicoya, 60 miles north. The dog man and his shepherd have helped to capture their current suspect, now inside with the detachment corporal.

Of the four porch chairs under the veranda, three are occupied - two by the young constables from Samara and the third by the dog man. There is a small convenience store right next to the police detachment. And it is small. Also, it has never been robbed. The two constables and the dog man each sip on a Coke. They are leaning back on their chairs, watching the people and tourists go by, to and from, and up and down the beach. Their police vehicles are parked off to each side in the sun, two pick-ups and two SUVs for the corporals. There is small talk.

Inside the detachment, the Samara corporal is questioning a young man of about twenty-five years old. He is sitting straight up in the chair in front of the corporal's desk with his cuffed hands sitting squarely on his lap. He is trying to be cool, but it is easy to sweat in Samara at noon.

"You are not denying that you broke in to the Hyundai and stole the cooler, pack sack, and what else?" asked Eduardo with his eyes brows raised, and his brow up, waiting for a response.

He liked to ask questions that included an implied agreement of guilt. It was something he could build on, or backtrack to in his questioning. It was his style.

His prisoner sat motionless, seriously facing him, his eyes wide and looking straight back at Eduardo. He revealed nothing in his look or expression. In this circumstance, it was his - Manuel Ramirez' - his style.

"No," Manuel replied simply.

"And in your vehicle, you were also in possession of stolen property. I am sure you do not carry that many coolers, backpacks, a camera, and a laptop computer to the beach," said Eduardo.

"No," Manuel replied as simply again.

"Do you know how many car thefts we face each year here along the beaches?" challenged Eduardo. "Hundreds," he added, not waiting for a reply. "Hundreds! It is guys like you that ruin our good tourist industry, and keep me busy trying to keep up with complaints, not letting me focus my time and effort on more serious crime."

Manuel maintained his profile and nodded as taking the corporals point seriously.

"So who do you sell your stuff to? A fence? A dealer?"

"I don't sell my stuff," replied Manuel. "I trade it."

"And, with whom do you trade it?"

"Friends," replied Manuel again.

"Some friends," says Eduardo, with a grunt showing his disgust. "And you will tell me the names of your friends?" now adding an exaggerated dumb look.

Manuel continues to look straight at him.

"Well I have a problem here Manuel," again starts Eduardo. "I have you, damaging vehicles. You, damaging our economy. You, with stolen property. You, giving our town and our people a bad name. You, giving the police a bad name because I don't protect them better. And you, keeping me from directing my efforts at fighting more serious crime and making a good name for myself!"

Eduardo pauses, considering his many options.

"So how are you going to help me with my problem? He pauses again then adds, "Manuel?"

The expectation is clearly on Manuel for some reply.

"Well maybe I can help you fight more serious crime!" Manuel bursts out.

Eduardo leans back in his chair, somewhat surprised, exaggerating his gesture for effect, and smiles with something of an impish grin.

"Well tell me," he directs Manuel.

"It's a long story," says Manuel.

"I am sure you can tell me in one minute or less," replies Eduardo. There is only a brief pause.

"My sister," starts Manuel. "I can phone her collect in San Jose. She has a good job there. She tells me to call her every week. Sometimes I do. Yesterday, she tells me she is going out with some new boyfriend, some older guy who is a security guard for a fancy jewellery store. She says her boyfriend told her some guy from here in Samara came in and sold them $20,000 worth of gold. $20,000! Now that sounds like bigger crime to me! Where does he get $20,000 worth of gold? And my sister tells me I should look into getting in to a business like that! Some business I tell her. Doesn't sound legal to me. You?"

Manuel challenges Eduardo. "You have to work how many years to get that kind of money?"

Manuel is relieved to get this off his chest. He is glad to be able to point a finger at someone else and take the attention away from himself.

Eduardo is listening. After a pause he asks, "So where does this gold come from? What kind of gold does he have?"

"I don't know," replies Manuel. He is talking freely now. "She didn't tell me."

Eduardo pauses for a few moments, thinking. Some noisy vehicle is pulling up from the beach and there are a few shouts back and forth between his constables and the vehicles occupants. They sound like they know one another.

"So what does this man look like? What is his name?" asks Eduardo. He hardly ever asks just one question.

"She didn't say his name. Some tall American guy. Older, with a grey ponytail. And a big white Mercedes truck. I have seen it here. You probably have too."

Eduardo sits for half a minute, thinking. Manuel has gone quiet and is staring at Eduardo expectantly.

Eduardo stands and walks around to Manuel.

"It is lunch time, and I will get something to eat. We will talk when I get back, about your future."

Eduardo assists Manuel over to the cells where a door is open and he unlocks and removes the handcuffs before he closes the door.

"Just sit for bit and I'll be back," says Eduardo. "Think about your future."

It's been the best part of an hour when Eduardo walks back into the detachment office, and one of his constables is sitting at his desk reading a newspaper. He quickly picks up his paper and folds it over under his arm and crosses to the front of the desk. He tells Eduardo that the dog man has left for his detachment in Nicoya, and the other constable has gone up to the highway for an hour on traffic duty.

"I know just where he will be parked," quips Eduardo. "Right on the crest of the hill to Carrillo."

They both give a chuckle of recognition. They both know the spot well. It is on the highway south to Carrillo, a good stand of trees and a pullout where travellers stop to look out at the view of the coastline and the bay into Carrillo. It is not the best spot to ticket speeders, but it does have a good view, good breezes, and good shade.

Eduardo bids his constable to come out to the front porch where they have a small conference out of earshot of their prisoner.

Eduardo comes back in after a few minutes and goes directly into the cell block and addresses Manuel.

"Well have you had time to consider your future?"

Manuel is back to his profile of not responding unless it is necessary.

"Manuel!" Eduardo says more loudly, ratcheting up the intensity of his approach. "When I ask you a question I expect a reply!"

Manuel immediately becomes compliant under this authority and stands to face Eduardo.

"Yes sir. I am only thinking too serious about my future." For a moment Manuel fumbles for his words, but is looking straight at Eduardo showing his respect and that he is taking Eduardo seriously.

"I am being less than a man, and I know I have let my behaviour go bad. But sir, I promise you I want to be a better man. I can do better. Can I come and report to you every week and tell you of the things I am doing better?"

Manuel's face gets a distressed look, and he continues.

"Sir, my sister will be so ashamed of me." He pauses. "Sir, I need you to give me a break. I will not let you down."

It is now Eduardo who is not revealing more than he needs to in his exchange with Manuel. Eduardo looks down to the floor and takes a couple steps towards the way to the cell and snaps his head up to again face Manuel.

"To be a better man are you ready to help me fight bigger crime?" asks Eduardo, now looking expectantly at Manuel.

Somehow there appears to be only one correct answer.

"Sir, I will do all that I can to help you. What is it that you think I can do for you?"

They stare eye to eye for a moment and Eduardo turns and walks over to his desk, pulls open the top right-hand drawer, and pulls up what is obviously the cell key. He returns and opens the cell door.

"Let's go for a ride," says Eduardo as he holds out one hand and places an open handcuff on Manuel's right wrist and closes it, not too tightly.

Getting Manuel into the open Jeep, Eduardo closes the open side of the handcuff onto the brace for the roll bar that has been welded into the frame and cab of the Jeep. He goes to the driver's side, gets in, backs out, and pulls away slowly from the detachment building.

"What I need you to do for me, Manuel, is not that difficult. But I need you to do it exactly as I say. Are you ready to do what I ask?"

Manuel nods. Eduardo continues.

"What I need you to do is in cooperation with the law, but nonetheless illegal. It is no more or no less than what you already do. I need you to break into a house. Make it look like you are there to find something or steal something. Nothing more. Gold, let's say. Or a map. Or jewellery. But you have to make your presence known. Make some noise. Make a mess. Pull down a bookshelf onto the floor. If someone comes I will honk two beeps on my horn like this."

Eduardo is slowly driving up and down each street progressively away from the police detachment as he turns another corner and honks his horn with two quick beeps and waves a small acknowledgement at a business owner sweeping the sidewalk in front of his store. He continues his instructions to Manuel.

"Steal some money if there is some, but it is not necessary to steal anything. Maybe it is best to steal nothing as you are now going to be a better person. I will be close by and watching you. When I honk like I did, you run out the door and run away as fast as you can. Run down the beach away from town. That would be the best. I will chase you but I will not try to catch you. Keep running and don't stop. Manuel, you keep running and don't stop. And don't come back to Samara. Is that clear?"

Manuel is looking bewildered.

"So you want me to do a break-in to a house, to look like I am stealing something and then try to almost get caught?" Manuel asks, still looking bewildered.

"Yes. That is correct," says Eduardo with a nod. "Do you have any problems with that?"

"So how am I helping you fight bigger crime?" asks Manuel. "Doing this," he adds.

Eduardo looks around at people on the street and turns up another corner heading back up towards the highway. He is questioning himself in his thoughts. There is no good reason to say more, no good reason to justify his plan. The less Manuel knows, the better. The less chance he can open his mouth and implicate him in any way in the future.

Eduardo sees that Manuel is acting uncomfortable. He decides to leave it like this. This is to his advantage. It drags on another thirty seconds or so. The discomfort seems longer to Manuel.

"So how do I get my car back?" asks Manuel.

Eduardo faces Manuel with a thin smile, an acknowledgement. The deal is done.

"Let's go get your car now and leave it in Carrillo. Then we will come back. Screw up my plan and you will have no car by the time you make it to Carrillo. Manuel! This is your big chance." Eduardo pauses then adds, "Deal?"

CHAPTER SIX

The ocean is quiet as the tide is heading out. The water is out a hundred yards from the palm trees where Phyllis is laying back in one of the big wooden recliners that they have set out for hotel guests in the shady areas. There is a nice breeze at this time of day coming in off the water. It is 4:30pm. A couple of young boys have started fishing. Having waded out into the surf up to their waists, they whirl weighted lines over their heads and cast out as far as they can throw. They use a weight, hook, and bait, and cast out, letting the line strip off a spool that is fixed on a stick handle. They retrieve their hooks by simply hand winding the line back onto the spool. There will be another ten or twelve men join them as the sun gets closer to setting. All are here hoping to catch dinner. The pelicans diving in to the water just out front of the two boys indicate that there are fish here. That is why they have all picked this spot.

Phyllis has done her work for the day and, in the last half hour that she has been relaxing here, the sun now finds her under the shade of the palm trees as it approaches the western horizon. She has had her book and a good moment to relax. She thinks of the part case of Smirnoff Ice she has in her refrigerator. Cold. It is Saturday. Bill, Jess, and the boys have been away four days now and should be home soon. Time to get up and make plans for dinner. Anticipating all the noise makes her stiffen for just a moment.

The hotel has been quiet, with only three units rented out. But there is a family spread out across their patio area in front of their unit. The mom, dad, and two girls have left towels hanging over chairs and water toys in the pool. The girls look to be maybe six and eight years old. They are local tourists from San Jose. They prefer the pool over the ocean.

Over the laughing and splashing, and calls for dad or mom to "watch this!" they wave at Phyllis walking by to her house. She smiles and waves back. Phyllis has a most pleasant smile.

She walks around the side of the last hotel suite on the side-walk out to the semi-circled parking lot that only has one minivan parked in it. Their own Jeep is parked in front of their porch and patio area. Their residence is a stand alone, single story bungalow that is only spitting distance from the rear of the hotel units.

Climbing the three steps up on to their porch area approach-ing the door, Phyllis is surprised to see the front door open. She didn't remember leaving it that way. A moment of ques-tioning. There seems to be some ruckus and motion coming from inside.

For Phyllis, recognition of what is happening comes into her consciousness like it was in slow motion. She finds it hard to believe what is happening! It's like it is happening to some-body else. Phyllis never does recall the two short horn blasts from a vehicle up the street.

Reaching the doorway, Phyllis is almost bowled over as a man, at least her own size, charges through the wooden framed screen door, partly crashing into her, frantically running past her, down the same way that she has come from - the beach.

Phyllis regains her balance with shock and surprise written all over her face. Distress. She doesn't try to pursue her assailant but pulls open the screen door and half steps inside. It is a mess. Drawers have been pulled out and dumped out on the floor, cupboard doors left open. There are cushions and books on the floor. She walks in a few more steps only to see more of the same, then she turns around and walks back out onto the porch. Realization slowly dawns on her. She has been robbed!

Consciously taking a full breath, Phyllis tries to re-orientate herself to what is happening. Her speed of recognition is picking up but she is still bewildered and in slow motion when she sees a police Jeep slowly approaching down her front street. She stands tall on the edge of her porch and waves her hands over her head to get his attention.

"Hey!" she hollers out, still waving.

The police vehicle lurches forward as its driver steps on the gas and speeds in from less than a hundred yards away. He skids to a stop in front of the porch area where Phyllis is standing.

As the Corporal scrambles out of his Jeep, Phyllis runs down the few steps right up to him. Her face is flushed.

"I've just been robbed!" Phyllis blurts out. "He just ran around the corner!" she points.

"What did he look like?" the Corporal asks catching the seriousness of the moment.

"He's my height, young, lanky, short black hair, and a thin black beard. He was just heading down towards the beach!" exclaims Phyllis pointing.

The Corporal bolts around the corner, and, as he encounters the family in the pool area he slows a little and just points down the pathways to the beach. They point the same direction. He bolts again full speed.

The Corporal runs down onto the beach far enough that he can see Manuel running midway down the beach where the sand is hard from the ebbing tide. He is making good speed a hundred and fifty yards ahead of him. The Corporal pulls out his semi automatic, hollers "Stop! Police!" and fires three shots at Manuel.

Manuel hears two separate bullets going by. Not that close but close enough!

Manuel runs faster than ever and heads up to the cover of the brush along this undeveloped area of the beach.

"That guy is crazy!" he says out loud to himself. He runs as fast as he can.

Manuel looks back over his shoulder and sees he is not being pursued. He knows he needs to get to his car and get away from here as fast as he can. He can't trust this guy!

Phyllis is excitedly relaying the events to her guests at the pool area. Though Phyllis is upset, she is trying to act calm, as to not overly alarm her guests. Eduardo emerges back through the palm trees up from the beach.

"Are you okay Ma'am?" he asks Phyllis, and dropping his head slightly, "Are you hurt?"

"No, I'm okay," assures Phyllis.

"Are you all okay?" asks Eduardo of the group.

They all indicate they are okay.

"You didn't shoot him, did you?" asks Phyllis with a look of disbelief.

"No Ma'am. He was too far away. I just fired a warning shot to see if he would stop."

Eduardo makes eye contact with each of the adults in search of recognition for his efforts.

"Then let me set up some patrols and get my men working on this. I will come back in half an hour and get more information from you," states Eduardo authoritatively. "Do you need any help?" he adds.

"No. No," replies Phyllis. "My husband should be home anytime now. Go do what you can. I'll try and clean up and see what is missing."

"Did you see him carrying anything?" asks Eduardo.

"No, nothing. He was pretty intent on getting away."

"Now you said he was your height. Five nine? Five ten?" asks Eduardo. "Short black hair? Unshaven? Slim build? Costa Rican?"

"Yes. Yes," replies Phyllis.

"And, what was he wearing?"

"Tan shorts." Phyllis shakes her head a bit trying to put together the fragments of her memory.

"Knee length," Phyllis adds. "A shirt. A regular shirt."

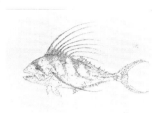

We are all glad to make it home. It is not late, but later than they had expected. We are hungry. When Bill travels, he does not like to stop any more than he needs to. There had been some tie-ups that stopped traffic for over an hour on the way over to the Nicola Peninsula. There is only one highway. Now here in Samara, it is dark around 6pm. Here near the equator, year round. Turning down off the highway to our street, a right, and then a left, we all see the red and blue flashing lights of the police vehicle at the end of their road.

It is at the hotel!

"What on earth is going on?" exclaims Bill.

"Dad!" says Mom with some alarm. "What is happening?"

Bill steps on it and accelerates. In these next few moments he only hears muted sounds from Saul and I.

He pulls the big Mercedes right up beside the police Jeep. He climbs down and steps up onto the porch as Grandma comes out the front door onto the porch. She heard us coming. She grabs Bill with an embrace.

"Bill," is all she says.

Bill is taller and can see over Grandma, into their lighted house. He sees the Corporal sitting with his note pad and folder at the edge of the table. He holds onto Gram. She needs his strength, his assurance.

"So what happened?" asks Bill after a few moments.

"We had an intruder. We've been robbed," Grandma tells him quite calmly, resigned to this reality.

"You're okay?" asks Bill, holding Grandma's face up to him in his hands.

Grandma closes her eyes for a second, as though all the events have raced through her head once more. She speaks as she opens her gaze to Bill.

"I'm fine. It's all fine. It is probably not as bad as it looks," reassures Grandma.

Mom stands a few feet away, her bottom lip trembling. Grandma turns to her and gives her a big hug and more reassurances. I'm looking around, surveying the scene. Cautious. The red and blue lights are flashing across our faces. Saul has already gone into the house. We all follow.

"Mr. Platten," says Eduardo, standing up from his note pad at the table as he greets Bill.

He extends his hand.

"Corporal Morales," says Eduardo, introducing himself.

"Yeah. Just call me Bill."

They shake hands.

Bill is not pleasant with his greeting. He looks disgusted with the whole situation.

"Well nothing appears to be missing," declares Eduardo. "And Mrs. Platten has given us a reasonable description of who she saw." He pauses. "And, by experience, it may take you a day or two to realize what is missing."

Bill looks around the kitchen, dining area, and family room. Grandma had been picking up and is placing items back where they belong, looking in drawers and cupboards to see if she can tell what is missing.

Grandma pulls out a grey metal cash box from the small desk by the telephone and places it open on the desk for all to see.

"Everything is there," she declares, picking up a small handful of U.S. and Costa Rican bills. She raises her brow and shrugs, closes the cash box and returns it to the drawer.

Eduardo stands and closes the cover to a clip board with his notes. He looks like he is ready to leave.

"Nothing stolen," he remarks, almost as though talking to himself. "Well. Maybe you will notice something in the next day or two. I will drop by."

"If you notice anything unusual please call us," continues Eduardo. "Best to keep your doors locked. And, of course, if you see anyone?" Eduardo's voice drops off leaving the sentence unfinished, directing this last comment to Grandma.

Bill is looking twice as disgusted as before as Eduardo heads towards the door.

"If he comes back, I will call you to tell you, you have a dead Costa Rican on your hands!" says Bill angrily.

Eduardo turns to face back at Bill.

"I understand you are angry," Eduardo says sympathetically. "It is natural."

He turns back toward the door and excuses himself.

"And I will increase our patrols of the area."

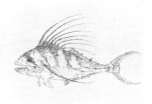

Eduardo gets in his Jeep and turns off the rotating red and blue beacon lights, returning the street to normal. He starts his Jeep and pulls away. He is pleased with himself. He has accomplished what he has wanted to do. He now has reason, good reason, to keep an eye on Bill's coming and going. And even stop to ask questions from time to time if it suits his purpose. He knows that Manuel will not be seen around here again. He knows that Bill will have more plans, with time, for more gold. More gold. Something to maybe confiscate if it has not been acquired legally. Maybe something to liberate if the opportunity arises. It takes Eduardo years to make $20,000.

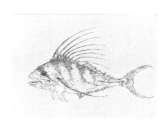

The street is back to normal. It is late. The house has settled. Everyone is in bed. Bill is sitting on the porch step, in the dark. One dog is barking a few blocks away. Even further away, a truck gears down on the highway as it climbs the hill south to Carrillo. Bill's cigarette glows redder as he draws on it, sitting alone in the dark.

CHAPTER SEVEN

I am still trying to understand how everything happened the way it did. I think I have a sense for some of what Bill was feeling, what Bill was dealing with.

I can only understand myself so much, never mind another, like my grandfather. I was having difficulties getting along with my grandfather. He would walk right over me sometimes, like I wasn't there.

I'm not good with this. This is not good. I am trying to get along with this man.

What do I need to do?

I was trying to understand then, and as each year has passed I have realized that there is more to understand. Understanding evolves.

So, coming to this understanding seems to be something I need to do, but something I feel I need to be careful about. And, truly, we never 'understand' anyone totally, yet we can approach understanding. We learn to understand people, acknowledging that it is an acquired skill, a learned behaviour, so that, as with any other acquired skill, some are better at it than others. And when it comes to understanding people, we are better at understanding some people better than others.

You see, I have my doubts. I doubt myself. This is all difficult to talk about. I know I understand a lot, but not everything. I don't understand everything that I faced, never mind what Bill faced.

I understand that it is a learning process. There are many things I do not know. I have run all this through my head a thousand times, over and over again.

But there are many things that I do know.

What I have come to understand, where I can now look back, is that people we were raised with, our relatives, we might never have chosen to associate with, had we only met them later in life. Especially if they were not relatives. Think about it.

Maybe I was too trusting. Maybe my mom was too trusting. We certainly needed my grandparents' support after my father died. But there are things here that are not clear, things I guess I do not understand.

So I keep asking myself: How much do I understand Bill?

There are a lot of things to consider.

This is what I've been able to put together from bits and pieces that I heard over the years. It was just after Kennedy's assassination that Bill's father had given Bill the strongest directive ever. Bill's dad was doing his best to guide his son from his own life experience. And that experience included a career military background spanning World War II, Korea, and many years after doing various smaller missions. He had been away for several years of Bill's early childhood as he came and went with new assignments and postings across the country during the more active part of his career. Bill was raised as any middle class kid living in Seattle through the 1950's and 1960's with a military dad who was home some of the time.

Bill's father had been places and had done things that needed to be done. He was not a glory seeking veteran, nor a crying-in-your-beer veteran either. He kept putting his life back together. That was Bill's dad. And all of this was a part of Bill. Putting things back together that maybe did not work out quite right.

But after watching Kennedy's funeral on T.V., Bill's dad sat for days and days watching media events of Kennedy, the assassination, Oswald, Ruby. He got quieter and quieter and would shake his head slowly. Bill says he would say, "You don't believe all this crap they are telling you do you? It is just all too contrived." Bill's dad got gloomier with every new twist the media presented.

Late one evening, coming in from an evening with friends, Bill finds his dad sitting alone in the dark in the living room, smoking a cigarette.

"Bill," he started, really seriously. "There hasn't been much that I have told you to do or not do. But now I am going to tell you two things."

"One: I will not allow you to be a policeman."

"And two: I will not allow you to serve in the military."

"I do not believe in the society we live in. Its values, its corruption, who is running things, or what the media tries to cram down our throats. Are you listening to me? This country is not worth dying for!"

Bill has spoken of this moment. Bill has said that he thought his dad was as sober as a judge that night. Bill knew some of the turmoil that his dad seemed to be going through. Everyone was feeling some of it after Kennedy's assassination. There was certainly a feeling of betrayal, uncertainty, and violation. Bill's dad was feeling all this. He had become disenchanted with much he had believed in, much of what he had devoted the struggle of his life towards. It was way more than broken dreams, more than a crisis of values. He felt betrayed. It was as if the milk had gone sour. For him, there was no going back. He resigned himself to a life that was less than he ever imagined it before, in a country that was less than he ever imagined it before.

Was Bill listening? I think he was. When he speaks of his dad telling him this, he always maintains a certain reverence for the moment. Though I have never heard him say it, I wonder now if Bill wished he had taken this advice more seriously. What would it have taken?

It takes time to listen.
It takes time to hear.
It takes time to understand.

Then came the Vietnam War. It was one of the most complex of wars for people of Bill's generation to decide what to do. What was right? Serve your country? Bill was certainly exposed to movements to oppose the war on campus, at the University of Seattle. He had been part of several events. Bill had been reluctant to get too involved with the anti-war protests, but was also reluctant to go along with the established thinking that if you are called, you go. And then, how much choice did you actually have?

Nothing was clear. There was as much argument for, as there was against, at the time. It depended on who you listened to. Those were the days. Friends that Bill grew up with, some were for, some were against. Some were going, some were talking of leaving and going to Canada. Those were the days.

Everyone keeps telling us as we grow up that we are going to have to make choices. Well we do. And, from where I see it, it seems that we have to make choices that direct the course of our lives much earlier that we realize. I believe we are making serious choices much earlier than we understand.

And I hope to impress this on any children I may have.

So, a thousand, thousand choices have been made, shaping what we are like and who we are. We all are making them. Yet we are only aware of some of the decisions as we make them. The rest we don't even notice. Most of our choices are just embedded in what we call a day, as each one goes by. But they are choices made.

So this was a key time in my grandfather's life, if I try to understand. He was making big choices.

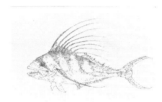

Bill, now in university, taking Anthropology, meets my grandmother.

Phyllis was a beauty. My grandmother was - is still - a beauty. It is a moment I have never talked about, when and where I noticed her picture on the mantle in their dining room. They had three framed pictures of themselves, and others of my mom as a baby, and growing up. There was one of me of my first birthday, with my dad and mom. And one of my dad and mom's wedding.

Of the three pictures of themselves, one was of Bill in uniform before going to Vietnam, one of Grandma with her cap and gown at her convocation at the University of Seattle, and one of Bill and Grandma together in the university days.

And as much as we like to see ourselves in pictures, I realized to the point of astonishment, in these pictures, that Phyllis, my grandmother, was beautiful. It is interesting that it just hit me like a bolt out of the blue. I had to go back and have a second look. And it was very clear. I have noted this many times since. Phyllis, my grandmother, in her university years, was beautiful. I think I should tell my grandmother that I have noticed how beautiful her pictures are, and I think she might take note that I said so.

My mother is pretty and very nice looking. She has an easy and pleasant face with more features of her mother than her father. I am glad for her. Somehow, mothers always extract from you some acknowledgement that they were, and are, pretty. I remember my dad being so proud of my mother. Proud does not cover it. He was pleased with my mom. He liked her. A lot. It showed.

Bill and Grandma were going out together in University.

I have had moments when I watch their interaction, and at times their difficult exchanges, and I wonder. I wonder how Bill was able to court this girl and hold her attention, including being away two years in Vietnam. I wonder about it. All I can come up with is that Bill must have had his special charming ways as a young man. He doesn't strike me as though he was overly handsome, though the moles and blemishes on his face were not as prominent then. They have always struck me as something less than attractive for all the years I have known him.

And I guess I would only be being honest to say that I have seen him be considerably persuasive at times, sometimes even what could be charming, towards Grandma. He has his ways, when he chooses to.

Phyllis' family were Howards. That was Grandma's maiden name.

They were Baptists and stronger hearted than most when it came to the war, both the last and this one. Their family was not a career military family, but a family with a strong sense of patriotism, and an ability to openly talk about values. They held it true. They believed what this country stood for, and they believed in what they did. Their family had a strong presence. They did well at all they believed.

Now, lets look back at Bill. Give it a minute's thought.

Bill's father, a career veteran, told him this country was not worth dying for.

Bill enlisted. Bill went to Vietnam.

The only way I can figure it is that Bill wanted to win Grandma, and win her family. And that included earning their respect by "doing his duty" and serving his country. Grandma, for Bill, was worth the risk - worth dying for.

Bill went. Bill survived. Bill came home undamaged for the most part. Bill had a thousand reasons to come home well. Nine hundred and ninety-nine had to do with the love of his life.

Other guys in 'Nam had the same reasons to come home. Some didn't come home. Most did. Some did not come home whole.

As any man in a conflict will tell you, they were different people then. Bill was different and wanted to be. And he said so. He didn't volunteer for extra duties. He kept his head. He didn't get into the crazy drug haze. He learned to trust his instincts.

He killed. He said that too. He said little. That he had helped men, helped wounded men, across where they dared not go, to the hope of an unknown site, an evacuation, a more defensible spot, maybe just a little safer place. He had carried men who lived, and he had carried men who had died in his arms. He had carried that weight.

I believe these choices, these events, have played a major part in shaping the rest of Bill's life. And I keep asking myself: Did Bill listen to his father's advice?

I'd say Bill did take his father's advice, maybe a few years later than he might do again, given another chance. Bill is an ex-patriot.

So with each decision made, everything seems to become yet more complex.

Here in Costa Rica, Bill depends more exclusively on his own skills to care for himself and his family. There is not that sense of community, lifelong friends, and family support like back in Seattle.

But, in cutting yourself off from broader social context and values of your family and established friends, you can also become more extreme in your own thinking, and more off-balanced. There is no one there to tell you they think you might be wrong, or that they disagree with you. There is nobody to kick the wheels straight for you. Sometimes it is only people that are really close to you who can get through to you when you need some serious advice.

Now, as I get older, I may get to know more details, get to understand more about Bill and Grandma's life together, and what must have been the so many reasons why they moved from Seattle and the U.S. There must have been so many things that were considered. Again, so many choices made.

Bill is a good man and has been a good father to my mom, Jessica. He has been a good husband to my grandmother, to the best I know. Though here you must realize that these are things I believe. Maybe I don't really know. Maybe some day, my grandmother will talk to me more of such things. I know their relationship is not perfect, but tons are revealed in how they get along. So I feel that I know some things. They get along well. They seem to like one another.

It has its completeness, and its complexities.

Bill is not perfect. Bill is not always gentle. Bill, I believe, will always be a bit of a wild card.

And it seemed to me that there was an underlying anger inside of Bill, a feeling of disenchantment. He wasn't a naturally happy person. Grandma was more naturally happy with every day. Bill had his longings. I believe he wanted to be a happier person, but things seemed to keep him from it, somehow just out of reach. There were the things that happened, like the crash in property prices which kept him from the dream of fortune to be made in selling his hotel. There were the things that didn't happen, that he had planned. To understand was to see that sometimes Bill seemed to be desperate for a chance, for that break, the chance to make something big, the chance to make one more good thing happen. It wasn't luck he was hoping for. He had certainly worked hard enough, risked enough, been through enough. And somewhere in the expectations Bill held for himself and his life, there, somewhere, were my mom, myself and Saul. Our dependency on him and Grandma was never part of the plan I'm sure.

And, looking back, maybe some of what happened was just all an episode for Bill. That Bill can be better than this. He can be better than what he was. It was maybe like having a bad day, which we all do, except that this was many days. Maybe a time of his life. I don't know. But he could be better.

I am still trying to understand how everything happened the way it did. I think I have a sense for some of what Bill was feeling, what Bill was dealing with.

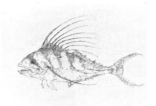

Bill is trusting his instincts. Bill knows there is trouble.

The street is back to normal. It is late. The house has settled. Everyone is in bed. Bill is sitting on the porch step, in the dark. One dog is barking a few blocks away. Even further away, a truck gears down on the highway as it climbs the hill south to Carrillo. Bill's cigarette glows redder as he draws on it, sitting alone in the dark.

CHAPTER EIGHT

Johnny told me that the morning started no different than any other. He was at the hotel at 7:00am to start his day's work: clean out the drains, check the septic system, vacuum the pool, top up the water level, clean out the sand from the outdoor shower basin, weed the flower gardens, prune the poinsettias and cut back the massive bougainvillaea, sweep, and clean up.

Best to get started early to take advantage of the coolness of the morning.

Best to get this work finished before the hotel patrons want to use the pool.

Johnny was spraying out the pool shower basin, down on one knee with the hose full blast, forcing the sand down the drain.

He said that he only saw Bill coming at him from the corner of his eye a second before Bill was on him. He said he didn't even have time to stand up.

Johnny was dressed in khaki coloured shorts to the knee, sandals, and a dark blue T-shirt. He had been told to always wear a shirt when working on site.

Bill was dressed about the same. He came along the edge of the swimming pool and, had you been watching the whole thing, Bill headed directly for Johnny as soon as he saw him. Bill flicks the half-smoked cigarette directly from his mouth with a snap of his arm to the right, and with a matter of a few quick deliberate steps he is over Johnny. Bill is much bigger than Johnny, and grabs him by the back scruff of his T-shirt and yanks him to his feet, actually off his feet, and hauls Johnny around the corner of the last unit of the hotel. It is on the beach side, and still in the shade, palm trees overhead and the poinsettias and decorative shrubs in the flower beds. Bill has Johnny pinned up against the wall, Johnny's feet a foot above the flower bed, Bill pressing Johnny against the wall with his left hand around his jaw and his right hand holding him by the front of the crotch of his shorts. Bill's nose is just about touching Johnny's and Johnny's T-shirt is split open at each shoulder seam from the strain of Bill grabbing him. Johnny is a picture of fear, struggling little, trying to get a breath, his mouth grimaced under Bill's grip, and his eyes wide and intense with fear.

"I thought I told you not to talk about the gold!" 'The gold" is stretched out as Bill says it in a very menacing way.

"I thought I told you not to be talking to anyone." 'Talking to anyone' is stretched out the same way - like strangling the life out of each word.

"But you had to go and shoot off your mouth to your friends. Being a big shot."

Johnny is trying to shake his head in denial, but it looks more like a shudder. Under Bill's grip around his jaw he can't get a word out. Johnny's face is flushed red under Bill's grip. Bill's face is flushed red from fury. Bill is still nose to nose with Johnny and Bill is moving his head from side to side with each word, delivering each word slowly, with such intensity they are like body blows.

"So you shoot your mouth off to your friends and we get broken into. And they were looking for the gold!" The last word of each phrase is stretched out for its intensity and menacing effect.

"So now I have the police down my neck and every rat in the territory thinking I have a stash of gold in my house."

Grandma came around the pool and picked up the hose that was spraying wildly in every direction as it snaked around. She turned off the nozzle and, in the quiet, she could hear the commotion and in a matter of a few steps, she sees Bill has Johnny pinned against the wall.

"You have put my home and family in peril," Bill says with his wife looking on. She has assessed the situation almost instantly. "I ought to wring your neck."

"That's enough Bill!" says Grandma, clearly and deliberately. And in the next moment, she adds again.

"Bill! I said that's enough!" She raised her voice only slightly. "Let him go Bill."

Bill steps back and literally, drops Johnny to the ground. Bill takes in a huge breath and takes another step back. Johnny has not collapsed to the ground but staggers, still on his feet. He looks at Grandma like she was some kind of foreign object, and then like a cat let out of a bag, he scrambles off toward the beach. There is no fight in him, just the urge to flee, to escape.

"And don't come back!" Bill yells after him.

"Bill!" says Grandma. It is not a question; it is not an exclamation. It is exasperation.

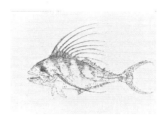

I guess half an hour has passed. I am vacuuming the pool, being told by my mom that I had to help out today, that Johnny wouldn't be in today. I always help out when I can. No big deal. I don't mind doing the pool. But I do let Johnny do the more unpleasant tasks, like checking the septic tank and system, cleaning the solids filter. It is a job I hate.

Mom is in the storage room, piling clean folded sheets on the room cart and checking out her cleaning supplies. Grandma scooted from around the corner into the pool area, then quickly turned and went back. Nothing is said. It seems nobody is very happy here today.

Finishing the pool and double checking for the bad spots to be sure they are clean, I disconnect the attachments and coil up the corrugated hose and hang it by the storage bodega. Mom is just finishing up supplying her cart.

"So what is going on here today?" I ask with an exaggerated display of bewilderment.

Mom looks at me with a mixed expression of frustration and dismay. I've seen it before.

"Dad has had some kind of meltdown with Johnny," Mom pauses. "He's fired him again, and told him not to come back. Again."

I start to ask what this is all about. Johnny is my friend. I am sure my face is showing my reaction.

"It's about the break-in," Mom interjects. "Dad thinks Johnny has blabbed about...." Mom stops without completing the sentence. "Come with me," she says as she nods her head toward the beach. "We shouldn't talk here."

"Well, Johnny hasn't said anything!" I retort.

Mom puts up her index finger between our eye contact. "Wait," she directs.

I shake my head in disbelief as we head around the pool. Several guests are sitting at tables enjoying the peaceful sunny morning, drinking coffee. I control my reaction for the moment.

Mom takes us over the levee of the sandy beach and walks us right down to the waters edge. It is low tide. That makes it another hundred yards. The breeze is picking up. That is good. Nobody's within half a mile of us either way. I scan the surface of the lagoon, searching out the tell-tale fin of a rooster fish. A few pelicans are diving at feed-fish another hundred yards out. A picture of Johnny and I fishing here on the beach runs through my head.

At the water's edge, mom stops and holds out her hands from her sides. She looks uncertain about what to say.

"Dad thinks that Johnny has bragged to his friends about the amount of gold you found. He thinks that because of this, word has spread and that a friend of Johnny's, or a friend of a friend, broke into the house to steal it," she pauses, "or the money. Who knows."

"No way!" I say, shaking my head. "Johnny isn't saying anything. He doesn't even know how much the gold was worth. He knows we found some gold, and that Bill was excited about it, but that's all he knows."

Mom stands there looking at me for a moment.

"Well you know any amount of money like that, gold or money, is a big deal down here. It is dangerous. You could get killed over it. Grandpa's upset about the break-in. He is worried about our safety. You know what he thinks of Costa Ricans."

"But that doesn't make it right though!" I protest. "Johnny isn't saying anything."

"You don't know that for sure Derrick," Mom says as a correction.

"Yeah I do Mom!" looking intently into her eyes. "Bill treats Johnny terribly. He does!" I insist. "Everything that goes wrong is always Johnny's fault. Anything that quits working, any equipment that wears out, it's Johnny's fault. It's not right, Mom."

There is a pause before Mom answers.

"Your grandfather is hard on Johnny," she concedes. "But he will settle down in a few days."

"Or maybe he won't," I throw in.

"Derrick, you don't fight with your grandfather, "she admonishes me. "He may not be perfect but he does care for us all. This isn't an easy place to make a living. Things haven't been easy. We have been our own burden."

"Johnny's my friend Mom. He is a good friend. This just isn't fair."

"Derrick, you can't fight with your grandfather." Mom pauses again, looking for words. "He has tried to be a father to you since your dad died. To you and Saul. He is so good to you. He maybe doesn't do everything right, but he does more than most of it right." Mom pauses again. "I am asking you to stay out of this for a few days and let Dad cool down." Mom looks deliberately to make eye contact. "Can you do that? Will you do that?"

Mom keeps looking into my eyes, waiting for an answer. I feel as uncomfortable as can be. I roll my eyes.

"Yeah, I can do it."

Mom slowly nods her recognition, though guardedly.

"We had better get back," she says.

We start walking.

"I just don't think it's right," I protest once more.

Mom puts her arm around me and pulls me in close. She gives me hug as we are walking.

It takes me by surprise. The tears well up in my eyes uncontrollably. It takes every bit of effort and resolve I have to hang on to the moment. I hope Mom doesn't see. I have to wipe away the tears before they run down my cheeks. I hope she doesn't see.

Dinner is late.

Bill is off balance. Rather than subdued, he is giving each of us directions as to what we are going to have to take care of without Johnny. Bill never mentions that he has fired Johnny, nor does he mention their altercation.

We are still all at the table, though finishing.

"It's your night to help with dishes Derrick," Grandma announces. I think she was sensing that I was ready to get away.

Bill takes Grandma's cue and adds, "and I guess I do not have to remind you Derrick, that we do not talk to others about what goes on in this family. Especially the gold dredging. Or money. Or anything else that's none of their business."

I start to get up, excusing myself from the table, acknowledging my grandfather with a deliberate nod, and a moment of eye contact.

"Just a minute," Bill says. "Just sit down for a minute." to which I drop back down into the chair showing some frustration at being cut off from my escape.

"I don't know if you realize the danger we've been put in. We are all at risk if it gets out that we may be keeping gold or money in this house. It's an easy way to get your throat slit, day or night. Do you know what the average income of a family is down here? Sometimes we have cash here and, until we get it into the bank, it is more than a year's income for most. For some, maybe several years' income. We can't trust these people. And Derrick, you don't trust Johnny either. You may think he's a good friend but he's just another Costa Rican."

"Bill!" warns Grandma, that he may be going too far.

"Well I trust Johnny," I throw in, hoping not to get too big a reaction. "Johnny hasn't told anybody anything."

"Derrick," Mom says slowly, giving me the look, and cautions me with that gaze. It says we made an agreement.

"Well it's obvious we've got trouble," adds Bill in his own defence. "And if it didn't come from Johnny talking, then where did it come from? You?" directing his comment to me.

"Derrick isn't the problem here Bill," Grandma adds, again as a caution to Bill.

"Well who else knows!" Bill throws out. It is not a question.

"I know," pipes in Saul claiming this territory and recognition. "I tell all my friends."

Every one is set back with this outburst. And it takes a moment to sink in.

"What have you told your friends?" Mom asks in a non-threatening manner.

Saul is obviously pleased with the attention.

"I tell them that Grandpa found $100,000 in gold in one weekend," he says proudly.

"You told them what?!" I challenge.

"I tell them that Grandpa found a ton of gold and that we are going to be rich. Real rich!"

Saul is quite pleased with himself.

There is a long pause, everyone staring at Saul. Grandma starts the first comment.

"Well I guess we overlooked the babe in the woods."

"Saul!" says Mom, exasperated.

"Saul," starts Bill. "Have you heard what I've just been saying to Derrick. You can't say things like that down here."

"Bill, they're just kids," adds Grandma.

"Kids or not," Bill continues. "If things get talked about, eventually somebody will hear it who shouldn't. You guys seem to think this is some kind of joke. It's not. Whoever gets the notion that there is something here for the taking, these people will steal it from you. And you could bloody well get killed in the process. These people have tons of contempt for us, and they would slit your throat in a second if you get in their way. I know if anyone of them is ever caught in here, there will be one less Costa Rican."

"Bill, please don't," Grandma admonishes him.

"Saul," adds Bill. "You stick around after dinner. I need to know that you are hearing what I am telling you. You stick around."

"Maybe you fired Johnny too quickly," I throw in, but I don't look up to face anyone. Bill doesn't come back at me over it and everybody goes quiet. After a moment I stand and start picking up dishes around me, then head over to the sink.

Saul has lightened the atmosphere. I think everyone needed some relief to the intensity of the day. Mom goes with her dad to talk with Saul in the living room, and Grandma and I are working on the dishes in the kitchen.

"So how bad was it with Johnny?" I ask.

"Pretty bad," Gram says, giving me a sideways glance. "Pretty bad."

"Well I'll go see him when we are done and see how he is doing."

"No, I don't think that's a good idea," she replies. "Not yet. Give it a day or two. Give me some time to talk to Grandpa."

"Well why can't I go? I see him everyday the rest of the time."

"Well let's say not today," Grandma replies. She is trying not to be hard on me. "Johnny may need some time to settle down too."

I think it over for half a minute. Maybe Grandma is right.

"He didn't do anything," I declare again. "Why does Grandpa hate him so much? Why do we live here if he hates Costa Rican's so much?"

Grandma turns to look at me, her hands just hanging still in the dishwater. She is thinking what to tell me.

"You know Grandpa was in Vietnam. You know some of his stories. But you don't know all the hardship he faced, the constant danger, not being able to trust the people. For two years Derrick, they were the enemy. So many were killed and wounded for life. He saw terrible things Derrick. So many were his friends and men he served with. I think there," she pauses, "he learned to hate. It helped him face the struggle."

Gram paused for a few moments paying attention to the dishes, then stopped again. "And it seems that once you have learned to hate, it doesn't leave you."

We both stand there looking at one another, still for moments, before we pay attention to the dishes. We are both quiet. It seems nothing more needs to be said.

Derrick felt restless before going to bed for the night. He stands out on the beach, facing out to the ocean, in the dark.

Alone. The waves are running up just short of where he stands. The ocean has a glow, maybe the moon coming through the clouds with its almost phosphorous light. Stars are not visible. The surf is building in the wind. Replays are running through his head of how the evening had transpired. Bill's power. And his overbearing way. He was proud he had stood up for Johnny. His reply to Bill. "Maybe you fired Johnny too quickly."

And that Saul. What a guy! Always a wild card.

The air is very warm, blowing hard and steady, slightly from the south. Very warm, blowing through his hair, and blowing his shirt collar up into his face. A gust of wind, with it's magic fingers, blows the last button open on his shirt and the tail of his shirt flaps against his back. The warm wind caresses him, blowing through his hair, his head held up and his face set into it, and his shirttail flapping like a flag. This warm wind, its intensity, feels good. He feels strong.

And it is going to blow tonight.

CHAPTER NINE

Waking slowly, Derrick realizes it's Saturday. He was allowed to sleep in today. He remembers the wind blowing hard enough last night to blow a few coconuts crashing onto the roof, waking him for only a few moments each time. But it is quiet and sunny this morning and warm already. He hears music playing and as one song ends, Derrick knows the next one about to play before it starts. It must be his mom, playing one of the CD's he remembers well from years ago. It was their favourite once. His mom and his dad's.

He notices the picture on his dresser of him and his dad, and that big grouper they caught. It must have been 50 pounds! Derrick smiles to himself. They had caught it down here, offshore, just outside the lagoon, back when they were here for just a visit. Dad loved to fish. Derrick loves to fish. Maybe today. Maybe he can get together with Johnny and see how he is doing. He knows Johnny will be glad to see him.

There are a few chores to do today, like vacuuming the swimming pool, cleaning the skimmers and checking the chlorine, but a light day. It's the weekend.

Derrick finds his mom sitting by herself on the veranda, with a book open on the table, her music in the background, and a cup of coffee. Fresh pastries had been brought to the door for sale this morning, and the basket on the table has less than its original dozen. There is a plate of fresh fruit, some cut and peeled, ready to eat.

His mom gives him a big smile.

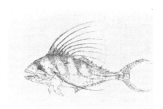

"Well look who made it," she declares. "I was afraid you had maybe been knocked out by one of those coconuts last night. Don't tell me you slept through all that racket!"

"No, I woke up a couple times."

"Well it blew," Mom adds. "There will be a bit of picking up to do today, and of course the pool will have picked up half of it. I'll help you after you eat. Sit down and I'll get you a plate."

Mom comes back with a plate, a glass of juice, and sets a coffee mug in front of me and offers me a cup of coffee.

"This is new," I proclaim to the offer of a cup of coffee. It's a first.

Mom just stands there deflecting my remark and standing like a waiter she asks, "Sir, would you care for a cup of coffee this morning?"

I can't help but smile. "Yeah! Please."

"Boy, things sure seem different than yesterday morning around here," I add. "What's happening here today?" I ask.

Mom sits down after she offers me a pastry and fruit.

"Well, everyone seems a lot happier this morning," says Mom. "It seems that Saul let the air out of the balloon last night. But I am sure we will get a few whiffs of unburnt Napalm as the day goes by."

"Napalm," I repeat after her, smiling, and laugh.

"Okay, don't repeat that." Mom says, giving me the look.

I try to take a sip of my coffee like it's not a new thing, but old hat.

"It's nice to hear your music Mom," her eyes meeting mine. "Boy, sometimes I sure miss Dad."

Mom's eyes are fixed on mine, but I notice that she drifts inside her own thoughts, and it's her thoughts she sees - not me.

"Me too," Mom says, as she sits back in her chair. "Me too," she adds again like its a brand new statement. "If you only knew."

We both wander in our thoughts for a few moments.

"So where is Grandma?" I ask. I notice the Jeep is gone.

"She's gone into town, shopping. Groceries and stuff. I think it's steak tonight. Your favourite."

"And Grandpa?" I ask.

"He's driven up to Nicoya for something. He asked if he should get you up to go, but I said to let you sleep. But I should get Saul up. What time is it?" Mom asks.

"Ten thirty," I reply.

Mom picks up her plate, cutlery and coffee mug, and starts toward the door.

"There is all the fruit peel in the kitchen sink if you want to feed it to the Iguanas," Mom says as she is going through the door.

"So when I am done around here, can I go fishing this afternoon?" I holler after her. Mom doesn't answer.

I enjoy sipping the coffee. It's good and strong, and seems to give me a bit of a buzz. After a minute or so Mom comes back through the door.

"I think that boy could sleep forever," Mom declares. "Yes, go fishing. I'll help you with your chores. I haven't gone around to see how much of a mess there is. Have you tried out that fishing rod yet?"

"Not yet." I make a fake cast and pretend to reel in a big fish. "But I am dying to."

Mom smiles.

"Derrick, make sure you thank your grandfather and give him a report on that rod," She says. "And it would be good if you would spend a few minutes with him and try and ease some of the tension from yesterday." Mom pauses. "Okay?"

"Okay," I answer. "So I can see Johnny today?"

"Sure, do that. But I don't think you should have him over yet."

"Don't worry. I don't think he will want to come over. He's probably afraid to come over anyway," I add.

The big iguana comes down to the edge of the roof where I

have placed the peels for him. The two girls, guests, and another young boy are watching as I put away the step ladder in the bodega.

"Why does he live on the roof?" the boy asks.

"I don't know," I answer. "I guess because it's nice and hot up there."

"Where does he sleep?" the boy asks again.

"I don't know," I say again. "Maybe we'll have to stay up late one night and watch him," trying to make it sound like something really dangerous and scary.

I pick up my fishing rod and a small tackle box I can just slide into the big pocket of my shorts. I have on an old pair of running shoes I wear into the surf. Most of the locals go in barefoot. I do sometimes, but I'd rather wear shoes. At least flip-flops. The last thing I want to do is step on a stingray. Deadly. Well, deadly painful anyway. And the dry sand on the beach can get so hot it burns your feet.

The tide is coming in, which is good. The fish feed on the bugs the waves catch on the beach. Nobody is fishing yet.

Several of our guests are tanning in and out of the shady spots in the palm trees. A father and his boy are catching the waves on boogey boards. Other than that the beach is deserted except for a few people walking. The weekend crowds are staked out closer to the town site under beach umbrellas. The surfing schools are busy for sure. The surf coming in today is good, because of the winds last night.

Then I spot it. A rooster fish! His tail, actually his dorsal fin, is out of the water. The tourists usually think it's a shark fin with all the commotion that causes. He's out a couple hundred yards and feeding, making that sweeping arc back and forth as he works his way in with the surf. I watch him for half a minute and run up the beach to be nearer the centre of the arc he is feeding on. I tie on a four-inch-long silver spoon that has a really bright reflective red pattern on the other side. I wade out into the surf, stuffing my tackle box in my shorts pocket. I wade out to waves up to my waist. My first cast is good. Boy, it goes out far - at least twice the distance I can cast with a toss line. Maybe more. I try different motions for casting, getting a feel for the rod action and the reel. Johnny is wading in ten yards over from me, whirling his toss line over his head. He lets it fly and then starts winding in.

"Hey Derrick. Saw you out here," he calls.

"I was coming to get you when I saw this guy," I say, nodding my head towards the rooster fish. "How are you doing. You okay?"

"Yeah I'm okay," Johnny answers after throwing his line out again and making his way over to put a little more distance between us for casting room.

"Sorry about all the trouble. Grandma said it was pretty bad."

Johnny doesn't answer.

Several pelicans are diving into the school of fish that the rooster fish is corralling toward the beach. He is coming right at them.

"Are you sure you are okay?" I ask again.

"Yeah," he says nodding and looking over my way. "You are sure getting good distance with your casts."

"Yeah, this is good," I call back. "Maybe I can drop it right on his head."

The rooster fish is breaking the surface regularly and I try to lead in front of where he seems to be heading with my casts. Johnny has hooked a snapper and is backing out of the surf to land the fish on the sand.

"Any size?" I holler.

"He's okay," Johnny yells back.

I make several more casts and keep checking the tension after the lure hits the water each time. I set it fairly light. I can always tighten it if I have to. The pelicans are sweeping back and forth, searching for the feed fish. The rooster fish hasn't broken the surface for a couple minutes. I don't know where to cast but I try using both hands to cast, like swinging a baseball bat, to get the best distance I can. My cast is farther right than I intended, but good distance. As I feel the line tighten, reeling in the slack to the lure, I see the rooster's fin break the surface and head straight for it. The twenty feet is covered in seconds. My heart is pounding as I feel the line tighten, then slacken. I reel in quickly to pick up the slack and then it happens. It's like you have dropped a brick tied to the end of your rod. It goes where it wants. The line starts stripping out way faster than I've ever seen before. I go to tighten the drag a little but as the rooster fish heads away from me up the beach, I loosen it slightly. Too tight and he'll break the line. Too loose and I might not be able to control him, or worse, run out of line. I start backing up to the beach.

"Johnny! I've got him!" I holler as I keep backing up. Johnny runs out beside me.

"How much line have you got?" he says excitedly as we make our way back.

The rooster has headed in towards me and I stop to reel in as fast as I can. The line tightens again and I can see his tail as he arcs his way back, parallel to the beach, giving it all he can. I start backing up again.

"Three hundred and fifty yards," I call out. "Twenty-pound test."

I'm stepping high to get back into the shallower water.

I've never caught a rooster fish before, but I have seen several brought in. The Frenchman is an old guy who fishes here, usually just as the sun is going down. He's done the best. He uses a rod and reel. In the only English I've heard him speak he boasts loudly, "Six-pound test," he says proudly, shaking the rod like a warrior's spear once he has landed the fish. He landed a forty-pound rooster a few weeks ago. It took him over an hour. He would run up and down the beach as the rooster fish would make its many runs so as to not run out of line. He would patiently reel in, oftentimes running back into the water as the rooster made a dash seaward, and then as the fish would tire, steer it back in and do his best to recover line. A crowd usually draws. With his forty-pound rooster, a Costa Rican man ran into the shallow water that the rooster was grounding himself on, and above the shouting in French, obviously calling him off, he grabbed the rooster fish by grabbing in to his gill plate and dragging him up onto the beach. The Frenchman was pleased enough with himself that he patted his helper on the back, and gave the Costa Rican a sympathetic look at his bleeding hand. His hand must have got snarled in the hook, or the rooster's teeth.

A forty-pound rooster fish is a big fish to land.

I am half running at times as the Rooster heads up the beach. I still seem to have lots of line, but I don't want to take any chances of losing him. I want this fish.

"Stay with him. Stay with him," Johnny excitedly coaches me, as he keeps right along with me.

"How big do you think he is?" Johnny asks.

"He's big. He feels like fifty pounds sometimes," I call back.

Rooster fish have a tail like a tuna, and are deep in the body with a blunt head. This makes them fast, powerful swimmers, and they use their vertical profile to plane against the line at right angles to it. I know that when he runs, he has to keep his gill plates closed, and isn't breathing. It's like holding your breath when you are straining at something. He has to stop to regain oxygen. Not that he really stops, but I know to recover line every moment I can. The length and flex in my rod help absorb the shock of his fight, and keep tension on the line. The locals, with toss lines and a handheld spool, give the fish more of a chance to break free. Many still play the fish out in the same way, tiring him out, and others simply run up the beach hauling in as fast as they can until the rooster is grounded. If the line breaks, all you get is a sympathetic pat on the back from your friends.

My arms are tired and I hold the rod as close to me as I can to ease the strain.

Another big run.

Johnny stays right with me excited, and full of encouragement. There are at least a dozen people on the beach now, watching. The kid's eyes are wide. Their dads or moms are smiling at them, pointing out at the rooster tail fin as it breaks the surface in its fight for freedom. The dorsal fin is really a set of seven wide spines that fan out and stick about eighteen inches out of the water. Sometimes the rooster will jump right out of the water, shaking like some big sport fish, a swordfish or marlin.

With my twenty-pound test line, I am not having too much trouble steering this rooster around at the end of his runs. The runs are getting shorter, and I get more time retrieving than running. I know my next big hurdle to overcome is when the rooster hits bottom as I get him into the shallows. The trick is to run him up as far as I can on a wave and then ground him out.

"When you run him up, I'll hook him with my line and help

109

you pull him up," calls Johnny holding his hook in his hand. He is thinking the same thing I am.

"We should make a gaff," I call back. "Next time."

"Tell me when you are ready to pull him up," Johnny says, continuing his coaching.

The rooster has picked up a fair bit of breathing time and makes another strong run to the ocean. I run fifty paces into the surf before he starts to tire out again, and I get him turned around. I start to back out again. Johnny is right beside me, coaching me.

I know the rooster is using his runs parallel to the beach to the best of his advantage. But I know he is tiring out. He is not breaking the surface any more. There is another short-lived dash away, then I get to retrieve a lot of line.

"Johnny, I'm going to bring him in," I call.

I back up onto the wet sand and, reeling in quickly, I feel the rooster hit bottom and then I pinch the line down against the side of the rod and back step up the beach as quick as I can, pulling but hoping not to pull too hard and break the line. The rooster bottoms out on his side and his thrashing lets me pull him up quickly without dragging him in the sand. Johnny makes an effort to set his hook into it, but jumps back as the rooster fish thrashes about. It's all over too quickly for Johnny to do more.

"Get me a stick to hit him with," I holler down to Johnny.

Johnny runs up as I reel in the slack, keeping tension on the line, as I wind up to within ten feet of the rooster.

The rooster fish is played out. It tries to fight but can't. There is no more oxygen to revive him.

I plunk myself down in the wet sand, keeping tension on the

line and try to catch my own breath. I can feel my heart beating hard.

Johnny runs down past me with a sturdy three-foot stick and squaring himself alongside the rooster, gives it one hard smack across the head. The rooster flutters, then lays limp, gill plates not moving. It is over.

Johnny turns towards me and jumps up punching his fist up in the air and hollers "Yes!" just as loud as he can.

He gives me a hand up and we are both laughing. Can't get the smiles off our faces.

Most of the people who were watching have made their way down to have a look at the rooster. Its dark blue stripes stand out from its sparkling silver scales. A rooster fish is a very beautifully coloured fish. The sun reflecting off him is just making his colours sparkle.

"How much do you think it weighs?" asks a man with his two boys.

"What's it called?" asks one of the boys.

"It's a rooster fish," I answer.

The father is showing the dorsal fin to his boys and explaining how it sticks up like a rooster's tail feathers.

I pull up on the gill plate and cautiously slide my right hand into the opening, wanting to get a good hold but not run into any teeth or splines. I pick it up.

"It has to be better than twenty pounds," I pronounce, as proud as can be. "I'll bet you it's twenty-five pounds," I add again.

"Twenty-five pounds easy!" adds Johnny.

I take a few steps toward the surf with a good grip on the

Rooster's gill plate. I let a wave wash over him, washing off the sand. I walk my catch back up and show him off. He looks better than ever.

"That's a beautiful fish," the man declares.

"That's a beautiful fish," Johnny says in agreement.

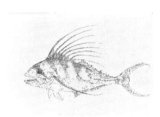

Mom has rushed to the bodega to grab a sack to lay the fish on. I lay it on the sack on a small patch of grass next to the veranda.

Everybody is all smiles and Grandma has gone for her camera.

Saul is closely checking out its rooster tail dorsal fin.

Bill is just coming over from the road finishing a conversation. Corporal Morales pulls away in his police jeep. Bill doesn't look too happy, but his face breaks into a smile when he sees the rooster fish.

"Hey Derrick! That's a prize!" says Bill, like everything was all right or something, like nothing had ever happened.

CHAPTER TEN

Derrick steps down the steps of the front veranda. The front porch light is on and a motion detector light snaps on as he crosses the parking lot. It is dark enough. A Howler Monkey growls from the branches above him and Derrick quickly swerves hard to the right to avoid him. The outside light is on at Bill's shop, across the road. The shop yard and vehicles flash bright in different patterns like so many lightning strikes emanating from inside the shop. Bill is welding inside and the big shop door is open.

In the shop yard, Derrick walks by the big Mercedes, and past the Zodiac on its trailer. The white on both vehicles reflects the shop light and the welding flashes.

As Derrick walks in the big doors, Bill flips up his welding mask. He takes a pointed hammer and gives several good raps to knock the slag off the joint he is welding. It looks like some kind of framework. The smell of the welding fumes and the smoke make the hot evening air seem closer than ever. There is no breeze tonight.

"Time for a break?" I call out.

Bill lets out a big "Hmph," with his big breath.

"Yeah, maybe," he adds. "Too hot in here."

He kicks off his boots, crawls out of his coveralls, and steps into his flip-flops. There are sweaty patches showing wet on his T-shirt. Tapping a cigarette part way out of its package, Bill clasps the end of it in his lips and pulls it out. He lights it, and waves Derrick into the shop where he was working. He wants to show him something.

"Have you got a few minutes?" asks Bill.

"Yeah," I reply, shrugging. I work my way over to beside Bill.

Bill reaches back toward the workbench and pulls a stool over and plunks himself back on it.

"There's another right there," Bill points further down the workbench.

"That was a nice fish you got there today," says Bill as I pull up and sit up on the stool. "Nice fighting fish, though not my favourite for eating. But your Mom did it up nice with those peppers and onions. I think she soaked it in lemon juice first. It helps take away the strong flavour."

"I hear they are good if you slice the fillets thin, salt them and dry them in the sun for a couple days. Then fry them," I tell Bill. Johnny's mother told me that is how she likes to cook them, when Johnny and I would talk about the Great Rooster Fish we were going to catch.

"Yeah. Well down here they will eat anything, but yeah, I've heard that too," Bill adds. "How did that rod work?"

"It worked great!" I answer enthusiastically. "Sometimes it felt like he was going to yank it out of my hands. But the drag on the reel is what works the best. I don't think I could have got it in without that. Not with a hand line."

Bill smiles.

"And casting," I add. "I can cast two or three times the distance of the hand lines. You should have seen him take the hook. He just attacked it! He must have been twenty or thirty feet away and on the surface. He just went for it."

Bill is smiling and nodding in agreement.

"Well it's the biggest fish I have ever caught," I add again. "How much do you think he weighed?" I ask.

"I would say thirty pounds. It was a beauty," Bill replies. He pauses for more than a moment.

"You know, we need to have a chat Derrick," Bill says.

The alarm bells go off inside my head and a wave of anxiety crashes over me. Now I am going to get it, I think to myself.

Bill starts again after a few moments pause.

"I am going to need some help here, hey?" Bill starts. "I am going to need your help," he emphasizes, again pausing, looking for words. "I've been thinking how to go about it."

Bill pauses again.

"Thinking about what?" I ask cautiously. Another pause.

"You see," Bill holds out his hands, about a foot apart in front of himself, and shakes them like he was slowly shaking a piggy-bank. "I can make a lot of money with my gold dredge. More than I can make doing anything else right now. Pay off what we owe on this place, and if we are lucky make a lot more. The trouble is," Bill lifts his brow high, and his eyes wide, looking at me, "is that it is dangerous. Well, it can be dangerous," he corrects. "But I think I have it figured out, a way where it doesn't have to be."

Bill breaks off for a moment. My anxiety level starts to settle out, but it will take another minute for my heart rate to settle down.

"Are you with me on this?" Bill challenges.

"Yeah I'm with you," I say encouragingly. "Really. What do you want me to do?"

Bill clasps his hands behind his head as he leans back.

"Well first, don't say anything about it to anyone. I need somebody I can trust. No Johnny's."

I tilt my head sideways with a look of exasperation and a hint of a shrug. Almost like it's painful.

"I won't say anything," I add.

Bill is watching me, and takes another pull on his cigarette, and continues.

"What I have figured I can do is conceal what the equipment looks like so that it is not so obvious. You see this frame I am working on? It will bolt onto four of those water tanks and I can mount the dredge pump and a clearing box on it, with room enough for you to work. The sluice box will be on separate floats that we can attach like a trailer when we need it. And I can quickly disassemble everything after we use it. So, as long as nobody sees it working, no one will know how it all goes together and what it's for. Now here's the trick." Bill points his finger at me like it was a six-gun. "The rest of the time, when we are not using the sluice, we will look like we are doing an Archeological dig. A recovery of artifacts. I am an Archeologist."

Bill jumps back lifting up his hands to protect his face like a small explosion has just gone off in front of him. He is being dramatic.

"I am an Archeologist. Master of Science Degree, Seattle U, 1972," he says melodically, mimicking reverence. "And I am recovering artifacts from what we believe to be historic village sites of the early native peoples. I'd have papers and permits along that say we are from the University of Panama, put big door decals on the truck and everything. I am sure it would satisfy any local curiosity we run into, and probably let us squeak through if anyone more important came along."

Bill pauses. "Are you following me?"

I quickly nod a few times, with probably what looks like a silly grin on my face.

"Well I can talk the talk," Bill keeps going, "and make it look like it is all approved work that we are doing. The documentation and permits I need I can get forged down in Panama City with all the proper letterheads and logos. Big decals on the doors of the truck will make it look like a University vehicle. I'll put a vehicle number on it and everything. Even Panama plates. If we just watch how we go about it, the deception is complete."

"Several more things I have thought of," Bill continues. "One of the rivers I would like to try is over the border in Panama. We can only access it from the Costa Rican side. But once we are over the border, nobody will be clear on who has jurisdiction. The Costa Rican Police aren't going to bother us, and the Panamanians don't have any road access. The more we can avoid anyone snooping or asking questions, the better. And for the gold. I have figured this out." Bill smiles broadly. "You know those big plastic barrels I picked up in San Jose? We put everything we get from the sluice box into them, and leave it there till we get home. No extracting. Just the heavy sands and gravel that we keep the artifacts in so that they are packed in a safe medium to transport back to the University."

Bill tweaks his fingers in the air like making quotation signs as he says "gravel" and "artifacts".

I can tuck away my panning machine to sample what we are

getting, but I can just pour the gold we are getting back into the barrels. It hides everything. I can even have fake newspaper articles printed up that talk about what we are doing. I think we could fool just about anyone. Then when we get home, we'll do the extracting. I am sure we can get away with it at least once, and maybe more. We can get away with it probably as long as nobody asks questions. And I can pick up a collection of items that look like artifacts, pottery pieces, arrow heads, and maybe a piece or two of jewellery, just to show anyone who is too curious."

Bill has become more intense as he explained his plan. His eyes are sparkling and he is lit up with excitement.

"What do we have to do?" I ask.

"Hey, now you're talking," says Bill. "The trouble is that I now have that police corporal snooping around. He stopped by today 'just doing his rounds,' but it was easy to see that he was scoping out what was in my yard here. I am not sure if he is keeping an eye out for me, or on me," he emphasizes.

"I saw you talking to him," I add. "What did he want?"

"What he says he wants, and what he wants aren't necessarily the same thing. He says he was just making his rounds - regular patrols, looking out for us. But he asked if we were able to discover anything taken from the break-in. I told him there was an envelope with U.S. Cash in it, maybe a hundred dollars, that we realized was missing. It's a lie, but I know he thinks that a break-in with nothing stolen doesn't sound right. So if he ever asks you, you know the answer. I told Grandma and your mom that that is what I told him, so we can keep our stories straight. I guess I had better tell Saul."

Bill pauses and shakes his head in dismay.

"That Saul!" he adds. "At any rate, Corporal Morales is someone we don't need hanging around. I don't trust him."

"Maybe you should close the big shop doors so he doesn't see you welding," I suggest. "Maybe paint the windows black. But I guess you need ventilation."

"No Derrick. You're right," Bill agrees quickly. "That's probably a good idea. I can weld during the day when it doesn't show up so much."

"What I need to do," Bill adds, "is put a couple days into fabricating the platforms for the dredge and sluice box, and then drive out some afternoon and try them out. I can make the grizzly head on the sluice box collapsible so that it will look more like what they would use in Archeological digs. Make it so we can change it in a matter of moments. When we know it all works right, then I will head down to Panama and get the documents I need. I know a guy from the Army who set up a print shop down there. He will either do the work for me, or at least know somebody who will. Once I have all that done, then we would be ready to go."

Bill pulls out another cigarette.

"So how does it sound?" Bill asks as he lights up.

"It sounds like you have it all worked out," I answer. "So do Archeologists wear uniforms or anything?"

"Good one Derrick," Bill comes back at me. "University of Panama T-shirts all around. I can pick them up when I am down there."

Bill drops his head down on his chest, nodding his head slightly, thinking, enjoying his cigarette and the moment.

"So what do you think? Let's close things up and call it a night," says Bill as he gets up. "What do you say Derrick? Does it sound good?"

"It sounds good," I reply convincingly.

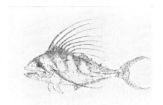

We pick up a few tools, grinders and cut-off saws. Welding rods go in sealed containers. I help Bill move long pieces of square tubing from the bed of the Mercedes into the shop.

I feel like I have lost some of what I thought I had gained yesterday. I had stood up to Bill, saying that I didn't think Johnny was the problem. Now, trying to get along with Bill, I have let him walk over me again. I feel like I have let Johnny down. I feel like I have let myself down. Johnny didn't come to the house when I carried the rooster fish home. I didn't encourage him to either - I guess I was afraid of creating a scene. Johnny was avoiding it and I guess I was too. I need to talk to Johnny more and see how he is feeling about everything. I'd like to hear what he has to say about what happened when Bill blew up at him. Too late tonight to head over, but we usually spend some time in town together on Sundays. Check out the surf school, the internet store, shops, and the beach. We'll have time to talk. Bill seems happy enough, and excited about his plans. He seems happy with me. It's been a big day. It seems that a lot is happening.

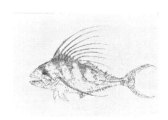

·

Bill and I swing the gates to the compound together and Bill wraps the chain around and snaps on the hefty padlock.

"So you'll get this all arranged with Mom?" I ask. "You might want to make it sound more like a fishing and camping trip."

"Yeah, I think I can take care of that," says Bill. "Leave that part up to me, will you?"

"It's all yours," I agree.

We head across the road into the parking lot of the hotel.

"You know, I don't think Johnny is the problem you think he is," I throw out.

Bill gives me a look. After a few steps, he says, "Yeah?"

"Yeah," I say.

And we make it into the house without saying more. I am glad to see Mom and Grandma there, and I head over to them to put some distance between Bill and myself.

"What have you two been up to?" asks Mom.

"Just hanging out," I declare. "Talking about fishing and stuff. I think I have some bragging rights today."

Mom laughs. "Yeah you do," Gram agrees.

Bill heads over to the fridge and grabs a beer.

"You want a Coke, Derrick?" he hollers from out of the kitchen.

Everything seems good.

CHAPTER ELEVEN

I do my little knock on Saul's bedroom door.

"What?" drags out the voice of a twelve-year-old, soon to be eleven. "What are you doing disturbing me?" is what he would call out if he was to say what was on his mind. Or worse.

I open the door, and step in. It smells like Saul's room in the morning. It's messy enough - clothes scattered on the floor, comic books on the undisturbed corner of his bed. Saul stretches around under his light covers.

"Mom says it's time to get up," I announce.

Saul's runners are lying on their side on the floor. The heels are crushed down and they look like something he found in somebody's trash bin. They are dirty and tattered, the laces only tied through the bottom half of the available holes. If I was told I had to pick them up, I think I would go look for a pair of gloves first.

Saul groans as he stretches again.

I remember when Saul and I used to share the same bedroom - his shoes, his socks, his feet. I remember one night when we were getting ready for bed. Saul was sitting on the end of his bed, and his shoe clunks on the floor as he pulls it off without undoing the laces. His sock has a big blotch of blood on the sole.

"What's the matter with your foot?" I asked, looking at him like he is my weird brother. Which he is.

"Nothing," is all I get for a reply.

"No. What is it?" I asked again. "Why is your foot bleeding?"

"I don't know," he comes back. "Probably a rock in my shoe."

I reach down, pick up his shoe, and tip it over. Nothing comes out. I pick up the other, tip it, and a round pea-sized rock bounces on the floor. I look at it and then look at Saul.

"You mean you'd walk all day with a rock in your shoe until your foot is bleeding?" I asked in astonishment. "Without stopping to take the rock out? Are you crazy?"

Saul ignores my questions.

"It didn't hurt," he replied like it was just some off-hand remark.

"Let me see your foot," as I reached down.

Saul cooperates, and I twist his foot around one hundred and eighty degrees, rolling Saul onto his stomach on the bed. I lift his foot up and there is a hole in his foot the size of the rock, and it is bruised and bloody around the wound.

"I'm going to go get Mom," I said. "She is going to want to see this. It could be infected."

At any rate, Mom came to look and wanted to put some iodine on it since it seemed sure to infect otherwise. I offered to put the iodine on but Mom insisted she do it, and I sat on Saul's legs, Saul face down on the bed. She said it was going to hurt. But Saul never really flinched, but kind of rolled his foot around by the ankle, like to try and improve the flexibility or improve circulation. I have put iodine on cuts before, and it hurts. Really hurts. But Saul? It didn't seem to phase him.

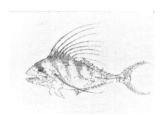

"It looks like you need a new pair of runners," I say. "Ask Mom. She'll take care of it. And Saul, I need you to help me carry that rooster fish over to Johnny's place. Mom says it's just too much for us to eat. We'll put it on a plank and the two of us can carry it over. They'll be glad to get it. 'K?"

Saul makes it to sitting up on the edge of his bed. That is confirmation. I wander out and head back to the kitchen.

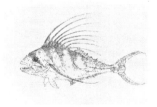

Johnny lives about a block away, and I am carrying the front of the plank and Saul is at the rear. We turn into Johnny's yard, through the entrance which has two rock pillars and a two-foot fence of rock around the yard. There are similar houses on each side here, a block from the beach. Saul has one of his stray dogs following him, not appearing too interested in the rooster fish. I knock on the door.

The house is quite small, made of cinder block and wood trimmings, that have aged in the sun and salt air. The door is strong and solid. The windows are not large, and set midway in the block walls. The shape of the house is like a simple bungalow, where the living room and kitchen are a larger sized area from the bedrooms to the rear. It has a corrugated steel roof that is supported by the steel framed trusses that form a small eve around the perimeter. It is a very standard home in the rural areas of Costa Rica.

The door is opened by Johnny's mom, and Saul and I are greeted with her big smile. It is a pleasant smile.

"So this is the big rooster you caught, Derrick. You brought it here to show me?" she asks.

Of course, I'm all smiles.

"No, I brought it for you. Mom says it's just too much for us to eat."

Johnny's Mom has a puzzled look on her face.

"Are you sure for certain?" she asks.

"You can use it can't you?" I ask. "Johnny tells me how you dry it in the sun for a couple of days, and then fry it with spices and vegetables. I'd sure like to come over for a dinner like that if I could. I think I would really like it."

"But this is almost your whole fish Derrick. Are you sure?" she asks again.

I smile and nod. "Yeah. I'm sure."

"Come in, come in," invites Johnny's mom. "And Saul, you are growing by big amounts. Look at you! Here. Set it on the counter here."

Saul and I slide the plank and rooster fish across the sink and counter top, pushing back a few dishes to get the clearance we need. We step back and neither of us knows what to say next.

"Are you going to fillet it yourself?" I ask.

Johnny's mom smiles broadly. "Yes Derrick. I have filleted many, many fish. And I'll dry it some in the sun, like you said. But tonight, I think I will make a fish soup. Johnny loves it."

I am just about to ask where Johnny is when he walks in the front door carrying a plastic bag of groceries in each hand.

"Hey Derrick. Saul," he greets us. He walks over and sets the two bags on the counter next to the rooster fish, pushing more things aside to make room. He is just back from the supermarket. The supermarket is small by American standards, being about two and a half thousand square feet. Not too bad for such a small town.

"Isn't it good that Derrick has brought us his rooster fish?" Johnny's mom says.

"Really?" exclaims Johnny. "Why?"

"Nobody really likes rooster fish at our house, except Derrick." blurts out Saul. "It's too strong. They like dorado."

"Well, we don't know how to cook it properly," I say defensively.

Once we are ten feet out the door I give Saul a slight cuff to the back of the head.

"That was my fish I gave to them, and I wanted them to feel good about me giving it to them. Not that we didn't want it. Way to go Saul," I say shaking my head in disgust. "Why don't you try not to be such a creep all the time."

Saul shrugs it off and he lets me know he doesn't have to listen to my scolding by just wandering off on his own, toward one of his friend's houses, the stray dog in tow, licking at Saul's fingers. I know by the dog that Saul was touching the rooster fish. Its red meat had bled out some on the plank. Saul.

Johnny pops out the door.

"Hey. Where you going?" he beckons.

"I don't know," I shrug. "You feel like walking back in to town?" I ask.

"Sure. Why not."

Johnny pokes his head back inside and blurts out his plan to head out with me. We almost always walk down the beach, at least when we are heading into town. If we are carrying things back, sometimes the shortest route is the best. But usually the beach has the best breezes. It is just another sunny, hot morning, and being Sunday, there are quite a few groups setting up on the beach - blankets, towels, umbrellas, coolers, beach balls, and frisbies. Lots of families. Then there is the surf school with its group, and the local surfers who like to hang out and show off to the girls. And the language school, the dive school, and several small hotels like our own, whose patrons group out front on the recliners and sun chairs.

I unbutton my shirt to let the breeze cool me better. Johnny pulls his T-shirt off up over his head. That is when I see the big bruised patches coming from under his arms up to his shoulders. I look at his back in disbelief and it is marked the same.

"Is that what Bill did?" I exclaim.

Johnny goes to put his shirt back on and I stop him. I take a good look at the bruising.

"What did he do to you?" I demand. "That's terrible!" I say in disbelief.

"He yanked me right off the ground by my shirt," he says defensively.

Johnny doesn't want to talk about it and pulls his shirt back on over his head. But I want to talk about it.

"He almost tore my shirt right off me," Johnny starts. "That's what caused the bruising. He's a strong man. And, was he mad!"

Now that Johnny is talking, he keeps going.

"He says that I blabbed about the dredging and that somebody broke into your house. That it was my fault. I didn't do anything. I didn't talk to anyone. For serious," Johnny protests.

"This is ridiculous," I protest.

"It looks worse than it is. It doesn't really hurt. Just a bruise," Johnny adds.

I am obviously disgusted, and still shaking my head in disbelief. We keep walking.

"You didn't tell anybody what we were doing," I state as a

known fact.

"No. Nobody. Why would I? I wanted to go out with you again. It was fun."

"I told Bill you didn't tell anybody. And I'll tell him again. And I'll tell him what he did to you."

Johnny looks at me seeming not to know what to say next.

"The worst is that he fired me," he finally adds. "I need my job Derrick. Where am I going to find another?" It isn't really a question.

"I'll talk to my Grandma," I say after a moment. "And I'll talk to Bill too."

After saying it, that I would talk to Bill, I spent half a minute wondering just how I was going to go about that. Bill is busy fabricating his equipment in the shop. He is busy and intent, and putting in long hours, but he likes to show me what he has done. I can tell him I have talked to Johnny and that I know I am right. He will have to listen. He will have to listen, I repeat to myself, trying to convince myself, I guess, as much as anything.

"Lets go up to the internet shop. I'll use my time card for both of us," I say, the time card being a discount card where you pay for ten hours and you get twelve.

"At least it will be cool in there," I add. It is air conditioned.

"I'll talk to them," I say again to Johnny after a few moments have passed.

"Should I come and see Bill, and tell him I am sorry?" asks Johnny.

"Sorry for what!?" I retort back. "You didn't do anything." And after a pause, "No. Let me talk to him first."

I don't want to tell Johnny how poorly Bill thinks of him. Him and all Costa Ricans. I am ashamed and afraid to say so. I don't want Bill and my family to be seen in such a poor light. I want to be doing something to make things better. It scares me. I am not sure how to be going about it. Especially without making things worse.

We turn from the beach, up the main street that comes into Samara from the highway. Shops and restaurants line both sides of the street, except for the full block of the playing field. And the police station. Corporal Morales is sitting in the shade of the veranda on the porch of the station, he and another policeman, each with a Coke in their hand, both leaning back in their chairs. I give him a small wave of recognition, not wanting to make a big deal of it, and he nods back at me. Johnny and I continue on across the big playing field and the breeze from the beach just seems to vanish. By the time we make the few hundred yards, I am just about ready to melt. Entering the internet shop is like walking into a cooler. The air conditioning is turned right up to keep all the computer equipment cool. I pay for two half-hour sessions with my punch card, and there are two computers side by side that are free. Time to cool down.

Johnny and I both enjoy time on the internet. Most of the time. Stepping back outside from the internet shop is like stepping into an oven. After the air conditioning, it makes the heat worse than ever. There is no breeze making it up this far from the beach. We head back to the main street and pull in to the first shop where I can buy us a couple of Cokes. I decide to buy half a dozen. There were no drinks allowed in the internet shop. The Cokes are ice cold and taste great. Johnny's watching his money. I don't mind buying them. We each finish our first in less than a minute, and pop open a second.

Today we take the shortest route back to home. The streets

are quiet. It is Sunday, and kids and families are enjoying time in the shade wherever they are finding it. Many yards are empty. Families are at the beach and, I guess, people who just stay indoors. Johnny and I are seen together a lot, and we wave once or twice at people we know. Johnny is known better than I am, but then he has been here his whole life.

Many trees native to Costa Rica shed their leaves as the weather gets drier, to not need so much water. Others must have bigger root systems and their foliage stays full and green. A block ahead of us is a big green tree with full foliage and hanging branches. The tree is in yard, but hangs over the road allowance and the stretch of sidewalk you don't often find in Samara. Two kids are scrambling down its branches and drop to the ground. They are making a racket, calling out to one another. That catches our attention. Something seems to have their attention in the grassy ditch between the yard and the sidewalk. One boy gets up from his crouch and looks around. Spotting us, he waves with both arms over his head and calls for help.

Johnny picks up his pace, then starts to jog up to them. I follow his lead. The one boy runs up to meet us part way. He is out of breath and visibly distressed.

"We need your help! Our friend has fallen out of the tree."

He turns and runs back and we follow.

I stand in disbelief only for a second. It is Saul laying in the grass. The two boys with him are telling their separate versions of what happened and what they each saw. Both at the same time.

"Ricky is like a cat. He goes up trees and then gets scared to come down. Saul climbed up to help him down. And sploosh! Down he fell."

"He did help me down," the other boy pipes in. "He helped me down and then he fell."

Saul starts moving with a groan. His face, first looking flushed, seems to clear. I kneel down right beside him face to face, less than a foot apart.

"Saul. Can you hear me?" I ask cautiously.

In a moment, Saul nods slowly.

"Are you hurt?" I ask again.

Saul starts to roll over on to his back and groans.

"I think I knocked the wind out of me," he says in a hoarse voice, almost like the groan.

"Does anything hurt?" I ask again, starting to look him over. There is no bleeding, and his legs and arms look like how they are supposed to.

Saul pulls up one knee, and a then the next, and takes a big breath.

"Saul is tough man," exclaims one of the boys.

"He fell from that branch up there," says the other, pointing up to a big branch fifteen or twenty feet up. "Boy, I thought he was going to be dead."

"How are you feeling Saul?" I ask.

"I'm okay," he says slowly, still with a hint of the hoarseness.

"Do you want to try and stand up?" Johnny asks.

"In a minute," Saul replies, answering more quickly now.

"What happened Saul?" I ask.

"I don't know. I guess I lost my balance," he answers. He takes another deep breath.

"I saw you. You looked up at the sun and then you fell over backwards." Said the one boy who had told us that Ricky had to be rescued.

"Do you want to sit up and lean against me? It'll help you catch your breath," I say. I had a teacher who did that in the school yard when one of the kids got the wind knocked out of him in a soccer game.

I sit and lean my back against Saul's. He has propped himself up to lean back against me. Immediately I feel the heat building as our two bodies are together back to back.

"Do you want a sip of Coke?" I ask Saul. The two last cans are lying in the grass where I dropped them.

"Yeah, that sounds good," says Saul.

Johnny grabs him one and flips open the top and hands it to him.

"You two want to share the other one?" I say to the two boys.

Johnny hands the last one to the boy who isn't Ricky. He opens it himself.

"Saul, you're going to get yourself killed if you don't start to watch out," I say admonishingly. "Really," I add.

"Saul's one tough hombre," says Ricky, reaching up to the other boy for a turn at the Coke.

"Hombre," I say. "Yeah, Saul's an hombre," I say as though it's impossible. At least ridiculous.

The heat between us is uncomfortable, and Saul stirs and starts to stand.

"Let me give you a hand," says Johnny, there to assist.

Saul makes it up to vertical, a moment after me.

"Are you sure you're okay?" I ask again.

Saul tips the Coke back to drain the last of it, and he teeters a bit but regains his balance.

"Lets help him home Johnny," I say as we maneuver in close to Saul and join an arm behind him and hold Saul's arms, one over each of our neck and shoulders. Saul cooperates. We walk up onto the sidewalk.

I stop and turn back to Ricky and his buddy, and Ricky is finishing the last bit of the Coke, and throws the can down.

"You two are okay?" I ask.

"Yeah," they both chime in.

"Pick up the pop cans will you," I say, getting after them.

"Thanks for the help Saul," Ricky pipes back.

We step onto the road as the sidewalk isn't wide enough for the three of us.

"Hombre," I say again, like it is the most ridiculous thing anyone could say about Saul.

"Well, remember that fight last year when Saul cleaned that Paul guy's clock?" remarks Johnny.

Yeah. That Paul guy.

It was something.

About six months ago.

Ana Elina. The girl with the pretty name. She passes me a note heading out of class for the day. I flip open the note as I step out into the schoolyard, and quickly I catch what the note says. Ana Elina thinks I'm cute. All very well, but this Paul guy grabs the note out of my hand and starts reading it out to everybody, making fun of me and Ana Elina. This Paul guy is

Costa Rican, and so is Ana Elina. I tell him to just shut up and mind his own business. Paul gives me a shove.

He is bigger than me, a little taller, a little heavier, and a little older, though we are in the same grade. He is a local hotshot, being the Captain of the school soccer team. Of course, he likes Ana Elina. It is not just her name that is pretty.

A small crowd gathers quickly, mostly guys, the girls gather behind the guys as I stand facing Paul. I know I am going to get hurt here, and I am struggling with the fight or flight scenarios going through my head. Paul is doing the Yankee Go Home routine and gives me a hard shove which knocks me back into the stand of boys.

As I am recovering my balance from being knocked back, Saul quickly steps out from the crowd and, with his arms swinging wide like a cat, fights. He clobbers Paul with three punches, each one on the nose. Bam-Bam-Bam! Each punch hits Paul across his nose, first from one side, then the next, and again, the punches as quick as you can count. Facial injuries, I think a broken nose. The blood is everywhere. Paul is holding his face with blood running down his hands. Saul steps back and kicks him up the crotch. Paul gives a good grunt, and bends well over forward, still with his hands on his face and nose. Saul delivers an uppercut that hits him in the throat. That was it. Paul was down.

I break free of the boys holding me back and grab Saul by the arm. For a split second I thought Saul was going to clobber me too, but he recognizes me through his rage soon enough and lets me restrain him back. I hold onto Saul by the shoulder and the crowd that has gathered parts, and lets us through. The crowd has a buzz to it though I can't hear what they are saying. I steer Saul towards home as quick as I can without breaking into a run. I check behind us to see if we are being followed.

There is no one but Johnny running to catch up.

Saul is settling down.

Now I don't know. Were they just lucky punches? Maybe. Maybe not.

But what I do know is that Saul executed his attack like he had been training for it all his life. This Paul guy was probably a foot taller than him.

I remember that Bill was talking to a group of hotel patrons late one afternoon, after many cocktails, all sitting around the pool, and I was listening intently to his stories of the Army, and Vietnam as he answered questions and shared stories. Bill said that you can train a man to fight, and you can train a man to kill, but for a true warrior, it was 99.9% instinct. You don't need any training.

It seemed that Saul had this instinct Bill was speaking of.

Nobody picks fights with Saul. Nobody has ever picked a fight with me again. It seems that they figured we were trained in the martial arts, with our "military" family, C.I.A., or whatever. If Saul was as good as he was, nobody wanted to check out what I was capable of.

The spin-off for me was great.

Legends are made like this.

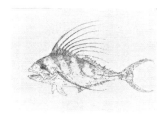

Saul is about ready to shake Johnny and I off as we step up onto the veranda at the house. We don't let him, and I prop the screen door open with my foot as we step Saul sideways through the door. Bill is washing at the kitchen sink with some hand cleaner, and Grandma is scrounging through the fridge to put some lunch on the table.

Saul plops himself down on the couch with our help. He stretches out and pulls a comic book up over his face. Johnny stays quiet as I bring the adults up to speed with what we just encountered. As the questions come, Johnny gives me a small wave and steps out the door.

Saul seems okay to everyone, and brushes off any concern as only he can. Saul says he only knocked the wind out of himself. Any concerns I raise over Saul fainting or whatever are dismissed by Bill as the heat, dizziness, or as growing pains.

Saul slips off to bed a little early, and I poke my head into his room on my way.

You okay?" I ask. The room is dark.

"Yup," is the extent of his answer.

"Well I've reconsidered," I state. "You are one tough hombre," I tell him.

Saul doesn't answer.

As I pull the door shut, leaving his room, I turn back and add, "Just try not to get yourself killed. Hey?"

CHAPTER TWELVE

I wake up to a dream of Saul driving the big Mercedes, and he is out of control. I am yelling at him how to get the brakes to work, which he can't seem to get right. The hill we are racing down, ever faster, is twisty, with gorges and valleys whizzing by on either side. I know we are going to get killed.

Awake. It is a good thing. I settle to the reality of my room, and the welcome awareness that it is all real. My dream is fading, like it happened to someone else now. No longer threatening.

I don't mind lying awake. I sweep out the last remnants and debris of anything that re-emerges of the dream of the crashing Mercedes. Interesting, isn't it? That we never get killed in our dreams.

The clock radio on my night table says it is 5:20am. Soon to be light.

I don't know if you have ever been in a tropical country when day breaks. It is something. I remember being woken up by all the noise and clatter, when we would visit, when we were younger. After living here for the last couple years, like so many things, I got used to it. But to someone who is not used to it, as I said, it is something.

Somewhere on the Eastern horizon there is a hint of light that arrives with the moment. I have always wondered whether it is the first bird that notices the light, that makes the first sound, that wakes up someone's rooster, so that it crows, or is it the rooster that wakes up first and crows to wake up all the other birds. I guess you have to be lying in bed at 5:20am to be thinking about such things.

However, it happens, someone's rooster makes the first loud noise, to which several other roosters, in different yards, all reply, with a sense of one-up-man-ship to herald the first light. That wakes up somebody's dog who joins in, barking at the roosters, and all the neighboring dogs join in the competition to be heard. Then the tropical birds start, their names too plentiful to list. Literally hundreds of species. And the birds get louder and louder with all their different calls to one another, again joining in the competition to be heard, it all building to the crescendo. The symphony of the jungle. Then the Howler Monkeys join in to broadcast their territory to one another. Of course, that gets the dogs going even more. And as the noise builds, it seems that each group turns up their call even louder, just to be heard over the rest.

This racket lasts for twenty minutes to half an hour, before it settles down and every living thing gets on with the rest of their day. Someone, a block over, starts a truck, that could use a new muffler, sure to be heading off to work, and the dogs take their turn barking at that. Whoever is up, his alarm is surely this first-light racket. No other alarm is needed.

And if your usual routine is to start your day later, you get used to the racket and just sleep through it.

I decide to get up and, after a glass of juice from the fridge and a quick note left on the kitchen table saying I am out for a walk up the beach, I unlock the front door and ease myself through the screen door. The hinge springs are rusty and squeaky from the salt air.

The early morning air is refreshing. Everyone is still asleep. Nothing, yet, has had to face the bleaching effect of the sun and heat of what will be another hot day. I love it most when there has been a shower during the night and all the dust is washed into pools of water that will help cool the morning. The bougainvilleas and poinsettias are all washed clean and bright, and whichever flowers give off a fragrance, they have had their energies renewed.

The beach is near deserted. A couple are holding hands and walking to the south end of the lagoon, walking briskly, probably half a mile ahead of me. Another lady, a few hundred yards to my right, is jogging back toward the town site. Early risers.

I scan the water surface for tell-tale signs of feed fish, and see the pelicans gathering far out toward the reef. Several are diving, and like they have been called for dinner, the rest are heading out to join in on the feed.

It takes an hour to walk to the south end of the beach and back. I know I'll be hungry when I get back and breakfast will probably be on the table by then. The suns first rays are just clearing the ridges of mountains to the east. It feels good to be up and out early. It feels good to walk.

Near the south end of the beach, there is much less development, and fewer homes. The homes there are poorer looking, like they have had rooms added on haphazardly, and have more junk left in their yards than most places in town. There is a dirt road that comes down onto the beach, used mostly by the fishermen, those with boats. A commercial prawn boat is anchored out and they are using a smaller boat to ferry in their catch from the night. The prawn boat, with its big booms and gathered nets, looks like a wreck. Its hull is rusty and everything looks poorly maintained. The exhaust from its engine, probably running to keep generators and coolers going, is black and sooty. A commercial buyer is parked down on the beach, a nice new truck with a refrigerated box, the buyer probably down from Nicoya. He will have a route to sell the seafood to the hundreds of restaurants up and down the coast. The buyer and his helper are busy with several other boats and their fisherman, and the tail-gate lift on the truck has a balance scale mounted on it where different catches are weighed and paid for.

I like to look at the catches. There are big and small fish. Red Snapper, Grouper, Dorado, Ocean Perch, octopus, squid, prawns, and an eel. Pelicans, doing their wobbly walk with their big bills held down on their chest, looking for a handout. Several frigate birds are diving and swooping to catch morsels thrown up into the air by the men who are filleting fish on planks laid across the gunwales of their beached boats.

An old fuel truck is backing down the beach, with a trailer attached that carries a wide flat-bottomed aluminum boat. It has a tank aboard the aluminum boat that they will fill from the fuel truck once it is launched and floating in the water. It will be used to make the trips back and forth to fill the tanks on the larger boats. The big boats all use diesel. The smaller boats, with their mostly outboard engines, have their tanks on the beach to be filled with gasoline that is kept in a smaller tank on the fuel truck. There is no wharf at Samara, and the only towns big enough to have one are a considerable distance away up and down the coast. The owner of the fuel truck has made himself a job by adapting his equipment to service these local fishermen. He makes a reasonably good living I am sure, for himself, his sons, and maybe a relative or two that he employs.

The sun is well up over the hills and mountains to the east. Its heat is starting to be felt. There is no breeze yet, but maybe soon. I head back.

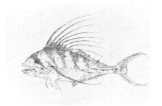

Bill, Grandma and Mom are all seated at the table on the veranda. I get a cheery welcome as I walk around the corner of the hotel, coming up from the beach.

They even have a place set for me, and there is juice, fruit, and muffins, which I heartily get into. Mom offers me a cup of coffee. It all tastes great after that morning walk - especially the coffee.

"Is it really that important that you go now?" asks Grandma of Bill.

I am not caught up with the conversation as yet. I eat, and listen.

"It is. And if I take the Mercedes," says Bill, "I can pick up the fridge, mattresses and furniture pieces we need to replace here from the duty free shops on the border. It saves a bundle compared to buying anything from around here, as you know."

"But we don't usually replace anything like that until the fall Bill. You know that," says Gram. "You're the one who says not to replace things with new until the winter tourist season starts, when our rates are highest. Why wear it all out now with all the kids in the summer?" Grandma is almost scolding Bill.

"Well then I can leave that part until Fall. You can come with me then. Things are usually pretty quiet later in September. We will pick out the new furniture you want for us then too. And if I just take the Jeep, well then it will cut down my travel time and expense, and I'll get back sooner. I should only be a few days."

"That's a few days without travel time. Right?" Grandma is obviously not thrilled with Bill's plans.

"Well look," says Bill. He is staying calm and is trying to play down Grandma's concerns. "If I leave tomorrow, I should be back by the weekend. How busy are we this week anyways?"

There is a pause and everyone is quiet.

Mom stands up. "I want another cup of coffee. Does anybody want more?" she asks.

She turns and starts back into the house. Bill and Grandma each take a turn responding.

"Yes Dear. I'll have one."

"Yeah. I might as well have one too," adds Bill.

"You want another Derrick?" Mom yells back from inside.

"Yeah sure," I holler back. "It tastes great after that walk."

"Has anybody seen Saul yet today?" I ask of Bill and Grandma.

"No, not yet," Phyllis replies.

"Well. Today, he will probably feel like he was hit by a truck, if he fell as far as they said," Bill adds.

Grandma looks right at me and says, "You thank Johnny for us will you, for helping Saul home."

Bill is on his good behavior. He doesn't flinch, or say a word to that.

Mom comes back out with a pot of coffee and pours it around to each of us. She empties the pot pouring what remains into her mom's and her own cups.

"Do you really like it black Derrick? She asks me.

"Yeah," I say nodding. "It tastes good."

"I checked the guest register when I was in," Mom adds. "Everyone who is here will be here through the weekend. No change-overs." There is a pause.

"Oh things are quiet enough I guess," says Grandma. She waves her arm in a dismissive gesture, like she was going to back-hand a fly that is buzzing around her. "Do what you want Bill," she adds.

"Well, it's not just what I want..." he answers back. "It's a serious trip, something I feel I need to do, and this is a good time to do it," he responds. No anger. A little frustrated.

"Who will help out around here?" asks Mom.

"I'll help," I say as I am about to take a sip of coffee.

I think it was the early morning walk and the buzz of the coffee. And that Bill seemed to be on his good behavior.

"And why don't we get Johnny back," I throw out. "I keep telling you he didn't do anything wrong. And he needs his job. And he knows how to take care of everything."

Everything goes quiet again for a few moments.

"Yeah. Get Johnny back," Bill says, throwing out his hands like he is out of control of the whole situation. Resigned.

Everything goes quiet again.

"Do what you need to do," Bill adds, and looks at me. "You'll talk to him?"

"Yeah." I nod. "I'll do it right away."

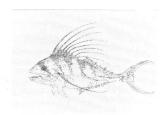

Bill and Corporal Morales. There is one thing they both had in common. Their common love, their common delight, their common affinity . Gold.

Morales wore a gold butterfly around his neck. The butterfly was a crude image, not ornate, most certainly carved from a larger piece of gold. Maybe from a gold nugget that held the general shape of a butterfly. Though crude in shape, it was beautiful in its simplicity. It was unique. Maybe some detail that it had been given by its original sculptor had worn away from the years of wear.

The butterfly had one hole drilled through it at the tail that stood for all that is basic in a man. Two holes at the top of the body were drilled for eyes, representing our capacity to see. Three holes were drilled through the left wing, representing understanding of our world around us, and four holes drilled through the right wing, symbolizing the powers and mystery of the Bri-Bri's beliefs. These powers, and their mystery, are believed to be greater than the reality of the visible world.

At least that is what Morales' father had told him when he was a child and, supposedly, his father's father had told him before that.

Yes, the butterfly was being worn around Eduardo Morales' neck. The jewelry piece had had its repairs by a goldsmith, and probably repairs by generations before, to keep it wearable. It had been handed down from father to son for generations. It was Eduardo's great great grandfather who rode up to trade with the Bri-Bri, he who traded for this jewelry piece.

And it was in his saddlebags when he did not return.

Eduardo wore it proudly. He wore it with delight. And as with his father, and his grandfather, and that father before him, Eduardo wanted more. Gold could be seen to sparkle in Eduardo's eyes whenever he spoke of his butterfly necklace, it's history, his great grandfather, or whenever gold became the topic of discussion.

Now Bill, he wore his passion for gold differently. He had designed and built his own dredge. It gave him a certain command over gold. He knew where to find gold and how to capture it. Now, Panama. There is much he had done, and much more to do. The trip he had to make to fabricate his deception. Panama.

His plans. The deception. Why would a man go to these extremes? They are extremes. So, why would a man go to these extremes, except that he loved it so.

And I had seen, and could see, the gold sparkle in Bill's eyes whenever he spoke of it for more than a moment. And he had been speaking of it for more than a moment many times lately.

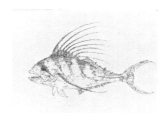

Corporal Morales had parked his police Jeep in front of the hotel, in the parking lot. He walked up to the front door and knocked, the knock answered in moments by Grandma.

"Has everything been quiet for you here?" asked Morales. "No problems?"

"No, everything has been great," replied Grandma "No problems."

"Your husband said that you realized an envelope with cash in it was missing. Isn't that right?" he asked. "How much money did he say was missing?"

"A hundred dollars U.S.," replied Grandma. "But we know you will never be able to track that down," she added.

"No, you are right," agreed Morales. "It probably meant more to your robber than you can imagine. Enough money to get out of the area. We have had no further break-ins or complaints of a similar nature in recent days. No one showing up who has matched your description. He has left the area for sure, I am certain."

Grandma nodded in agreement, but added nothing to the conversation.

"Is your husband around today?" asked Morales.

"Yes," replied Grandma. "He is over in the shop I think," she directed, pointing across the road. "Give him a holler from the gate. He doesn't like people sneaking up on him."

Morales looked a little surprised at that comment and excused himself and made his way over to the shop.

The gate is open and Corporal Morales looks over to the shop to see if he can see Bill. No sign of Bill. He walks to his left as he enters the yard, walking along the fence line. He bends down and tries pulling up the base of the chain link fence, but there is no give, and the fence seems to be secured to anchors in the ground. He walks to the middle of the next section and tries it again. It is also well secured to something in the ground. He squats and picks up what looks to be a crumpled up note, and unfolds it to read. It looks like somebody's grocery shopping list. He re-crumples it in his hand and throws it back down.

He stands up and turns around and almost collides with Bill, who had been standing over him. Morales is startled, not having heard Bill approach.

"Can I help you Corporal?" says Bill in almost a menacing way.

"I am sorry," apologizes Morales. "I went to the house to see you and your wife told me I would find you here. I was just checking the security of your fence. It seems to be well anchored. No one can easily crawl under it. That is good."

Bill stands there looking at him like more explanation is necessary.

"I have driven by many times since your break-in, and there has been no indication of suspicious activity. Would you agree?" asks Morales.

Bill folds his arms on his chest and takes a step back to the side. Corporal Morales takes the opportunity to start walking back towards the gate.

"Yeah. Everything seems to be fine Corporal."

"As I said to your wife, whoever it was who broke into your home seems to have left the area. Maybe there is no longer need for concern," adds Morales. "We have not experienced any further suspicious activity."

Bill walks Morales right to the door of his police Jeep.

"No, I am not worried Corporal," answered Bill curtly. "Probably best if you direct your energy to something of greater urgency. Really. I think that is what you should be doing."

Corporal Morales pulls out a business card from on the console of his Jeep and hands it towards Bill. "Well. If you see anything or anyone that causes concern for you, you can give me a call," he says to Bill as professionally as he can.

Bill declines the card.

"I have one," Bill says curtly with a nod. "You are the only thing happening out of the ordinary Corporal," says Bill.

Morales gives a momentary puzzled look in response to Bill's statement. He is thinking that it could have more than one meaning. Their goodbye is polite and quick, and Corporal Morales drives away, slowly.

Morales is seeing that this Bill guy is a wary creature. Not one to approach without considerable caution, considerable strategy, and possibly only when things are considerably in your favor. Morales will think about caution and strategy and how to keep things in his favuor. He will think about it a lot. As a matter of fact, it starts to consume him. He thinks of little else, except when more serious events demand more from him.

Bill pulls the gate closed to the yard, and starts over to talk to Grandma. Bill contemplates his trip to Panama, leaving early tomorrow, and Corporal Morales still sniffing around.

Bill knows he smells a rat.

CHAPTER THIRTEEN

Approaching the Bridge of the Americas is incredible. The bridge spans the Pacific entrance to the Panama Canal at Balboa, just to the north of Panama City. The bridge is huge, at just over a mile long. The bridge has a long ramp-way on each end to gain the height clearance for the sea traffic through the Panama Canal. Freighters, tankers, container ships, and cruise ships all must fit under it's 200-foot vertical clearance. Ships are designed specifically to fit the bridge clearance, and the Canal's lock chambers. They are referred to as "Panamax" and they literally fit the locks of the Canal with less than two feet of clearance around the entire vessel. The maximum vessel size capacity of the Canal lock system is 950 feet in length, 106 feet in width, 190 feet of height, and 39 feet of draft.

Tankers, freighters, and container ships are anchored out on the Pacific side of The Bridge of the Americas, in Panama Bay. There can be a hundred ships waiting to clear the inspections, pay transit fees and meet the numerous regulations and protocols necessary before moving through the Transit List. This is the only shortcut through the western hemisphere and it saves thousands of miles of sailing.

There are numerous marinas within view along the city coastline. They are filled with an array of pleasure craft. Sailboats, with their masts standing tall, cruisers and yachts, big and small.

The skyline of Panama City stands out with its high-rises and business districts.

This is a vital, vibrant centre. One of the Wonders of the World. Its history is as rich as the economic activity it has spawned. From its ancient peoples, Spanish Conquistadors and pirates like Henry Morgan, come stories of sunken treasures, buried treasures, Canal history, free trade zones, military traffic, wars, and revolutions. Images of old black and white movies, with the likes of Humphrey Bogart, and smoke filled, dimly lit bars, slow ceiling fans and an array of seedy characters. Panama hats, spy thrillers, arms dealers, and smugglers of anything worth smuggling. Murder and intrigue. This is Panama.

All of this around you as you try to concentrate on your driving across The Bridge of the Americas. It is all right there around you. It is hard to take it all in. You can't, and drive too.

Bill has to concentrate. Even to light up a cigarette seems to be more than he can fit in right now. The local traffic is, of course, used to it all and passes by, changing lanes, skirting to an exit, trucks and cars merging in, all at a pace that seems reckless to the newcomer, one who has become accustomed to the 40-50 mile per hour traffic around Samara.

Bill spots the exit sign to the Santa Ana Business Park. His old friend Dave has had his printing business here since the mid-1970's, is one of the countless Vietnam vets who had trouble settling back in to the American Dream. When Dave's father died, younger than a man should, Dave left the States and re-established his family business here in Panama. He had the business equipment loaded into a semi-trailer, and that was it. Panama probably has one of the largest ex-patriot populations per-capita anywhere in the world. Sometimes it seemed that nobody was from Panama, that everyone had come here from someplace else.

Bill pulls over and stops his Jeep once he is in the Business Park and looks at the Google Map he printed for himself. Adviser Graphics is up about three blocks and then south a couple more.

Bill pulls up and parks in the designated parking in front of Adviser Graphics. It is a commercial district, but all relatively new construction, that was obviously planned as a commercial district sub-division. All the buildings are a stucco exterior, all architecturally compatible, though many different shapes and sizes, and all the same dusty rose colour with red Spanish roof tile and each yard with parking areas off the street area. There are ground level air conditioning units on cement foundations surrounded by shrubbery and flower gardens. The standard is practical, neat, clean, and well maintained.

Bill walks into the reception area and what first strikes him is the powerful smell of the shop - inks, solvents, toners, and cleaners. He approaches the counter that has several staff at their desks, each with a large screen computer and an assortment of printed materials crowding the desk surface. A lady in her thirties approaches to serve Bill.

"How can I help you Sir?" she politely asks, with a smile.

"I am here to see Dave. He is expecting me," answers Bill.

"Is that Dave Gonzales or Dave Rideout you are wanting to see?" she asks.

"That would be Rideout." Bill nods and smiles.

The lady retreats back into a hall that seems to have several offices, and in moments returns to Bill before returning to her desk.

"Mr. Rideout will be with you shortly."

Dave Rideout comes out of the hall with the offices wearing a big grin on his face. He walks fast. Before he makes it around the counter he calls out.

"Hey Bill! Good to see you!"

He reaches out and they shake hands.

"How was the trip down? The traffic on the Pan American highway didn't drive you bonkers?" asks Dave.

"No, not quite," answers Bill. "If you can call it a highway," he adds.

"Well come on. Come on into the back," bids Dave.

Dave is not quite a foot shorter than Bill. He was a redhead with hair as loud as a bougainvillea in bloom in his younger years. There is still considerable red, but there is also considerable grey. He has the complexion of a redhead, and the more than half a life time of sun near the equator has accentuated the variegated pigment of freckles and near freckles, and spots with no freckles. Still in good shape, the feisty, friendly manner, sparkling eyes and a radiant energy tell you that Dave is a character - has always been a character - and was certainly trouble for most of his grade-school teachers growing up.

Dave's office is a good size and nicely furnished, though not pretentiously, unlike a lawyer's office. It is primarily functional, with a large round wooden table (teak by the looks of it), in a work area ahead of his desk. Dave slips into one of the chairs and pushes a few articles aside and gestures for Bill to take one opposite.

"Good to see you," welcomes Dave. "What brings you down? Where are you staying? Is Phyllis with you? Sorry - too many questions," Dave adds smiling. "And please tell me when you get a chance, how your daughter is doing. When I last saw you her husband had just passed away. Just terrible Bill. How long ago was that now?"

There is a pause, and Bill settles in to a chair.

"Sorry Bill," Dave adds. "Too many questions. You just got off that crazy highway and ...."

Bill raises his palms out, up in front of himself, and pats the air as a calming affect, smiling.

"Yeah. Lots has been happening, "says Bill. "Seems crazy sometimes."

Bill spreads out his hands, palms up, and gives a bit of a shrug, giving a slight nod of his head to the side, still smiling.

"But that's life, hey?" adds Bill. "Seems harder every year just to keep up."

Dave nods in agreement.

"At any rate, Jessica is doing alright." Bill starts. "It's been three years, and her and the boys moved in with us. It has its moments, but it is generally alright. She is still on her own. It has been tough. Raising the boys down here, being on her own, living with her parents. But I think the move to Costa Rica was a good thing for them. It changed everything."

"Phyllis and I make it down to the border for shopping trips once or twice a year, but we haven't made it this far down since we last saw you. It's time to get her down again. Jessica and the boys can run the place for a weekend or so. The boys are sure growing up. Man," Bill exclaims, again, shaking his head slowly. "No, I am down by myself. So, how is Monica?" Bill asks.

"Monica's good. Really good," Dave says happily. "Life here has been good. Business isn't everything we would like it to be, but we keep up. It seems every new computer program that comes out takes away a piece of our business. And the technology in copiers and printing equipment keeps you scrambling to keep up. I mean, look at it! How many film developing shops do you see now? There used to be tons of them. Now it's all digital cameras and print your own. The printing business is going down the same path. A sunset industry, they call it."

Dave has always had facial expressions that, at times, gave away what he was going to say before he said it. It had caused him some serious trouble in the Army. His top lip would develop something stronger than a tremor, just before he was about to ask a question. If he stopped to consider something before he spoke, the tremor would again reveal that he was about to speak.

Dave's lip started to quiver. Bill felt the question coming.

"So what are you doing down here?" Dave asks with concern.

There is a pause. Bill takes in a breath, feeling reluctant to start.

Dave jumps in, like to recover from a bad move.

"No, wait. It is late. I'll call it a day here. Let's go down to the boat. Bring your gear. You can stay on the boat tonight. Or if you like, come up to the house after. It will be cool down on the boat. We'll go for drinks. Monica can join us. What do you say?"

Bill settles way back in his chair, and opens out his arms and hands. A big comfortable smile comes to his face. It is the answer.

"Sounds great to me," replies Bill.

Dave is already standing.

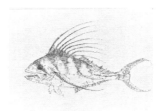

Derrick is standing back ten or twelve feet from Johnny, who is bent over the septic tank. Derrick is standing back to avoid the fumes. The hinged concrete lid is pulled up and lies open, the padlock that secures it is laying to the side. Johnny is cleaning the coarse metal mesh filter with a hose, wearing rubber gloves and scooping messy stuff into a garbage pail.

"Why don't you do that first thing in the morning and get it over with?" asks Derrick.

Johnny finishes up and shakes his hands off above the pail, then pulls the lid closed and washes his gloves off with the hose onto the lawn before taking them off.

"If I did it in the morning, I would have to wonder how clean my hands are all day. If I do it now, I can go home and shower and be done with it. Day finished."

"I see your point," says Derrick. "I had to clean it once when you were away. I hated it. Bill did it a couple times. He hates it too."

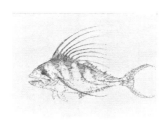

I thought it, but didn't say it, that it was probably part of the reason Bill took Johnny back.

"Well good. We're done," I say. "Lets go fishing."

Johnny coils up the hose and I pick up a rake and take it to the storage area. Johnny hangs his keys up on a nail on the wall that he can only reach standing on his tip toes.

I reach in the cooler and grab us each a Coke.

"Lets sit out for a bit," I say.

We walk out toward the beach and sit where there is a rough-cut bench Bill had made from a big piece of driftwood, with a chain saw. Mom is laying in a recliner, in the shade of the palm trees, settling in to a book. She has only just finished her work for the day also. We all enjoy the breeze coming off the water. Saul is goofing with a dog. Saul buries a stick in the sand and the dog digs it up.

I bang my shoulder into Johnny's and say, "Don't lick your fingers." Johnny gives me a shoulder shove back. I am glad Johnny is back.

"Aren't you two going fishing?" Mom asks. She seems glad everything is back to normal too.

"Yeah, in a minute," I answer back.

"Do I need to take anything out for dinner, or are you going to catch it for us?" Mom asks.

I gulp down the last of my Coke and let out a good belch. Mom doesn't get after me but shakes her head.

"We'll catch it for us. Can Johnny come over for dinner?" I throw in.

"Only if you catch dinner," Mom replies. I know she doesn't mean it.

"Tomorrow," I say to Johnny, "What do you say we go catch a crocodile? We haven't done that in a long time." I say it fairly loudly, showing off our prowess as great fishermen.

"Can I come?" butts in Saul.

Johnny and I look at one another like it is not that preposterous a request. But it is something new. Mom looks at me like she might plead Saul's case.

"Is it okay with you?" I ask Johnny.

"Sure. Fine with me."

"Saul," I say. "Tomorrow just after lunch. You can run up and buy us a bag of chicken heads tonight. They might be closed tomorrow. Mom, you can float Saul for that, hey?"

I get up and Johnny follows my lead.

"I'll meet you down there," I say to Johnny, meaning the beach. "I am going to get my gear."

As I start back up to the storage room, I call back to Saul.

"Get us about a dozen heads. They usually charge us one or two dollars. And Saul, don't bring your dog tomorrow. If he starts swimming in the slough he could get eaten by a croc."

Boy! Don't I sound like a hot shot today!

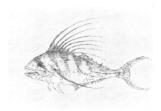

"Bill, Bill, Bill. You are getting my Irish blood running hot." Dave pauses. "You do have this worked out. Really. I am impressed."

Bill raises his martini glass and toasts Dave. Bill has said his piece, spoke of his plans and his need for a whole list of fabricated documents. Forged documents. He is talked out for the moment, and has left himself a little vulnerable. At least vulnerable to being thought a fool by a friend. Bill lets Dave mull over all that he has said.

"There are so many Archaeological digs going on in Panama," starts Dave. "They are everywhere you go it seems. They make the papers all the time. I have to say it is a clever ruse."

Dave, again, picks up the list Bill has given him of the documents he would like to get. He browses through it again.

"The University of Panama logo is easy. I have it on file. They contract out their printing needs to the lowest bidder. We do some work for them regularly. The drivers licence is not that difficult, nor the vehicle registration, but it is all detailed and time consuming work. You can steal your own Panamanian licence plates. Just send me the plate number and the renewal sticker number. The newspaper articles are the easiest. There is a software program that just requires us to type them up. You could actually do them yourself. Have you brought me photos of yourself and Derrick?"

"Yeah, I have a CD with tons of pictures. It's in my bag," answers Bill.

"And the permits and authorizations to conduct an Archaeological dig." Dave pauses and considers this for a moment. "Maybe you know what they should look like, because I don't. But then I guess nobody else does either, so just about anything should pass. Just make it look official."

Bill laughs in agreement, and Dave joins in, quite amused.

"Just make them look professional," Bill agrees. "On my list

I identify the 'National Environmental Authority', the 'Environmental Impact Agency', and designation as a 'World Heritage Site'. Give them each a Panamanian Seal and somebodies signature and that should have it."

They toast their martinis again, and the moments of time seem strained to fit in all that each of them has to say, and wants to ask, as their conversation drifts off to other topics. The time passes quickly, and the sun approaches the Western horizon. It will be a beautiful sunset. Bill eats his last olive from his Martini.

"So can you do it?" Bill says, then quickly corrects himself. "Will you do it?"

"Sure," Dave says. "I'll take care of it myself. It might be fun."

"And you know I expect to pay well for your work." Bill reassures.

"Well," Dave says, and pauses. His top lip starts to quiver. "It is a matter that the penalties for creating the forged documents are way more severe than being in possession of them. So, though you are taking risks in your adventures, you are asking me to take risks also. Considerable risks if it ever comes back on me." Dave shrugs and adds, "Though I know it shouldn't. It won't. As I said, it might be fun. Put a little adventure in my life."

There is a pause as Dave's comments strike a sobering note.

"And what is the cost of doing this kind of work, risks all factored in?" asks Bill.

Dave answers quickly, and his lip does not quiver.

"The price is usually determined, first by how desperate you are, the urgency of how much you need the documents and, next, by the demands of how sophisticated the documents are to produce. And last, by the quality and reputation of the man doing the workmanship. And, if you are the finest forger in the world then maybe the priorities for pricing get applied the other way around."

"Well I brought $10,000 cash with me," states Bill. "I will leave it with you. If you would like more, I am serious, just say so and it's yours."

"No, no Bill," says Dave. "How about half that. And if your project turns out as well as you hope, or even better, bring me a big gold nugget to put on a necklace for Monica. She would love it."

"How soon do you need it all?" Dave adds.

"You know," Bill tries to shrug off his question. "As soon as you can."

Dave mulls this over for a few moments. And this time his lip tremor again introduces his thoughts.

"Can you give me a couple of weeks?"

"Yes. Sure," says Bill. "Call me when you are ready, and I will come down and pick them up myself." Bill pauses. "You know how much I appreciate it Dave. It's like old times."

The ocean breezes are perfect. Dave's boat is beautiful. The rear deck has teak flooring, and heavily chromed, highly polished fittings. It is a newer model power cruiser, probably 38-40 feet. The sliding rear doors are open to the salon. Everything is placed perfectly, shining, and part of a perfect package. Dave returns from the salon and sits back in his deck chair after mixing a fresh shaker of martinis. He places a fresh cocktail toothpick with two olives in each of their glasses, and pours. He tilts his glass toward Bill, this time not standing or reaching to toast one another more formally. He sips and leans back in his chair, and holding his glass high he says.

"Now this is really living."

Dave has used this expression before with Bill. This toast. It was one Dave's father used, and Dave remembers it, and uses it with reverence.

Bill holds his martini glass high, and says, exactly in the same phrasing and tone as Dave, "Now this is really living."

The sun is just starting to sink over the Pacific. The light is changing. The air is cooling. Dave recognizes the sound of Monica's high heels walking down the wharf. It is going to be a fun evening. Just like old times.

CHAPTER FOURTEEN

Saul comes strolling into the pool area with a dog in tow, just as I am finishing up vacuuming the pool. He has the bag of chicken heads he was sent for. Johnny is coiling a good length of ¼-inch yellow poly rope, which he puts the binding turns to and stuffs it in a light pack sack.

"How many Cokes should I bring?" asks Johnny as he heads to the cooler.

"Half a dozen anyways," I reply. "How much did she charge for the chicken heads?" I ask Saul.

"A dollar," he replies. "She only had ten."

"Ten's good," adds Johnny. "Do you have a knife Saul?"

"No, Bill took it," he answers.

"Go ask Grandma for it," I say. "Tell her you need it in case you have to cut a rope that gets tangled. Just in case - to be on the safe side."

Saul starts off to find her.

"And you have to do something with that dog!" I holler after him.

I finish putting away the corrugated hose for the pool vacuum.

"I think we have to hoof-it today," I say to Johnny. "Bill took the Jeep for a couple days."

I know that I have not told Johnny where Bill has gone, and he doesn't ask. He is probably just happy not to have to face him. It hadn't come up with any specifics at dinner the previous evening either. We seem great at avoiding any issues. We did catch several perch and two red snappers. Dinner was good, and Johnny enjoyed watching the movie we got later.

Grandma is hunting through a drawer of Bill's clothes in their bedroom and I stop at the doorway. I presume she is looking for where Bill has put Saul's belt knife.

"Can you find it?" I ask.

"No, not yet," she answers. "Give me another minute." Grandma pulls out the bottom drawer. "Don't you have one you can loan him?"

"A pocket knife maybe. But they're not the best," I reply. "And what can we do to tie up Saul's dog? He can't come."

Grandma stands up, holding Saul's belt knife. This one was one of Dad's that Mom gave to him as a keepsake. Mine too.

"Put him in the compound, and I'll let him out a while after you've gone."

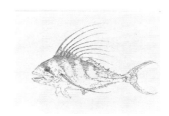

The Estuary, we call it, is actually a small river in the rainy season, and the water quits running if there hasn't been rain for a few months. The water, when it is running, creates a good-sized creek bed across the beach, but only when it is running. The berm of the beach, and the wave action, deposits enough sand to bottle it up as a back-water that turns a milky white in the heat. I don't know how deep it is because no one goes in it. There are crocodiles in there.

The water seems swampy, and there are sandy reaches of gentle sloping bank that lead back to the mess of mostly bushes, and the occasional larger tree. There are outcroppings of dead-fall in the sandy areas, trees washed down by flood waters that get buried in the mud and the sand. Most of the branches eventually break away.

It is more than a mile south of the hotel, and the area we like to go to is set back about a quarter or half a mile from the beach. It is what you would probably call a swampy flood-plain area, very flat, and the road the fisherman and gas trucks use to get down to the beach is just this side of it, set back far enough as to not get flooded out if there are big rains.

It is hot and muggy. The ocean breezes don't often make it into this undergrowth area. Walking in gets you warmed up enough. The talk has mostly been between Johnny and myself, about our crocodile experiences, and giving the low-down to Saul of what to watch for and how to do things. Saul has joined in, and has even asked some good questions on how to do things if something goes wrong.

"So what happens if you get a crocodile so big it starts pulling you into the water?" asks Saul.

"Cut the rope," says Johnny. "That's why it is good to have a knife."

"If you have to cut the rope, try and cut it as close to the water as you can, so we have enough left to keep fishing," I add.

"Can they really pull you into the water?" Saul asks sceptically.

"Pretty tough to do," answers Johnny. "Wrap the rope around a log and let him thrash around. Eventually the rope will get cut up enough by his teeth that it will break. Sometimes they will let go of the bait, but just leave it. They will come back for it. If they break the rope, you will know it. It snaps."

"But the best is to pull him up onto the banks so we can see him," I add. "Sometimes you have to let them swallow the bait to do that. Their mouth is pretty tough to take the hook. Remember that one you got last time," I say to Johnny. "Saul, Johnny got him up on the bank and he must have been five or six feet long. He would lunge at us! We finally had to cut the rope. He scared the pants off me."

Saul looks at me all quiet. Johnny is looking at me, quiet also.

"Okay," I say. "He had to be four feet long."

"Hey, let's do it." yells Johnny. "Do you want to go first Saul? We take turns."

"No, you guys go first. I'll watch how you do it."

I think I have put enough fear into Saul. We are all excited.

"What would happen if you tied a rope around his mouth." asks Saul. "Then we could maybe sell him."

"Not to me!" Johnny replies.

"How are you going to move him? He isn't going to follow you home like a dog on a leash." I add.

Saul pauses, then adds, "Well I think it would be neat to tie him up around his mouth. Maybe we could carry him, hanging from a pole."

Johnny and I look at one another, shake our heads and laugh. Obviously I haven't put enough fear into Saul.

"Don't be doing anything stupid like that today." I direct at Saul. Saul just goes quiet.

Johnny picks a site where a decent sized trunk of a tree is buried in the sand about thirty feet from the waters edge. He sets down the pack sack and pulls out his machete from it, and together we walk back to a thicket of bushes that has some long branches sticking out of it. Johnny pries himself in between the branches and hacks at the base of a long dead one that is probably twenty feet long and about three inches at its base. He adjusts around, forcing himself between branches to cut at it from another angle, and then adjusts back again to complete the job. As soon as I can reach it, I pull down on it to expose the branch to Johnny's hacking. The branch gives and I start dragging it over to the log where Saul and the pack are.

"Saul," I call. "Can you drag over any pieces of wood you can find to prop this branch up by the bank? Rocks are good too."

Saul is looking around aimlessly, not knowing what he is really looking for. I throw the branch forward and it lands over the tree trunk.

"Come with me," I direct Saul, walking away from the waters edge. "What we need is enough stuff to prop the pole up so it reaches out over the water. We can dig a hole in the sand to anchor the butt end. See if you can find something good to prop it up with."

Saul runs back to Johnny and asks to borrow his machete. Joining me, Saul points to branches in the thicket.

"If we cut two pieces of those we can use the fork on the ends to prop up the pole," says Saul. He holds his arms in an "A" formation and spreads two fingers out on each hand in a fork pattern to show how they could support the pole.

"It could work," I say. "You cut them. I'll find a piece of wood or a rock."

Johnny is working with the coil of rope and the bag of chicken heads. He ties a knot through the rusty treble hook. The hook is about the size of your fist. He forces one, then a second, chicken head onto the hook. I push the base of the long pole into the sand at an angle to hang out as far as it can over the water. Saul sets his two branches, with forks on the end, at angles to support the pole as a triangular brace.

"Don't get so close to the edge of the water," I tell him. "Crocs are known to lunge out of the water at anything on the shore."

Saul and I jockey around the base of the pole and get the long branch to balance on the braces Saul has cut and planted in the sand.

"Hey, that works well!" I say, and call out to Johnny who is finishing up with the hook, rope, and chicken heads. He pulls the knot several times to test it. "Look at this," I holler out to him, pointing at the braces Saul has cut to support the pole.

Johnny and I string the rope up the pole. We put a small loop on the end that hangs on the end of the branch. It takes us a couple of attempts to set the length of the rope so that the hook and chicken heads just to touch the surface of the water.

I try to tell Saul the strategy of what we are trying to do.

"What we want is for the heads to touch the water so their scent goes into the water. That's what the crocs will come after. When they see it, they will go after it."

"Who wants to go first?" Johnny asks.

"You go," I reply. Saul stays quiet. But he watches. He banks up some sand around the base of the supports he has cut.

Johnny uncoils the rope back to the log where the pack is and sits in the sand leaning against the log, the coil of rope at his side.

"Ready for a Coke?" I ask.

I fetch a couple out from the pack. Neither declines the one I offer them.

Johnny and I ramble on about our crocodile fishing experiences. We are bragging to impress Saul - how brave we are, how lucky we have been, and how dangerous it all is.

Saul jumps up. "Look!" he exclaims and points to the water surface fifteen feet from the chicken head. "Right there!"

I can see the water rippling on the surface, approaching the chicken head. I can't see the crocodile. Johnny grabs the line up in his hand but does nothing more.

Like a huge rat trap, the jaws of the crocodile break the surface and snatch the chicken head. The rope pops off the end of the branch and the branch falls down at the edge of the water from its braces. The yellow line is pulled into the water and we all run up closer to the waters edge.

"Close enough," I say to Saul.

Johnny coils up some of the slack of the rope in his hand, then gives it a big jerk backwards, stepping back from the water as he does it until the rope bites. Then Johnny is jerked forward and he plants his feet and starts pulling backwards, adjusting the line in his hands so he can let more out if he needs to.

"How big is it?" I holler at him.

I see the line thrashing about in the water and the water boils, breaking the surface. Crocodiles have a huge tail that makes them powerful in the water.

"I don't know yet," Johnny yells back. "Not too big."

"Can you bring him up?" I yell again.

"Lets see him!" yells Saul.

The crocodile is heading under water toward the ocean, then stops. Johnny runs ahead and tries to pull him forward up onto the bank in the direction he was going. Johnny is keeping a good six to ten feet from the waters edge. We run along with him, keeping our distance from the waters edge also.

The crocodile moves forward and Johnny steers him up onto the bank, and it emerges - its head and half of its body are out of the water before it plants its feet. Now there is a tug-of-war between Johnny and the crocodile. The crocodile gives a sideways toss of its head, instinctive to rip a piece of flesh from its prey. With its tail still in the water, we can't see his full size. Its mouth is about the length of my forearm, and its teeth look about an inch long, sticking up from its bottom jaw.

"He's probably four feet anyway!" yells Johnny.

Saul approaches toward the crocodile and it gives its head another shake. Johnny shudders with the jerking of the line.

"Saul!" I yell, warning him off.

Johnny resets his footing and starts to pull harder. He drags the crocodile up another couple feet up the bank, then they set again in their tug-of-war. The crocodile swings its tail to one side, then the next, and we get a better look at him. He has to be close to five feet long.

"He's a good one!" I holler at Johnny.

"What do you do now?" asks Saul.

"Wait," says Johnny, "and see what happens."

We all stand there in a Mexican Standoff, one crocodile against the three of us. Johnny keeps the line taught.

"Should I pull him right up on the beach?" Johnny asks.

"Yeah!" says Saul with emphasis.

"If he lunges at us, I am out of here," I say.

The crocodile uses its strong tail to help it pivot and lunges towards the water. Johnny strains on the rope.

"Do you want to try it?" Johnny asks Saul.

Saul has his eyes fixed on the crocodile and says, "sure," as he angles towards Johnny, keeping his eyes on the crocodile. Johnny hands the rope towards Saul. It goes limp for a moment. The crocodile lunges to adjust its hold on its prey and the hook and chicken heads pull out of its grip onto the sand. The rope goes slack.

The crocodile stares at us for a few moments, then lunges into the water. The water leaves a wake behind this water monster as it swims back to where it came from.

Johnny starts laughing and I join in.

"Wow!" exclaims Saul. "That was neat!"

Johnny pulls up the hook with the chicken heads into his hands and inspects it. The chicken heads look a little worse for wear, but they are still intact. Johnny holds the bait out to us.

"Look," he says. "One of the hooks broke off."

The treble hooks were discards given to us by one of the local fishermen who runs a bottom line - one they anchor out and leave overnight to catch bottom fish. The salt water deteriorates the hooks rapidly. Corrosion had eaten away the strength of the metal.

"You want to try it now?" I ask Saul.

"Sure."

"The scent of the bait," says Johnny, "and the thrashing of the crocodile will only bring in more. Maybe bigger ones."

Saul smiles.

Johnny rigs another hook, and puts on fresh chicken heads. He throws the broken hook into the bag with the chicken heads still on it, just in case we need it later.

Saul and I rig the line over the end of the long branch and reset his braces. With this setup, the chicken heads are now just barely submerged - maybe a couple inches into the water.

Johnny recoils the remaining line and hands it to Saul.

"If anything goes wrong, just let go," says Johnny.

I give the branch a few shakes that bounce the bait in the water.

"Come on up and have a Coke," I beckon Saul from the log where the pack-sack is and hold up the Coke cans.

Saul makes his way back, uncoiling the line as he comes, and sits and leans back against the log like Johnny and myself. I crack him open a Coke and hand it to him. Everyone sits for a moment and enjoys the cool Cokes.

"So what happens if you cut the rope?" asks Saul. "What happens to the hook?"

"The mouth of a crocodile would dissolve the hook in a day or two," says Johnny.

"Really?" says Saul.

"The croc would never notice it was there," I add. "Grandpa said they can go as long as a year without eating."

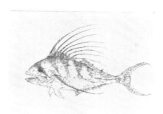

Phyllis remembers that she was supposed to let the dog out of the compound. She closes out of her internet program on her desk, having answered enquiries about the hotel and Samara Beach. Her keys are on the kitchen table and she grabs them as she passes by. Stepping out the screen door, she sees Corporal Morales' police Jeep driving away.

"Oh boy," she says with a frustrated sigh.

Morales didn't see her come out, she thought logically. He would have stopped if he had. Morales didn't see her. She doesn't have to make up anything about where Bill has gone. The story she and Bill had agreed on was that Bill had gone up to San Jose to an appointment with a specialist. No more specifics than that.

Phyllis picks up the padlock on the chain around the gate of the compound and the dog runs up from some shady spot he had found. As soon as the dog is out, it runs over to the hotel parking lot and sniffs around. Phyllis locks up, turns around, and sees the dog sniffing off toward the direction the boys went. He seems to pick up their scent and picks up speed, heading off in their direction.

"Oh great!" Phyllis lets out, but dismisses it in her mind and carries on.

Saul drains his Coke can, stands up, and coils the slack rope in his hand as he approaches the propped-up branch. He gives the branch a bob or two. That gives the chicken heads some motion in the water, and the rope and bait sink a little further into the water. He uncoils the rope from his hand as he makes his way back to the log and Johnny and Derrick. Just as he is about to sit back in the sand, his dog breaks through the bushes and runs straight at him, barking. Johnny and Derrick turn around at the noise.

Saul yells at the dog, then feels the jerk on his arm and the coil of rope bites into a knot around his hand. Caught totally off guard, Saul swings around and is jerked toward the water - dragged toward the water!

Derrick and Johnny are yelling at the dog and only after a few moments do they realize what is happening. Saul plants his feet and resists, but he is still being tugged in. His body jerks toward the waters edge.

Bolts of fear rattle through Saul. He realizes he is not holding his own in this tug-of-war. His stray dog jumps up at his face, the dog excited to find him. He bats at the dog with his free hand and the dog excitedly jumps at Saul and nips him on the hand.

Saul is jerked several steps closer to the waters edge. The knot is gripping tighter. It hurts his hand. The dog has bitten his free hand. Helplessness grips Saul. For Saul, it feels like a fatal grip. Fear and helplessness. He wants to yell for help, but it just doesn't come out. Saul shakes his head around in gyrations. He can't shake off the fear and panic he feels.

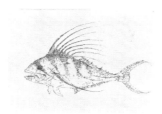

As Johnny and I are hollering at the dog, Saul is yanked right off his feet and into the sand by a good jerk from the line. It is only then that we see what is happening. Fear registers, along with reality. Every action now seems to happen in slow-motion.

The dog lunges at Saul's face, not biting, but playing a game of tag like Saul has played with him so many times before. Saul is being tugged, face-down in the sand, being pulled inches each time, toward the water. He isn't putting up any more resistance than a dead weight. He isn't trying to recover or get on his feet.

Johnny runs up and cuts the rope a foot from Saul's hand. The rope snaps back the rest of the way into the water and disappears. Johnny still has his knife in his hand. He turns towards me.

"That was close. Too close." he exclaims.

I drop to my knees in the sand beside Saul and put my face down close to his.

"Saul. Saul!" I call out to him, trying to shake him awake.

Saul seems to be unconscious.

Saul's face is flushed. I shake him again then roll him on to his side

"Saul, what's the matter?" I plead. I brush the sand off of Saul's face and Johnny unwraps the remaining line from his hand, which has knotted up. Johnny chases the dog back, but the dog is persistent, still trying to get close to Saul.

"Saul. Saul!" I call out again trying to shake him awake.

Saul starts to move. He starts to breath heavily, and his colour settles back to his usual complexion.

I start to prop Saul up and Johnny helps.

"Man that was scary," says Johnny.

"Yeah, no kidding." I answer.

Neither of us say anything for a few moments as we try to catch our breath.

"Lets try and move him - sit him up over by the log," I say to Johnny.

We get Saul up on his feet and prop him up to walk over to the log where the pack is. We settle him back to where he was previously sitting.

"Saul, are you okay?" I ask again. "What happened?"

Saul groans a bit and brushes more sand off from his face. The dog comes over and licks him in the face too.

"I don't know," Saul says almost grudgingly, pushing away the dog.

"Did you faint?" I plead.

Saul sits without answering for a few moments, seeming to gather his wits.

"I don't know man," he replies. "I guess so."

We are all still breathing deeply, recovering from all that has happened. Johnny starts to pick up the pop cans and what is left of the rope, bait and tackle, and puts them in the pack-sack. He sits on the log facing Saul and myself.

"Well that's enough of that," Johnny says. "That was crazy!"

I agree, slowly shaking my head, still in disbelief of what has just happened.

"Can you make it home Saul?" I ask.

"Yeah" Saul says with a big breath.

"This is twice we've had to help you home in a week." I add.

I help Saul get up and he starts walking on his own, a little shaky.

"I'm okay," he says. He brushes sand off from his shirt, shorts, and his leg.

We start back, exhausted, as if we have just lost a World Championship soccer game. We are each quiet. Each subdued. There is no bravado, no boasting of the one that got away. Maybe they will come later, the stories, but only after the intensity of these moments, and the fear, fades from memory.

We never even got a glimpse of the crocodile that took the bait. Time and again these thoughts come back to me. Time and again. And on many a night, as sleep approaches, I am jolted awake at the thought. How big was the crocodile? Having not seen it has made it all the more terrifying. There is no comfort in not knowing. The images of Saul being dragged to the water never fade.

The only comfort is in having cut the rope.

CHAPTER FIFTEEN

Bill sticks the Panama truck plates under the floor mat on the passenger side of the Jeep, then re-considers. Best not to conceal them. He moves them into a side pocket in the rear of the Jeep with some other tools. Border crossings, possible inspections, stolen plates.... He will say he found them, if asked, and say he was going to turn them in whenever he ran across a registration office.

Leaving Panama City is straightforward enough. He knows he will be back in a matter of a couple weeks. He was disappointed that it might take a couple of weeks to get the documents back from Dave. But what should he have expected?

Phyllis won't be expecting him back so soon, but that will be well enough received. Home for dinner is a pleasant thought. Last evening, Dave and his wife Monica – also pleasant thoughts.

Traffic is busy on the Pan American Highway. It is always busy, day and night. A day of travelling. Bill lights a cigarette.

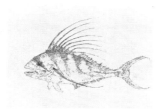

Bill pulls into the hotel parking lot and parks in his spot across from the veranda. The front door is locked, so Bill unlocks it and sets his kit bag inside the door, locks it again, and goes around to the pool area and the storage room to grab a beer from the cooler. Several families of patrons are sitting around the pool area and there are kids and adults playing in the pool. Bill smiles and waves, and heads toward the beach and the shade of the palm trees where he feels sure to find Phyllis. The breeze feels good. Phyllis is in her favourite recliner, with her book and a cool drink. She is surprised to see Bill.

"I certainly didn't expect to see you today!" she exclaims. She is happy to see Bill and he bends down and gives her a kiss.

"Did everything go okay?" she asks.

"Yeah, everything went fine," Bill answers. "It is just going to take a bit longer to pull things together - longer than I thought. I don't know what I was thinking. There was no point in waiting around. Stuff won't be ready for a couple weeks."

"Did you see Dave?" asks Phyllis. "How is he doing?"

Bill smiles at the thought.

"It was good," he replies. "Real good. We got to spend some time together - cocktails on his boat, and then Monica joined us for dinner. One of those oceanfront restaurants by the Marina. I've got to go back when he calls. Would you like to come with me? It would be good. I know you would enjoy it."

"Sure, we can talk about it," replies Phyllis. "I didn't expect you home for several days yet. You only left yesterday morning."

"Is everything okay here?" Bill asks.

"Yes," Phyllis answers. "No problems. Jessica and Saul have gone into town to pick a few things up. Derrick and Johnny are out there fishing."

Phyllis points up the beach a few hundred yards towards the town site. There are half a dozen men fishing, spaced even distances apart, Derrick and Johnny among them. Pelicans have shown them where the feed fish are located.

"Those two sure get along well." adds Phyllis. "Johnny has worked out well here. There don't seem to be any bad feelings. I am asking you to remember that Bill. And the boys all had an adventure yesterday. Crocodile fishing at the estuary. I'll let them tell you about it."

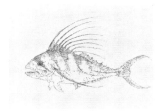

Dinner is going to be good. An all-American standard. Mom and Saul returned from town with fresh hamburger and buns, and I am trying my hand at the barbeque. Mom spiced up the hamburger and now she's making fries. Bill is sitting out on the porch until it is all ready, with Grandma, each with a beer, catching up on the events of the last couple days. Of course, everyone was surprised to see Bill when they returned. I sent his fish home with Johnny tonight, so they would have enough for dinner. Mom checks on how I'm doing, cooking the hamburgers, and brings me a plate of cheese to put on them and then calls everyone in. Saul is directed to turn off the T.V. when he comes to the table.

Saul and I finish relaying yesterdays crocodile fishing story to Bill. Saul has claimed his territory, and status as The Great Crocodile Hunter, and tells everyone how he would like to catch one and tie its mouth shut and sell it.

"Someone would pay you lots of money for it, wouldn't they?" he asks Bill. "Don't you think?"

"I don't know," answers Bill. "Not me. But I don't think you want to be taking such chances. Those crocs can really move when they get a notion to. You like having two arms and two legs, don't you?"

It wasn't really a question.

"It wasn't just the crocodile that scared me," I add. "Saul just seemed to pass out - faint, whatever - and that scared me. Seems like he had a heart attack or something."

"Yeah right!" declares Saul, like it was the most ridiculous thing in the world.

"Was it hot?" asks Bill. "Had you been drinking enough water?"

"Yeah," answers Saul.

"Were you wearing a hat?" asks Bill. "Were you?"

"No," answers Saul.

"It seems strange to me," adds Mom. "I should maybe make you an appointment to see the doctor."

"Well, you've been going through a growth spurt lately," declares Bill. "Your mom fainted a couple times growing up. Once at the Dentist office, and once getting her ears pierced.

Twice that we know about. Saul, you should try wearing a hat when you are out in the sun. You're not Costa Rican. And take a pinch of salt in the morning. Just lick it off your hand. Maybe your electrolytes are off. You sweat down here way more than you think you do. You lose your salt."

Bill changes topics and everyone is fascinated with his description of Panama City. We have all met his friend Dave before, and it is nice to hear of old friends.

"And Dave asked about you Jess," says Bill. "Asked how you are doing. His own daughter, Julie, is your age as you know. He is concerned. I told him life is going better, and that the boys are growing like weeds."

Mom gives a gentle smile. Dave's concern has touched her - a soft spot. But it also seems to have touched a raw nerve. Jessica, now having to spend moments to recover from unwelcome memories and feelings that she did not wilfully choose to visit.

"Tell Dave thank you when you see him, Dad. Thank him for his concern, but tell him life is good for us here. But tell him I would go back in a second. I think he will understand." Jessica pauses. "And if you would, tell him..." and she pauses again, "...tell him how good you have been to us. You and Mom. Really. Tell him how much it has meant to me and the boys."

The reflective smile Mom has had falls. In a moment, she appears to be distressed and, as quickly, she recovers her composure and stands up and goes off to the kitchen. The kitchen lights up as she turns on the lights and starts moving dishes on the counter.

Saul turns around in his chair to look over at Mom. Saul has heard and felt something that is new to him. I noticed.

I know myself that my feelings seemed to get caught on a hook, and I was wanting to break free.

"I'll also tell him what a wonderful daughter you are, and how proud we are of you and the boys," says Bill loudly, directing his voice to Mom in the kitchen.

We all remain silent. Grandma gets up slowly, steps behind Bill's chair, puts her hands on his shoulders, and gives him several gentle squeezes.

Bill pats her hand on his shoulder. He seems to know that a change in topic might be good. Grandma heads over to the kitchen.

"You boys, I could use your help," starts Bill. "I know you are helping here, but I am working with a few projects that I can't do by myself. And Saul, I could use your help too."

"What's up?" I ask.

"Well, Derrick. I have talked to you already about how I plan to conceal work we do with the dredge. In a couple weeks, I will be ready. What we need to do now is check out the equipment I have built and see how it works. Work out any bugs there are. Practice how to use the equipment effectively. And that is where you come in Saul - you can help. I'll teach you how to run some of the equipment. It would be good for you Saul. It would be good for you to spend time with me. I'll explain to you what I am trying to do, like I told Derrick. We will have to get our stories together."

Bill has done this before, many times. He takes Saul under his wing and has Saul spend a lot of time with him. When this is his mission, wherever Bill goes, Saul goes. Usually it was because Saul had been acting up - causing Mom trouble, talking back, not listening, being weird. Bill gives Mom a rest. Takes on more of a fatherly role I guess. Grandfatherly anyways.

"And Saul," Bill adds. "I want to be clear. You can not talk to your friends about the work we do with the dredge. No mention of gold, or where we go, or when we are going to go - nothing. Do you hear me?"

Saul nods convincingly. "I hear you."

"You seem to have enough adventures of your own to talk about," adds Bill. "You guys! Do you know that there are hundreds of people killed every year by crocodiles?"

"Here?" blurts out Saul.

"In the world Saul," Bill says staring into Saul's eyes to make his point. "But there are people killed here too, every now and again. And people mauled also. Some of those crocs get pretty big here. Just a few years ago there was a thing in the paper about a boy being killed - a thirteen-year-old, I think. From Tortuguero, here in Costa Rica. Him and his brother - they were swimming in an estuary. I think it was the younger boy who was pulled under by the crocodile. And then the croc surfaced again with the boy in his jaws, and the boy cried out 'Goodbye my brother', and then the boy was gone. Never seen again. It was probably a bigger croc than what we have in this estuary, but then who knows how big they can get here?"

"This was a big one," I say. "Wasn't it Saul."

"Yeah," answers Saul, with emphasis. "It was big!"

"I think there was another one in Mexico about the same time – a younger boy." added Bill.

I think Bill made an impression on Saul. But I know he made

an impression on me. Now I have pictures in my mind of Saul being eaten by a crocodile to add to what already jolted me awake last night. New pictures. Saul crying out to me, "Good-bye my brother."

I know I am going to talk to Johnny about it.

Everything started to build in intensity over the next few days, but smoothly. Saul and Bill spend lots of time in the workshop. I spend time there too - especially in the evenings, after dinner, when Bill would go back over to work some more. Saul would be back at the house then, watching T.V. Bill related his plans to me, told me what he was teaching Saul. He would show me ways to use the equipment he was working on, like the grizzly head, to clear bigger pieces the dredge pulled up. Bill told me what real artifacts could look like - what they might be. And I saw that sparkle on several occasions - that sparkle in his eye when he got talking about the gold.

"And I am telling you," Bill said earnestly. "There is nothing to say we won't recover gold artifacts. Jewellery, sculpted pieces, maybe nuggets that big - so big that they won't fall through the grid! They are out there. Really!"

He brushed a wisp of hair from his face.

"So you are going to have to keep your eyes open," Bill added.

I was keeping my eyes open. And I could see the sparkle in Bill's eyes. I knew it was the talk of gold.

Johnny and I were doing all the maintenance work for the hotel. We freed up Bill's time so he could devote himself to his projects. And things were going well with Johnny. Well enough, anyway. Bill and Johnny had crossed paths - Johnny, here, doing his work. It was impossible for them not to run in to each other. And I saw the first, and possibly the next few, incidents. I was watching out for them.

Johnny was up on a step ladder, reaching up onto the roof tiles with a rake to pull down a palm branch that had blown down on to it. My heart skipped a beat or two as I saw Bill approaching. My fear, and I guess my worst fear at that moment, was that Bill would kick the ladder out from under him. But that is not what happened. An irrational fear I guess. Bill simply told him what to do, like he would do on any other day.

"There are a couple palm fronds on the house roof. Make sure you get them too," said Bill, and kept walking to the storage room to fetch whatever and then back to what he was doing. He never said another word to Johnny.

I brought up the encounter with Johnny later that afternoon as we were heading up the beach together to the internet store.

"I saw Bill run into you today, when you were up the ladder. How did that go?" I ask.

Johnny's expression was flat, subdued.

"He was okay," answers Johnny. "He scared me. I didn't see him coming. He told me to clean the branches off of the roof of your house." Johnny pauses for a moment. "The last time I didn't see him coming, I thought he was going to kill me."

It is the first time Johnny is explicit with any details about his episode with Bill.

"Bill isn't going to kill you," I say, trying to be convincing and persuasive. Though I have my fears also, I don't say so.

"I think I would rather wrestle with that crocodile," Johnny adds.

I laugh, to lighten the moment. I had certainly thought about their first encounter. I was afraid for how Johnny would feel and react - that he might run away. I didn't know what to expect.

"Johnny," I say. And then I pause looking for words. "It's not you. You're not doing anything wrong. I don't think he treats you right. But stay out of his face. If he talks to you, just listen. Don't look him in the eyes. I'm sorry. But it is just the way it is. Bill doesn't like strangers. Bill doesn't trust people. Always keep your distance from him."

We walk a bit farther before Johnny responds to what I have just said.

"He doesn't like Cost Ricans," says Johnny with some degree of contempt to his voice. "I see it, how he treats guests at your hotel. If they are Costa Ricans, he treats them different. He is not friendly, like to Americans."

I look at Johnny, disgusted and ashamed with the truth being out in the open.

"Yeah, I think you're right," I say quickly, then add, "But so what? Who cares. All we have to do is get along with him."

I say it. It is effective. Johnny does seem to shrug it off, but I know that I do care. I haven't got the answers to my problems. I am struggling with it too.

"He's not all bad," I add. "He has his good points."

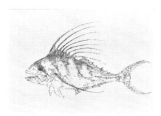

Things went smoothly enough the next couple of times Johnny ran into Bill. Johnny stepped off of the sidewalk and stood to the side as Bill went by, keeping his eyes down. Nothing was said. And the next time, Johnny was giving Phyllis a hand to load folded sheets into the shelves in the bodega and Bill came in, asked a couple questions of Phyllis, and that was that.

It wasn't great, but it wasn't out of control. And Johnny seemed to be easing with the tension himself.

Another night. Something has woken me up - some noise. I turn over, trying to rule it out, trying not to wake up. Then it is there again - the noise. Nothing serious. Two cats in a stand-off, shrieking at one another outside my window. I turn over. When I should be drifting off back to sleep, my mind tricks me and takes me where I don't want to go. Like, I know I shouldn't look at it, but I do. There: The images of Saul, again, too vivid in my mind, now indelible. Saul, being jerked into the water by the crocodile, being dragged down by the crocodile. Calling out to me.

I open my eyes and I back step, trying to recover reality. I am alright. Saul is alright. Johnny is alright. I remember how quickly Johnny reacted to save Saul. He cut the rope and saved Saul. He was good. I make a note in my mind to point this out to everyone. I make a note to point this out to Bill.

I make my way to the kitchen and pour a glass of orange juice from out of the fridge. I drink it, and set the glass quietly on the counter. Heading back to my bedroom, I pick up a couple of Saul's comic books lying on the end of the couch. In my room, I turn on the light by my bed and start to flip through the pages of one, then the next. One catches my interest and I start reading it.

The next thing I know, I am waking up to the muted conversation of Mom and Grandma in the kitchen. It is daylight. It is morning. I turn off the light by my bed and start to get up.

CHAPTER SIXTEEN

I get myself a cup of coffee, and pull up a chair with Mom and Grandma on the veranda. Bill is inside, talking on the phone. I had heard it ring a minute before. Bill sounds excited; Very animated.

"I took the last cup of coffee," I say. "Should I put some more on?" I ask.

Mom and Grandma are agreeing with one another that they should hire someone to help do the housekeeping at the hotel. They are intently discussing who to hire, so they ignore me. They each present different profiles of who they each consider desirable and the best match for their needs and the image of the hotel.

I help myself to fruit and pastries. It must have been the morning for the bakery van to come by again.

Bill comes through the screen door after a minute.

"That was Dave Rideout on the phone. My stuff will be all ready tomorrow," declares Bill. "I guess I am going to Panama tomorrow."

"Well that hasn't been two weeks," I say.

"No, it's only been a week," answers Bill.

"What's happening?" Grandma asks Bill, leaving the conversation with Mom, not having comprehended what Bill has said so far.

"That was Dave Rideout on the phone, and my stuff is ready to pick up. He says he got excited about doing it, that it's been years since he had a project like that, and so he gave it a few extra hours. So, it is done."

Grandma stares at Bill for a few moments, like she is trying to fathom the implications of Bill's news.

"So we can head out early tomorrow morning, spend an evening with them, and be back by the weekend," Bill directs to Grandma.

"Well," says Grandma, and pauses. "I can't be ready to go tomorrow."

Bill looks surprised by her response.

"No Bill," Grandma declares. "I can't go tomorrow. I am not going to run down there on some whirlwind trip and drive for fifteen hours to rush in a visit, and maybe get to go out for dinner." She pauses. "No Bill, you go. Take Derrick with you."

I look up from breakfast and coffee, this being the first I have been acknowledged so far this morning. And now my next few days are being planned for me.

Things go quiet for a minute.

"I'll put on some more coffee," says Mom, as she gets up. She knows there is more discussion, and coffee time to come.

"Bill," starts Grandma. "Lets plan to go down at the end of September. I'll go with you then. Then we can plan to spend a couple of days and enjoy our visit."

Saul has wandered out and sits in Mom's chair.

"Your mom's sitting there," Bill says to Saul.

Saul stands up and walks into the house. In half a minute, he is back with a glass of orange juice and a chair for himself. I make a little room for him and he fits in between Bill and I.

"Where are you going?" asks Saul of no one in particular.

"Panama City," answers Bill.

"Hey can I come?" throws in Saul.

"Would you like to come too Derrick?" asks Bill. He sees I am chewing a mouthful. He looks at Mom who has just come out with more coffee. "How about you Jess? Want to get away for a day?"

Mom sees the expression on my face. I am still chewing, and she answers for both of us.

"I think we all have plans on the go," Mom says, disarmingly.

Bill dismisses it. He is thinking, and checks his watch.

"Bill, I'd love to go in September," adds Grandma. "Let's plan for that."

Bill simply nods in agreement. He is looking a bit puzzled, like he is working out details in his head.

"I wanted to do a practice run with the equipment this weekend," says Bill. "But we'll look at that when I get back I guess. Derrick, Saul, you two could help me load equipment onto the deck of the truck. I mounted a winch at the head of the box to help us slide stuff up the loading ramps. I'd like to see how it works, just to see that we can handle everything ourselves."

Bill looks like he is ready to get at it.

"Bill," says Grandma gently. "Please sit down and finish your breakfast. I don't think you've had anything yet. You are all wound up."

She reaches across and pours Bill a coffee. I stick out my cup also. Bill settles back down.

"There's a lot I've got to get done," responds Bill.

"Bill," Grandma says as gently again. "There is always a lot to get done. You're going to be rushing off for a couple days again, and you have been going like crazy all week." Grandma pauses. "Tell me - since you are going to be gone for a couple days again, what can I cook you special for dinner tonight?"

Bill looks at Grandma, stares at her for a moment, then gives her a big forced grin.

"How about we do up some lobster tonight?" he replies, still grinning. "Ask Johnny if he can get us some. Hey Derrick?" Bill says looking at me.

"Yeah, sure," a little surprised how easily he brought up Johnny.

Everything settles down and a calm comes back to the conversation. Mom and Grandma are suggesting what would go with lobster.

"I had a heck of a dream last night," I say quite loudly, trying to catch everybody's attention. "It was about you Saul. I think I must have cried out in the night. Did anybody hear me?"

I have everyone's attention but no one is saying anything. They are waiting for me to carry on.

"It was that crocodile, tugging Saul into the water. It was dragging him. No exaggeration," I emphasize. "And it keeps dragging him and there is nothing we can do about it. And Saul disappears into the water, and the crocodile, huge, surfaces with Saul in his mouth, biting him in half, and Saul calls out to me: 'Goodbye my brother', and disappears. It was terrible,"

I exclaim.

"It sounds terrible," Mom says, agreeing with me.

"It does," agrees Gram.

"It was like the story you told Grandpa. The one of the boy who was killed in front of his brother," I say. "It was almost the same."

Everyone is quiet for a moment, reflecting I guess, on the brutal images in their own minds.

"Well it sure woke me up. Scared me half to death," I say, continuing my story. "But thinking about it then, if it hadn't been for Johnny, that's what could have happened. Johnny went down and cut the rope. He actually saved Saul's life."

I pause again. Then continue.

"But if that crocodile was big enough to drag Saul into the water, it was also big enough to kill him. It sure woke me up thinking about it. And if it wasn't for Johnny, who knows what would have happened?"

"You would have cut the rope," says Bill. "But it was good that Johnny had the presence of mind to do it. Maybe you guys should knock off the crocodile stunts for a bit."

"How about forever," Mom says.

"It was just a dream," says Saul. "I don't dream about it. I'd still like to catch one and tie its mouth shut."

"Please tell me you won't be doing that," says Mom.

"I won't," I say.

"Why not?" says Saul. "I think it would be neat."

"Yeah. Neat," says Bill. "Saul, how about the next time you start causing too much trouble around here we just send you down crocodile fishing?"

"Bill!" exclaims Grandma, drawing out her protest.

I laugh. And then I laugh some more.

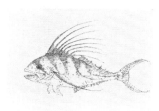

Bill has a hand-held control box for the winch, and Saul and I are helping to guide the big dredge pump on its floats, up the ramps, into the box of the Mercedes as Bill runs the winch. Bill has configured the frame that holds the dredge pump and floats together, so that it has four balloon tires protruding for moving on ground. Bill says the balloon tires keep it from sinking into sandy or gravel surfaces. We have to be able to move it ourselves. The winch really works well, and it helps lower the equipment down the ramp as much as it helps lift it all up. This is the heaviest piece of equipment. Bill uses a spray can of paint to mark the outline of where each piece of equipment should be loaded, so that everything fits and the load is balanced. Everything gets strapped down. Half a dozen dive tanks are strapped to the side. The barrels will be the heaviest, Bill says, when they are full of the silt and gravel from the sluice box. Probably seven hundred pounds each. But they will be filled gradually and will remain on the truck bed.

Johnny has come into the compound and is standing to the side, having dropped off a box of live lobster already at the house. I wave him over to come join us.

"Johnny can help us for a bit?" I ask of Bill, thinking I maybe shouldn't have waved him over just yet.

"Yeah, sure," says Bill.

"You know you have to keep it to yourself - everything you see, what we are doing," I say to Johnny as he joins us.

"Yes. For certain," Johnny replies.

Bill uses the spray can to mark the position of the barrels.

"How come I feel like I am being worked over here?" Bill directs at Derrick. "Here, help me move this in tight Derrick." Bill adds.

I don't give any comment to what Bill has said.

Johnny helps Saul with moving the sluice box on its balloon tires and floats out from the shop.

Bill feeds out the winch cable and I hook it onto the sluice box. Bill winches it up the ramps and we position it in place.

"You see what I have done here," Bill points out to me. "There are two sluice boxes, side by side, so one can be being cleaned out while the other one is still working. It will keep us from having to shut down. We can switch from side to side."

"It's sure going to keep us busy," I say. "But it is good."

"If you see we are getting gold sediments down near the bottom of the sluice, you can switch it over to the other side and empty the full side into the tub, wash it down a bit, and then it should be ready to go again. Just take a pinch of sediment from the lower part of the sluice and rub it between your fingers. You'll be able to see if there is gold in it."

"It sounds like a production line," I say to Bill.

"If I am under water," adds Bill "I won't know that you need to stop to clean things out. This will keep everything running," says Bill. "You are right. It will take a few hands, but you and Saul should be able to keep things running. Don't you think?"

"I think we would be pretty busy," I answer. "The dredge pulls up lots of stuff. I was really busy just keeping the grizzly head from plugging last time."

Bill stares at me for a few moments, lost in thought.

"Yeah, maybe more hands would help," Bill says. "I'll think about it."

I stay quiet. I know I have said enough, and Bill seems to be getting sensitive to my prompting him. He knows I want Johnny to come.

"We'll try it out next week," Bill adds.

We load everything up, and then everything back out into the shop, and Bill closes up the shop and locks up the compound. He is ready for his trip to Panama.

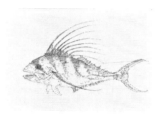

Bill and Saul got away early the next morning. And the next couple of days go by quickly - peacefully. Johnny and I keep up with the hotel easily. Everything seems to be working well and we are all caught up with cleaning, painting, trimming, and any other maintenance. We get to go fishing, and Johnny even hooked into a smaller sized rooster fish the following morning. But he lost it. They are hard to get in with a hand line.

Bill and Saul get in late the next evening, and Bill seems excited. He is pleased with what he picked up in Panama City. He spends time with Grandma out on the veranda, talking in low voices. Saul takes over the T.V. When I step out to say goodnight, Bill calls me over.

"I want to head out for a few days, maybe a week, probably the day after tomorrow," says Bill. "I had lots of time to go over details in my head, with all the time driving. I think you are right about needing an extra hand. Ask Johnny tomorrow, would you? See if he can come."

That is good news.

"Have you seen Corporal Morales in the last few days?" asks Bill.

No I haven't.

There will be no practice run. Bill has decided to not risk blowing our cover with less than a serious run. Everything will work. Bill is confident of it.

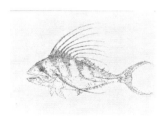

It is busy getting ready. In the morning, Bill and Grandma head up to Nicoya to do grocery shopping at the bigger shopping centres and pick up last minute supplies. Johnny can come. He is glad to. He, Saul, and myself pull together kit bags with clothes, rain gear, camping gear, sleeping bags - all with the help of Mom, of course. We even pack a first aid kit. We have fishing gear, belt knives, hats, bug spray, and Saul has his comic books. Stray dogs stay home. Mom gives us four new T-shirts each. They all have 'University of Panama' emblazoned on them with the University logo. Four are for Johnny too.

We load everything, again, into the bed of the Mercedes. Personal stuff goes in the cab. There are coolers of food, pop, and beer.

Bill keeps an eye out for Morales as we work. No sign of him again today.

The day has built up with the intensity of Bill's plans, and Bill. Later that evening, Bill spends some time reassuring Mom and Grandma that all is well. Their concerns have surfaced - that we will all be safe, that we are going to have time for fun, that we will come home if there is anything that is not going right. Bill reassures and reassures again.

It takes a while to get to sleep that night. And for the first time in my life that I can recall, I have this thought: I wish I had a big brother. Maybe I am feeling unsure of myself. But Johnny is coming and he is maybe something like a big brother.

It is feeling like an adventure about to unfold.

CHAPTER SEVENTEEN

Traffic is always busy here. Bill gets his chance to pull across the highway, makes a left-hand turn, and drives up the potholed road a mile before pulling over under a grove of shade trees. Bill has been briefing us about our deception as archaeologists. Johnny, Saul, and myself act as volunteers, hoping one day to gain admission to the archaeology program at the university.

Bill is Professor Davies if we are speaking to strangers, visitors, or whomever. Bill is still okay to use, but also use Professor Davies.

Each of us puts on a University of Panama t-shirt, and Bill has me change the vehicle licence plates from Costa Rican to Panamanian. Bill puts on the big magnetic University of Panama decals on each door of the cab with the university logo. Even a separate decal that he puts on the driver's side front fender - Vehicle No. 1012.

We all stand back and look at the Mercedes, and at one another. Other than the fact that Saul and I are a bit young, though Johnny is less so, the deception looks as good as it can get.

Bill continues to coach us on what we are trying to do, the work that needs to be done, and the roles each of us should perform. Johnny and I have done it all before so we are familiar with what he is saying, but Bill tells us again, of the various changes he has made to the equipment, both to make it work better and to conceal its purpose. Part of the deception.

After a good number of miles, Bill turns off the broken pavement, onto a dirt road that twists and turns down into a valley. There are places where the sun barely makes it through the canopy of trees above us. The road deteriorates with every mile, and there are creek beds we drive through - some dry, some with two feet of water pooled up. Bill has the Mercedes in four-wheel drive, and he is proud of how well it is handling the trail we are now on.

Bill says he believes we are now in Panamanian territory. We stop several times and walk down trails to the river. Bill says we might be able to drive down, but turning around can be a problem. Best to walk down first to check out each site. Bill points out to us the features of how the river has picked out its route, what the terrain may be like under water, and its chances of holding gold. Each trail leads to some semblance of a campsite at the waters edge, where people have stayed before.

Bill likes the look of the fourth site we walk down to. There are several outcroppings of bedrock that make the river pool and spill, from one level to another. There is a vertical drop of some thirty to forty feet, with three large deep pools forming, each spilling over to the next. The pools of water look deep and green. We all walk around the area where Bill points out what would make a good camp, where we could set up tents, and where we could launch our equipment into the river. The canopy of oak and ash trees provides a large shaded area; shelter from the sun. It is really quite beautiful. Bill says there is probably a million dollars' worth of gold down there. Johnny and I know we can catch fish in those pools.

But we don't stay. Bill says we will come back to it. Best to go as far up the river as we can before we start. We'll work our way back down, Bill tells us. Less chance of running into people, he says.

The road doesn't get any better, as we work our way mostly through forested areas; sometimes getting away from the river and then coming back to it again. Bill identifies two more spots he would be interested in working for a day or two each. Then we come to a spot where the road stops right at the rivers edge, and across (probably thirty yards), the road pulls up from the bank on the far side into a parkland area with big oak and ash trees, again, blanketing the area with shade. The water does not look too deep - the riverbed is wide here, and the water is not moving so fast. Bill takes a machete and cuts himself a six-foot sapling that is about two inches in diameter, and uses it as a staff to brace himself as he wades across the river. At its deepest point, the water comes up to Bill's waist.

The Mercedes crosses the river without a hitch. The three of us - Saul, Johnny and myself - are wide-eyed during the crossing. Bill seems to have done this sort of thing before. He says the Mercedes would still make the crossing if the river was another couple feet or so higher. But that would mean the flow rate of the river would be double or triple, he explains.

The terrain gets steeper with hills, gulleys, and creeks feeding into the river. As we climb and gain altitude, the river gets smaller and has more steps to it - more pools and fewer access points. The forest is denser and you cannot see into the darkness of its shadows. And then the trail stops. There is a rock wall covered with vines and ferns and all kinds of succulent plant life. The wall was created by some geological fault line and stands more than fifty feet high. Bill says there are only going to be horse trails above this point. And the mountain Indians who don't like people coming here, looking for gold. It sounds as ominous as the rock wall we are facing.

We spend some time scoping out this site - where we can set up camp, and the river. The rock face has a waterfall half of its height. The rest had been worn away into a small canyon. There is a good-sized pool of water at the bottom of the canyon and falls, emerald green in its depth. The river is not as big here, and the area where we are to set up camp is completely shaded. The dense canopy of trees above us probably only lets the sun through at mid-day. Bill seems happy to try here. We are all happy to stop. Being jostled around in the Mercedes for the last several hours has worn us all out.

"Stay in sight of the truck," Bill says to us all. "I am going to hike up to the top of the ridge above the falls."

Bill steps up into the Mercedes and reaches in behind the stash of kit bags behind the seat of the truck to pull out his M16.

"I shouldn't be long," Bill continues. "If this site has been worked over before by prospectors, they would have had to divert the water. It will be obvious if they have, if I take a look from above. The canyon should have prevented diverting the water, but I'll check it out."

"So we can go fishing?" I ask.

Johnny is with me. Saul is already climbing on rocks over the pools of water. This is a beautiful spot, and I am hoping we get to stay.

"Yeah, take a break," says Bill. "Keep out of the water until we have a good look at what's in it. Tell Saul to stay out."

Bill heads back down the road, looking for a way to get up to the ridge. He stops and hollers back to Saul.

"Saul, I have given Derrick instructions. You pay attention. Do you hear me?"

Saul hollers back just as loud over the sound of the water: "Yeah, I hear you."

Johnny and I find our kit bags and set them out to retrieve our fishing gear. We know to try the water at the head of the pool, where the water is pouring in.

Corporal Morales pulls into his driveway with a sense of anticipation and relief. He has been in San Jose for the last week, taking a special course in drug enforcement - a course that has earned him a badge that he gets to wear on his uniform. This course will add to his qualifications to earn the rank of Sergeant. Some day soon, he hopes.

The week was tiring, sitting in a classroom five full days, looking alert, taking it all in, asking the right questions to gain a standing and recognition among his nineteen peers - both Corporals and Sergeants. The instructors were American DEA agents, Costa Rican agents, and a specialist from Panama. The evenings, though a relief from class time, were spent with his peers. Though there was some fun to be had (a couple nights out at bars), there were also two separate nights when they worked into the early morning hours with drug enforcement specialists doing field work. Tedious. Being alert. Not enough sleep.

He turns off the Jeep's ignition, pauses for a few seconds, lets out a big breath, contemplates for a few seconds more, then starts the Jeep up again. He backs around, and heads back toward town.

Morales' house is a half mile out of town - not far, once an easy walk. But he never seems to walk it anymore. Driving is just quicker, and he tells himself that his visual presence in the police Jeep is part of the policing profile. His house is simple - stuccoed concrete block, a metal roof, ornamental security bars covering the windows, and a covered carport. The yard is neat and clean, and shady for the area due to the foresight of the previous owner having planted an array of shade trees many years ago. His house is at the end of the lane and as he guns the engine, he pulls up dust as he barrels past the two other neighbours before reaching the highway. He lives alone. He is not married. He has his friends, and lady friends. One close, one far. Policing seems to take up almost all of his time. Being a corporal and head of this small detachment keeps him busy.

All this last week it has been gnawing at him: the numerous parallels between drug enforcement and catching someone like Bill Platten. Morales' contempt for drug trafficking and drug crime was enormously greater than for the likes of Bill and his gold projects, though Bill was still getting something great for so little effort. Something for nothing. And he was onto Bill. He was sure! Bill was his pet project. Bill was in his town. In the drug enforcement classes, it seemed right. To catch him, just to catch him and enforce the law. Bill wouldn't go to jail, though he might spend a night in his jail. He would most probably only be fined when convicted - that is all. But it would rate as a star on his own job performance. And here, on his own territory again, maybe there was something in it for him. I mean, after all, he is risking his life fighting drug lords. If Bill goes free, is it wrong that his own life is made a bit better?

Morales did not pull in toward the detachment but drove a couple blocks farther, towards Bill's hotel before slowing right down, as if doing an early evening patrol. As he approached Bill's workshop and yard, he could see that Bill's truck and boat were gone. The compound was empty. He cursed out loud, and his heart raced trying to keep up with the speed of thoughts racing through his head. All the questions, all the possibilities. Annoyed that the week in San Jose had to be when it was, preventing him from keeping an eye on Bill's activities.

There were cars parked in the lot at the hotel. Time to make a courtesy call. He swung the police Jeep into the parking lot gently, controlling his swelling anger and frustration.

Phyllis answered his knock to the front door.

"Corporal Morales," she said pleasantly. A questioningly look on her face.

"I was in the neighbourhood and thought I would just stop for a second to see that everything here is all right," posed Morales.

"Well yes, things are fine Corporal," replied Phyllis. She raised her eyebrows expectantly and opened out the palms of her hands. You would have thought she was going to say something, but she didn't.

"I see Bill's truck is gone. I am assuming he is away," Morales said as innocently as he could make it sound. "I'll make a point of doing regular patrols while he is gone. That break in here happened while Bill was away before."

"Things are fine Corporal," Phyllis repeated. "There is no need to trouble yourself. Jessica and I do keep our eyes open. I'll call if I see anything that needs your attention," she added.

"When do you expect Bill to be back?" asked Morales, posing the question as innocently as he could.

"Bill took the boys fishing for a couple of days," answered Phyllis. She rocked her head back and forth, looking bewildered at the question. "He didn't say what day they would get back. When the boys start driving him crazy I guess. Or when they get tired of their own cooking."

Phyllis smiled and gave a little laugh to deflect Morales' attention.

"I am sure he will only be a few days," she added.

Morales gave a thoughtful nod.

"So where is the fishing good these days?" the Corporal asked, trying to sound friendly rather than probing.

Phyllis shook her head as she answered, "I have no idea Corporal. I am sure you would have a better idea where they would go than I would."

"Does he like river fishing or lake fishing?" asked Morales, sounding friendly, like he was ready to swap a few fishing stories.

"The boys love fishing and camping. Bill took the boat, so maybe they will do both," answered Phyllis.

"When did they get away?" probed Morales.

Phyllis' expression became more serious. She certainly remembered Bill's cautioning her about Corporal Morales, if he was to come snooping around.

She stared at Morales for a few seconds, blinking her eyes a couple times reflecting her thoughtfulness. Pondering the Corporals question.

"Just this morning Corporal. Why do you ask?" replied Phyllis coolly.

"Oh I am just curious. I have some time off coming. I would like to talk to Bill when he returns. See how he did. I'd like to put in some time fishing."

Phyllis did not reply right away.

"But, I would have thought in your line of work that you would talk to all kinds of people in a day," stated Phyllis. Again, coolly. "Certainly there must be a lot of fishing stories out there."

The pause was a few seconds longer than what was comfortable. Phyllis spoke first.

"Thank you for your concern Corporal. I'll mention to Bill that you were by."

Morales knew the conversation was over, and that there would be no more information he could extract from it. Police work. A lot of doors get closed in your face, and he knew this door was closing. Closed.

He quickly excused himself, saying that he had to get going. He reassured Phyllis he would do some extra patrols of the area, as he went down the steps toward his Jeep.

Phyllis closed the door.

Driving away, Morales thought to himself that she was hiding something. He didn't get much information from her. He kept mulling over the conversation in his head as it transpired. Bill had only left this morning. And she was not telling him what she knew.

And it is this information, running through Morales' head, over and over, that stirs up ever greater feelings of frustration and agitation.

Maybe it was just as an afterthought, needing to focus, settle down, regroup. Morales pulls up to the police detachment before heading home. His first shift back wasn't until morning. There is a note on the front door that the constable on duty would return in one hour. Morales unlocks the door, turns on the lights, and sits at his desk. There, sitting in the middle of his desk-top, like it had just been delivered, is a FedEx package addressed to him. He flips it over a couple of times as if figuring out how to open it. He opens the courier package and a letter drops on the desk top. It is a letter from the Ministry of National Security. Handling this envelope, the same as the courier package, he finally opens it.

Several expressions pass over Morales' face. First, a seriousness at which he furls his brow, then he flags his eyebrows like surprise, then a smile that trails off in to a questioning look, almost looking disturbed.

The letter has given Morales notice that he is to be transferred to the Drug Enforcement Unit in San Jose, effective in thirty days.

Many thoughts race through his mind. One was that, if he was ever going to get a chance to catch Bill, it had to be now.

CHAPTER EIGHTEEN

Derrick stirred. It was the noise of the morning, the thousand birds, monkeys, maybe the heat in the tent or a bug crawling on his foot.

The sun was blasting into his eyes, through a hole just on the edge of the roof panel of the tent, blasting like a strobe light as it made its broken path through the layers of branches and leaves to the floor of their clearing, and his tent.

Just a dim recollection of Bill putting the tent pole through that point while setting up camp, his lack of any care, or patience. Bill's way of doing things. Resetting his position in the cot to avoid the flashing beam of light, clinging to his drowsiness, Derrick drifts back to that level of consciousness where the sun, the morning and reality were less in his face.

He is in that zone, half asleep, half awake, where dreams and reality get to play together as children. Derrick revisits, pauses to reflect on a moments recall that he had just had from his waking dream.

His Dad.

The emotions swelled in him and left him feeling so vulnerable - the feelings of longing were incredible. Yet he knew not to chase these thoughts away like some other less-than-pleasant dream. The joy, the fulfilment. They were embedded in the building emotion as were the sense of loss, the longing for a moment to be with him, remembering his caring hand, his voice, his praise, laughter, his love. If there could be just one more hug.

The feeling of tears welling up came almost as a betrayal to the moment. Breathing more deeply, clearing a breath, reality now overtaking his emotions, the presence his dreams had now been swept aside by the brilliant beam of sunlight flashing in its staccato blast again through the hole in the roof of the tent.

Remember to sew up that hole today, Derrick told himself. Bill would have some thread and a needle for something like this.

Derrick adjusted his position in his sleeping bag. For just another few moments, reflecting.

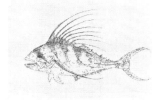

I guess it was Johnny asking last night, about his father, Derrick thought to himself. By the fire, a few, minutes after Bill had half-staggered to his own tent for the night. Johnny had asked, speaking low so not to upset Bill.

"Do you remember your father?" A few seconds passed, and again, "Do you?"

Derrick lifting his eyes to Johnny's. "Yes and no. Not as much as

I would like. My mom tells me lots though."

It was times like this when Johnny seemed desperate. Okay, not desperate but wanting to talk about things. After Bill had gone to bed and he knew he wouldn't be laughed at or scowled upon.

"How did he die?" Johnny asked.

Derrick lifted both elbows up off his knees from staring into the fire and sat up, adjusting his position. Johnny just sat there, looking at him.

"Mom says we were walking down the beach - all of us. I guess it was morning, just after breakfast. We were staying at a place on the west side. I don't know which beach. We were walking to a point and, about half way there, Dad had said he wanted to sit down and watch the waves. He had a bad cramp in his leg. Mom wanted to walk to the point, so I went with her and Saul stayed with Dad."

Derrick paused.

"By the time we got back, Dad was already dead - heart attack. They say a blood clot in his leg or something, had moved. I was seven, Saul was four." Derrick took a clearing breath, and settled back to looking into the fire.

Johnny, blinking his eyes as if the smoke had caught him, re-adjusted his position on the stump. Then he adjusted again. He pulled out his knife and played with the blade, checking its sharpness.

For all his inquisitiveness, now Johnny just sat quiet.

Derrick said, getting to his feet, "Well, I'm going to bed."

"Don't forget to pick up everything," said Johnny. "Or the monkeys will get it."

"Yeah. See you in a minute," said Derrick, picking up his flashlight, scanning the beam around to see if anything was left out, then headed into the tent he and Johnny shared.

Johnny stayed by the fire.

I am jolted back to reality by the sound of the dredge motor starting.

I check my watch. It is 8:30! I'm surprised that they let me sleep in this morning. I must have been sleeping hard, because they must have had to make some noise - Johnny getting up, making something for breakfast, Bill setting up equipment. Saul is not the quietest guy, but at least he is sharing Bill's tent. Not mine.

I pull on some shorts, and reach for my shoes. I had set them down deliberately last night with the soles facing up. It was Johnny who had taught me to do this. "It's the best way not to end up having a scorpion in your shoe," Johnny had coached. I bang each runner upside down before I put it on, just to be sure.

Getting out of the tent, it is clear and bright out. Saul and Johnny are putting a pack with water bottles and snacks on the pontoon platform, where the dredge and two sluices are already mounted.

"Boy, you sure slept in," taunted Johnny.

"Yeah, he was probably dreaming about Mellissa," adds Saul.

They both laugh.

"We've been up for and hour and a half already. Bill is wanting to get going, but he said to let you sleep. He is over there," says Johnny, pointing to the bubbles coming up from Bill's scuba gear, close to where the waterfall pours into the pool.

"Has Bill said anything about what's down there?" I ask.

"Not yet," answers Saul. "He just got into the water. Doing his reconnaissance."

"That's a pretty big word for a guy your size," I say, trying to get even for the Mellissa dig.

"Grab something to eat and come out with us," coaches Johnny. "I haven't run this thing by myself. Bill says he wants to tie the dredge off with a couple lines, so we can adjust our position in the water to stay with him. It would be good if you get him to explain it to you. It will probably take the three of us until we get good at it."

In a bit, Bill surfaces in his scuba gear and wades backwards towards us - the only way he can walk with his flippers on. He sits back on the edge of the pontoon platform, half leaning, half sitting.

"Derrick. Get me my cigarettes, a bottle of water, and bring down the M-16," Bill directs.

Bill takes a long pull on the water that Johnny handed him.

"There's at least one snake in there that I saw. Great!" Bill exclaims.

After he lights up his cigarette, Bill starts with his instructions.

"I want to start at the head of the pool, over there," Bill says pointing. "If we tie a line to the rack, let's say over there," pointing to a boulder further up on the bank, "and I tie a line into the rocks over there," pointing to the rock face at the waterfall, "we should be able to hold the position of the dredge. As you let out the line from the rock face, the rack should move in an arc, allowing me to cover more ground without having to re-tie everything. Stay behind my bubbles about twenty to thirty feet. One of you stand watch. If you see anything in the water, shoot it. If something is going wrong, shut off the dredge, and I'll come up. Just don't shoot me," Bill exclaims, with a clear emphasis on "me."

We all grimace at the suggestion. Bill continues.

"Lets try it for ten minutes, and I'll come up and check with you how things are going. I wish we had some kind of two-way communication built into this setup. It would sure come in handy."

With the lines tied off and the "rack" as we were now calling the pontoon boat, in position, we fired up the dredge motors again. Once Bill starts sucking up material, we are soon busy. Johnny is standing watch with the M-16 and Saul and I are clearing out rocks that stick in the grizzly head, helping larger pieces roll off into the water.

"Here, like this," I say, showing Saul how to lift the grizzly head up and dump all the rocks in the water when he wasn't able to keep up with clearing the grizzly head. I show him how to direct the dredge flow off to the side for the moment to do this, rather than have all the debris land in the sluices.

"Try and keep up," I add again.

That only gets me a grunt and a disgruntled look from Saul.

When Bill surfaces to check on us, it has been more than twenty minutes.

"How's it going?" Bill asks.

"You're bringing up lots of material," I answer. "It's keeping us real busy, and Saul isn't the fastest."

Saul gives me a look of contempt.

"Is there any sign of colour?" asks Bill.

I run my finger across the black sand in the channels at the top of the sluice.

"There's colour all right," I answer.

"Well, remember to switch sides to the second sluice, and clean this one into the storage bin when you need to. But don't let them fill up too much, or they just quit working," Bill instructs. "Okay. I'll go back until this tank is out of air, and we'll have a look at it again."

Bill is able to close off the intake on the head of the dredge, and as the water and material stop pouring onto the grizzly head, the dredge hose floats to the surface, and Bill also breaks the surface, right next to the rack.

I power down the dredge pumps and the world becomes quiet.

Bill pulls his diving mask off and sets it on the rack. We can't see his face yet, as the rack sits pretty high in the water.

"Could you hand me a bottle of water?" Bill calls out.

Johnny has it in a second and places it in Bill's hand. The bottle disappears over the edge of the rack.

All we hear is Bill's gulping, the plastic water bottle scrunching, and then a good guttural belch.

A quietness has settled in. There is the background noise of the water pouring into the basin, a few birds clattering away, and we can now hear one another without the sound of the pump engines.

Bill's water bottle, now empty, is flipped up onto the deck of the rack.

"Let that line out," Bill's arm waves out to the far shore to indicate which line, "and the rack should drift over to the shore." The shore he means takes us right to our campsite.

I loosen off the line, and as Bill said, the rack drifts toward camp.

"Saul," calls Bill. "Loosen off the other line until you reach the shore where you want to be." Bill pauses, watching us position the rack to the shore, "Now tie those lines off good."

Bill pulls along the large hose and the dredge head over to the shore. Again, walking backwards in his flippers, he hooks the dredge head onto the deck of the rack, and comes ashore.

Bill takes off his flippers and loosens off his air tank and buoyancy compensator and sets them on the ground. He drops his weight belt at his feet.

"Where are my cigarettes?" Bill asks, looking at each of us.

Saul points to the backpack on the rack.

Bill makes his way over and fishes through the backpack and comes out with a wet, soggy pack of cigarettes.

"Great!" Bill exclaims with some disgust.

Saul makes it back to the group from relieving himself at the edge of the camp.

Bill heads toward the truck for a pack of cigarettes.

"Well, it is awfully wet out there," I holler after Bill.

The boys laugh. Johnny catches himself and stops. He steps aside, making his way to the rack.

Bill is back in a moment with a cigarette already going, and makes his way onto the rack, lifting the screens up from the sluice boxes.

"You switched sides to the second sluice?" Bill asks me.

"Yes. The dredge was bringing up so much material, I was afraid it would overload the sluice box." Johnny comes alongside Bill to look at what is trapped in the steps of the sluice.

Bill runs his finger across the black sand trapped by the sluice box.

"There's gold in there alright," declares Bill. "Matter of fact, there is a lot of gold in there."

Bill whistles as he picks up one nugget after another, trapped in the second sluice. There were many, half the size of the end of his little finger. The tiers of the sluice all have a layer of granular and powdered gold - at least what looks to be gold. Most of it is in the top tiers and tapering off to the bottom tiers.

"This is good boys," Bill again declares, as a matter of fact.

Bill stands up straight and looks around, like he is looking to see someone who has called out to him. He scans around the site, three hundred and sixty degrees, and then says, "Where's Saul?" noticing him missing.

Johnny scans around, looking for Saul.

"Who knows," I say, with a certain indifference. "He will probably show up in a minute with another stray dog."

"Well you did good, switching the sluices over," declares Bill. "As soon as you switch over, clean the loaded one into the reservoir."

Bill flips the hinged lid back on the rectangular box below the base of the sluice and tilts up the sluice from its bottom hinge.

"Start the water pump up and hand me that hose," Bill directs Johnny.

Bill sprays a good flow of water to wash down the material in the sluice into the box below. He then flips the lid back over the reservoir box and lays the sluice back down into operating position.

"Like that!" Bill says. "Like that, we can probably work the dredge for most of the day, maybe all day, without having to come in and unload. It is a good design."

We both agree with Bill with enthusiasm. It is only now that my enthusiasm is dampened as it dawns on me - we might be working all day.

As Bill cleans out the other sluice, he starts giving Johnny and I directions.

"Derrick, you and Johnny can get some lunch going but I want you to go through the food and plan out our meals for the next number of days. Set some snack foods in a separate box so you don't have to go through everything to find something. Then we all stay out of the main food coolers. We don't want to end up with a miss-mash of odds and ends in a few days, that we can't put a meal together with. I'll tell Saul to stay out of the food coolers, except for the snack box. I'll set us up a latrine. It looks like we are going to be here for a few days. Let's get at it."

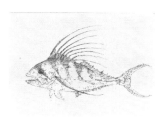

Saul shows up when lunch is ready. After lunch, we work the rack till mid-afternoon. Bill has changed out his breathing apparatus. He is now hooked up to the air compressor with an air line. His breathing line is one more thing to manage, but now Bill's time in the water is not limited to the air in a tank.

He is keeping us busy. It is work to keep track of everything on the dredge. Clearing the grizzly head, checking how full the sluice is getting, cleaning and flushing a full sluice into the reservoir, having to adjust lines to keep close to Bill's air coming up. Johnny and I are getting the hang of it, and we are pointing out to each other how to make everything work smoothly. Every now and again, Bill shuts down the suction head and we get to step back for a minute and look around, open a Coke. We are trying to show Saul how to do each thing since he has never worked the dredge before, but somehow he manages to be less than interested if we tell him too many things.

About mid-afternoon, Saul is taking a turn on lookout with the M-16 when he gets Johnny's attention by tapping him on the shoulder. Saul hands Johnny the M-16, turns, and dives into the water and starts swimming towards the camp. I am too busy to pay any more attention to him. Johnny keeps a close eye on him until he makes the shore and walks out, I guess watching for snakes.

Bill works the dredge until late afternoon, and then we loosen the lines and pull the rack back to shore at the camp.

Johnny and I are eager to do some fishing, and Bill is eager to get to the sluice material we have recovered for the day.

Once we have the material unloaded and the equipment covered over, Saul crawls out from his and Bill's tent and wanders over.

"What happened to you?" Bill asks as Saul approaches.

"Nothing," is all he gets from Saul as an answer.

Bill stands looking at Saul, clearly expecting more of an answer. He opens out his hands and says nothing, but if he had it would have said something like, "That's it?"

"I thought we were coming out for a camping and fishing trip," laments Saul.

"And to work the dredge for a bit," Bill fires back. "You can't camp and fish twenty-four hours a day."

"Grab me my cigarettes from over there," Bill directs Saul, pointing to the stuff unloaded from the rack.

Bill walks over and pulls out a gold pan from one of the equipment boxes. He goes back and scoops out a good sample from one corner of the first reservoir.

With his cigarette hanging out of the corner of his mouth, Bill shakes the material in the pan just under the surface of the foot of water he is standing in. Saul stands there watching.

"It won't hurt you to help out for a bit," says Bill, not looking up. "If you help me out, I'll make sure you get to do some things you want to do too." Bill continues to pan his material and in a moment, says, "Why didn't you go fishing with the guys, if that's what you are wanting to do?"

"They didn't ask me," answers Saul.

"Well if you want to be part of the group, maybe you have to try to be part of the group," says Bill. "And do your part," Bill adds, still keeping his head down, concentrating on his panning. "If you are going to be part of a group, your contribution has to be as important as any others."

Saul stands there and watches Bill pan his material for another minute or two. Saul could see the gold concentrating - probably enough to fill the palm of his hand. Bill worked the pan for another minute.

Bill looks up and meets Saul eye to eye. He leans the gold pan in Saul's direction and says, "Whoa!"

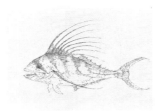

Johnny and I went downstream from the main pool and our camp. We are looking for a way to cross the river, to get to the far side of the big pool, but that is not going to be easy. It is hot, and we are both happy to be exploring and fishing, and to have some time on our own. There are smaller pools within the first hundred yards below the camp. Johnny has already caught two fish, and has a third one on.

I work my way closer to where Johnny is just landing his fish.

"How are you doing that?" I beg Johnny.

Johnny is grinning, unhooking his fish and putting it in his catch bag, tying it shut.

"What are they?" again, I ask. "They look like there is lots of meat on them."

"Tilapia," declares Johnny. "They're delicious. Like Red Snapper."

Johnny put a good-sized rock on his catch bag to hold it in place.

"I've been casting along the shallows there," Johnny says pointing, and sweeping his arm to show the arc he was casting along. "They seem to like the slower water that isn't so deep, under the trees. Reel in fast so you don't snag the bottom."

I cast across to where the water is welling up before spilling over the edge of the pool. I quickly retrieve my line to keep it from getting snagged in the rocks, and bang! I have one on.

"Got one!" I yell over to Johnny. I am grinning and look over to see Johnny giving me the thumbs up signal.

Johnny and I fishing. Always a good time. The sun is close to setting, and the camp is in shadows as Johnny and I come marching in. We have a good catch and we know it. I guess like any two guys, young or old, coming into camp with a catch of fish, we are proud – excited - and it shows.

Saul is pushing around the coals in the fire with a stick in one hand, and something from the snack box in the other as we approach. He adds a couple more pieces of wood to the fire and gets up to see our catch.

"Saul! You gotta come with us tomorrow!" I encourage Saul.

"I would've come with you today," declares Saul.

Johnny and I look at each other.

"Tomorrow Saul. For sure," I reply.

"Bill wants to get supper going," adds Saul, cutting me off. Saul isn't going to indulge our bravado and excitement.

"I'll start cleaning the fish," says Johnny, and he takes my catch bag along with his own, and heads down toward the waters edge.

Bill is putting some equipment away in the back of the truck as I approach.

"We'd better get some supper going Derrick," Bill directs. "But get up here and have a look at this."

I climb up onto the deck of the truck.

"We caught some nice fish for dinner," I say enthusiastically. "Johnny's cleaning them now."

"Good," says Bill in a quick reply. "Look at this."

Bill shows me a hand full of nuggets that are lying on a mat on top of one of the big barrels in the front of the truck box. In a bowl next to it is granular and powdered gold that Bill runs his finger through in little circles.

"This is from four samples from each of the reservoir boxes. Four pans from each box. Probably less than a tenth of what we pulled up today." Bill is intense. "This is better than I hoped for. This is serious Derrick." Bill is nodding his head slightly, staring in my eyes. "This is really serious."

"What do you think it is worth?" I ask, trying to show my enthusiasm.

Bill goes from gently nodding to gently shaking his head from side to side, as if it was a whispered no. And he stands there staring at me, maybe he is calculating how much the gold is worth.

Then Bill says, slowly and emphatically, "You don't need to know, and I don't want to tell you."

I stood there, uncomfortable, fixed by Bill's stare, bewildered by Bill's reply, not knowing what to think.

"And you don't need to be telling Johnny or Saul about this. Do you hear me?" adds Bill.

I feel like I am squirming in discomfort, looking helpless and hopeless, fixed in Bill's stare.

"I wasn't going to say anything," I retort back in my defence.

Bill finally drops his gaze, and starts pouring the extracted gold back in to the drum with the rest of the sluice material.

"It's safer in here," says Bill. "Out of sight. I'll extract it when we get home."

Bill replaces the cap to the drum and says, "So we'd better get supper going."

Then Bill stops again and fixes his stare on me again.

"Are you with me on this Derrick?"

I still feel like I am under attack and I respond emphatically. "Yeah Bill. Of course I am!"

I am sure I look annoyed with my reply. Bill starts toward the back of the truck deck, and we both climb down.

"So what is it worth?" I ask again, trying to gain Bill's confidence.

Bill looks at me with a look of defeat, a concession he needs to make.

"Lots Derrick," then adds again, "Lots."

Johnny is still excited about the catch and the full plate of fillets that he has breaded up and fried for dinner. Johnny has noticed that I am quiet, and Bill offered little comment on anything. I had lost any sense of jubilation about the day's fishing. I knew it was maybe time to be cautious around Bill and so I stuck close to Johnny. Bill volunteered Saul to do up the dishes, Johnny and I drying. Saul washes up a couple of jars and sets the jars and lids aside.

Sitting around the fire, Saul pestered Bill for some treats from the snack box, and questioned Bill as to what we were going to do the next day.

"We have some work to do tomorrow," says Bill, "and I want you to help out. There will be time for goofing around later."

Johnny whittled away at a stick with his knife. Saul seems to be the only one with any energy left.

"What is above the falls?" I finally ask Bill. "Are there any good fishing pools up there?"

It takes Bill a moment to reply.

"It is just a horse trail up there," says Bill. "It is wild and grown over. No need to go up there as far as I am concerned. It's safer down here, and the fishing seems to be good enough down here."

The conversation does not pick up, and after another few minutes or so I stand up and stretch.

"I am beat. I am going to head off," I say, still stretching.

As I am heading for the tent, Johnny gets up and follows.

Saul sits out with Bill for a little while longer, the crackling fire the only sound.

Bill finally notices Saul falling asleep in his chair, and gives him a little shake.

"You might as well head off," says Bill. "I'll be right there."

Saul makes his way from the light of the fire towards his tent. He can hear the quiet whispers coming from our tent, but shows no interest as he walks by.

"Is everything okay?" whispers Johnny to me.

"Yeah," I whisper back. "Things are okay. But maybe it's time keep away from Bill a bit," I caution Johnny.

"What did I do?" whispers Johnny.

"Nothing," I whisper back. "He just seems to be getting worked up about something. Best to give him some distance. Just do what he says," I again caution Johnny. "I think we should focus on working the dredge for a day or two."

Bill knew that rivers changed over time. They changed how they flowed, changed by flood paths worn new, and in a formation of bedrock like this, with the fracture that created the waterfall, the river and waterfall had certainly changed some over the centuries. There was gold here, deeper than old equipment, or men with simple tools could have extracted. His dredge was the perfect tool for the job. There could be pockets of gold that had been here for centuries, covered by overburden. Dredging out anything he could move down to bedrock was the key. He watched for formations of how the pool was formed, and how it had changed. The water coming over the fault formation made a huge trap for any gold that was pushed down the river from above. It seemed that he was the first one to be able to get at it.

Bill sat with a beer and a cigarette, staring into the fire. Quite awake.

CHAPTER
NINETEEN

"Let's get going this morning, hey," says Bill, tapping on the side of our tent.

The forest is loud with birds calling. Almost every bird sound possible. Sweet sounds to squawking. It means it is somewhere between six and seven in the morning.

"Are you awake Derrick?" asks Bill, tapping the side of the tent again.

"Yeah, I'm awake," I reply.

Derrick was coming out of a deep sleep. It seemed as if he had just gotten to sleep. He had tossed and turned for what seemed like most of the night. Bill's intensity had disturbed him, and Derrick felt a sense of foreboding that kept sleep from reach. Every time he dozed off he seemed shaken out of his sleep by some sense of urgency - some bit of a dream that made him feel like he was not keeping up, not able to sort things out, not able to make things work.

A monkey screeches at Bill, making a stand to ward off Bill's approach in the camp. The monkey claims some territory or possession, and now tries to protect it from Bill. Bill throws a stick at him, and yells at him and his tribe to clear out. The monkeys clamour and chatter away, and retreat to safer ground. Birds protest the approach of the scrambling monkeys into the trees, and then gradually the noise of the ruckus settles down.

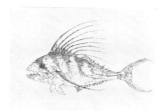

Johnny is up, dressed, and waiting for me to head out of the tent. He isn't engaging much, is quiet, and is waiting for me to take the lead to head out to face Bill. I figure Johnny is feeling the same sense of foreboding. Proceed cautiously.

"Let's just do what we can to get through the day," I say softly, catching Johnny's eye with an exaggerated grimace and shudder.

The day is bright and clear as we emerge from the tent. It is already good and warm. No breeze. And Bill is stoking a small fire. I can smell the coffee pot perking on the cook stove.

"A good day to get some work done," is Bill's welcome.

I open up the food box and pull out a bag of granola and set it out.

"I guess we eat it dry this morning," I say to Johnny, as casually as I can "Maybe with a cup or two of coffee. It isn't going to be a morning for a leisurely camp breakfast," I add.

"Saul! You coming?" hollers Bill.

So far, so good.

Underwater. Again, the sounds of Bill's own breathing, the water rushing up the dredge suction hose, and the clatter of the rocks and gravel rattling up to the surface. Bill is being methodical. He knows there is big gold here. When he first started, it was like gold panning and prospecting. But Bill clearly thought the gold was here. He could feel it. Now, he knows it is here. He is paying attention - close attention. He is focused on his every move. He is focused on what the dredge pulls in, and what it leaves behind. And, he is seriously watching the rock formations which he is exposing, and what this is opening up for him.

Bill's vigilance is paying off. He can see that he is undercutting a shelf formation of bedrock, formed by the erosion of the waterfall somewhere in its past history. Undercutting the shelf exposes material that has been deposited by some earlier event of circulation. It means he is pulling out the material that has been packed in there, since God knows when. Bill sets the dredge down, closing off its suction, and picks away at some difficult material. It has been packed down hard by so many years if not centuries. He pries out chunks, lets them fall to his feet below, then sucks them up with the dredge to include any debris around them, with the dredge. The suction and water flow into the dredge and help break up the chunks of material, bringing them up to the top. For the most part, the dredge is capable of breaking the material away from his excavation. Bill does not have to pry it away.

Bill knows he should be going up to the surface and see if there is some serious material coming up.

But just a few minutes more. And then a few minutes more. And then, again. Twenty minutes more, and then an hour more.

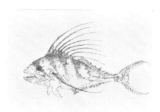

On the rack, I'm on lookout and am trying to bring Saul up to speed, coaching him on how to dump the sluice material into the reservoir box and wash down the sluice to get any remaining material. Johnny is working at clearing the grizzly head.

RON FOSS

We have to speak over the running noise of the motors. Not yell, but raise our voices to be heard.

I pick up the M-16 and gives the area a good scan for any danger.

"Some fishing trip!" Saul blurts out.

Johnny and I grin at one another, and an inaudible laugh lingers.

"Hey, we'll knock off this afternoon and take you down to where we were yesterday," I say invitingly to Saul. "Stick close to Johnny though. Do what he does. He out-fished me four to one yesterday."

"The Man!" boasts Johnny. "The Fisher-Man!" exaggerating his boast even more over the din of the motors.

"And I only caught mine, when I did what Johnny did," I add.

"I'm not coming out after lunch," declares Saul.

Johnny and I share a look, in jest of Saul's great declaration.

"Yeah?" I draw out with exaggeration. "Your going to go it against Bill, are you?"

Johnny puts on an exaggerated look of fright, like he is trying to shake something off his back, but doesn't say anything. Then, he quickly looks over his back to see that Bill doesn't happen to be at the surface, and can see him.

Johnny picks up a piece of rock stuck in the rods of the grizzly head, twists it in his hand for a moment, then hands it to me.

"What do you think this is?" asks Johnny.

I look the piece over and shake it in my hand.

"It's sure heavy," I comment.

"Here's another one," declares Johnny, shaking the piece in his hand to feel its weight. It looks like a piece of ginger root.

"Hang onto them," I say. "We'll ask Bill later," handing the piece of rock back to Johnny.

Johnny put one in each of the front pockets of his shorts.

"So what are you going to tell Bill?" I say over the noise of the motors, taunting Saul.

Johnny and I are grinning smugly, at one another again. Saul isn't grinning. We wait for more than a few moments for a reply from Saul. We both know that Saul can blurt out anything anytime. But he doesn't.

"Well just keep us out of it," I say, admonishingly.

Saul mutters something, under the noise of the motors that I can't hear.

Johnny is busy.

"What was that?" I challenge Saul to repeat what he has said.

Saul keeps quiet, working the clean sluice chute back in to position.

I put down the M-16 again, and give Saul a hand finishing putting the sluice back in to position.

When we are done, Saul picks up the M-16 and takes over the lookout position. He doesn't ask - he just does it.

Running the dredge and sluice boxes is not hard work, but it takes near constant attention to clear away rocks and debris and keep the system running as it should, sluices and all. Johnny and I work at it like it is almost fun. We make some small talk over the noise of the engines, commenting on what we are doing. And when it is going smoothly, we talk about going fishing later that afternoon, each of us looking forward to adventures. The sun is hot, having just cleared above the canopy of trees above us, and Johnny cups his hands into the clean water that is pumped in a heavy spray at the head of the sluice box and pours it over his head to cool himself.

"We might need to cover up from the sun a bit this afternoon," Johnny comments.

"What's that?!" hollers Saul, pointing to a long ripple forming in the water under some bushes along the bank closest to them.

The dredge suddenly stops pumping material for a few moments and both Johnny and I focus on what Saul is pointing out.

"Looks like snakes," says Johnny.

"Must be more than one," I add.

"Should I shoot them?" asks Saul.

We watch the ripples for a moment.

"They are far enough away. We probably don't need to," I finally reply.

"But I'll shoot them," declares Saul, lifting the M-16 up to aiming position.

"No! Don't!" I order Saul. "You will scare Bill if you start shooting."

"Shoot crocodiles," adds Johnny.

"There's no crocodiles in here," retorts Saul.

"Maybe not right now," replies Johnny. "But, sometime there will be."

"I'll check with Bill what he wants us to do," I add. "Bill already told us he saw one snake. He didn't tell us to shoot any snake we saw."

I know we do not want to upset Bill. Things are certainly strained, but they are going well for the moment.

"The dredge hasn't started up again," says Johnny. "I think Bill is coming up."

Johnny watches Bill's air bubbles breaking the surface and move towards them.

"Yeah, he's coming up," declares Johnny.

"Keep your eyes on the snakes," I direct Saul. "If they start coming this way, shoot at them."

Bill breaks the surface, and I help him get his breathing apparatus off and set it up on the rack.

Johnny shuts off the motor for the dredge, and the noise drops in half. Then he shuts off the pump motor to wash the sluice material, then the smallest engine running the air compressor for Bill's air. And it is quiet.

"Bill, there's a couple snakes in the water over by the bushes on the shore," I blurt out.

"Snakes. Great," answers Bill. But that was all he says.

Bill crawls up on the edge of the sluice. Bill's size makes it a little tipsy. We adjust our positions on the rack to stabilize it until Bill gets up.

"Do you want us to shoot them if we see them?" I ask Bill.

"Where are they?" asks Bill, straining his sight to where Saul is pointing over to the shadows under the overhanging bushes.

Bill takes the M-16 from Saul and lifts it up to aim. But he doesn't shoot. In a moment, he lowers his sights and hands the rifle back to Saul.

"They're not hurting us, I guess, or in a position to," declares

Bill. "And I don't want to attract attention with the noise of the rifle unless we have to. Probably wouldn't hit them anyway. It's hard to hit things in the water. You don't have a clear line of sight. The water bends the light."

Bill checks his dive-watch and says, "Let's head to shore - have lunch and gas up for the afternoon. I'd like to see what was coming in this morning. What did it look like to you Derrick?" Bill asks.

"You were keeping us busy enough," I answer. "There's colour in there all right. And you can see lots of nuggets in the sluice box - especially in the last hour."

Johnny and I adjust the lines to float the dredge back to the shallows close to the camp.

"And Johnny's got something to show you," I declare to Bill.

But everyone is too busy to do anything else at the moment, other than to pay attention to moving the dredge. Bill checks the sluice, running his finger across the ripples. He picks up a few nuggets and examines them, then drops them into the reservoir box. He then scoops his hand in the first reservoir box, probing his hand down into the corner. He pulls up a handful and examines it, trying to get an indication of the gold they are getting. He tries several handfuls from the first reservoir box.

We tie off the lines to the rack, once we get in close enough to shore to wade in.

Bill is the last to wade in from the rack, checking out the second reservoir box and sampling its contents. He then adds the contents of the two sluices so that they are clean to start again.

"So you said the nuggets were coming up good in the last hour?" Bill asks me as he approaches the cook site.

"Sometimes they seemed to come up in handfuls," I answer. "And you should look at what Johnny picked up."

Johnny and Saul are setting up some stuff for lunch.

"Show that piece to Bill," I say to Johnny.

Johnny reaches into his pocket and pulls out a good-sized piece and hands it to Bill.

"It's heavy," I comment, as Bill rolls it over in his hands, bouncing it to feel it's weight.

Johnny hands Bill another piece.

Bill takes them and walks over to get a sharp knife from the cooking utensils. He scratches at the piece with a knife to expose a shinier surface. He uses the sharp blade to make a deeper cut into the material to check out how hard it is.

He does the same with the second one.

"Where did you get these?" demands Bill of Johnny.

Johnny tries to keep working at getting some lunch together as he answers Bill, trying not to have to face him directly.

"They were stuck in the grizzly head," answers Johnny, "When I picked them up I could feel that they were a lot heavier than anything else for their size."

Johnny reaches into his pockets and pulls out another three pieces and hands them to Bill.

Bill takes them and stares intently at Johnny.

"Is this all you've got?" demands Bill.

"Yeah, that's it," replies Johnny. "I showed the first one to Derrick and he said to keep them to show you. So I did," Johnny says in his defence.

Bill is looking annoyed.

"Look, you don't own anything here," Bill blurts out. "Do you understand me?'

"Everything we find here is mine. Nothing here is yours," Bill says intensely, raising his voice.

"That's all you've got?" Bill demands again.

Johnny is looking real uncomfortable, being singled out and put on the spot. He knows Bill's anger.

"Yeah. That's it!" Johnny quickly answers.

"He's the one who found them!" blurts out Saul.

"But they're not his," snaps back Bill. "And they're not yours either. This is all my equipment. And it's my expedition."

"But he's the one who found them," I say in a calmer voice. "And if it wasn't for him, you wouldn't have them. He didn't do anything wrong."

Everyone is quiet for a few moments.

"And I thought we were coming on a fishing trip!" Saul blurts out, like only Saul can do.

Bill stands there for a moment, then reaches for his cigarettes and lights one up. Pulling hard. Looking disgusted.

"Look, I'll make it all worth your while," Bill finally says. "And we can plan another fishing trip. Right now, this is too good to give up. And I need you to help me," he says, calming his voice somewhat.

"There's no fun in doing this!" Saul blurts out again.

"Well, maybe it's time you quit acting like a spoiled kid Saul, and try and help out!" chastises Bill.

Saul looks straight at Bill for a few seconds, with his jaw clenching tightly, then takes the sandwich he is making and throws it straight at Bill. The sandwich goes to pieces in the air and never hits Bill. Bill lunges at Saul, but trips up on the camp chairs and stumbles for a bit. Saul stands there rigid, with his hands clenched in fists by his side.

"Bill!" I holler as I rush towards him. "It's only Saul!"

Johnny is standing back, and easing his way ever so slightly from the fray, trying not to attract attention.

I try to help steady Bill as he gets up. I grab his arm, and then hang on. Bill looks at me in disgust for a second, then eases his tension. I stand there. Then I let go let go of Bill's arm.

"Fine," Bill says, still angry, looking at Saul. "Don't help."

Bill goes over to a cooler and grabs a beer, and pulls a camp chair over to a piece of shade, cracks open the beer, and lights up a cigarette.

We start back at getting lunch together. Nobody says a word.

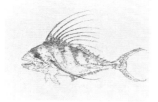

We manage to get through lunch. Everyone is quiet. Bill gasses up the engines, and to my surprise, Saul comes out with us. He had refused any lunch just because he was being ornery, as far as I was concerned. But he surprises me, coming out. Bill instructs us, before putting his breathing gear on, to keep a good eye out for those heavy pieces of rock. He never mentions the word gold, but by now I am sure that that was what they are, the way Bill has reacted and all.

As Bill goes down, I breath a sigh of relief. I think we all did.

"Saul, what do you think you're doing?" I ask.

Saul just gives me a quick sideways glance, looking annoyed at being challenged.

"Come on Saul. Like, that is just what we need. You having a big run-in with Bill," I continue. "You've got enough attitude to take on the world. But you can't take on Bill. You're not going to win. You just can't do it. Don't be crazy. You are going to ruin it for all of us."

Johnny is subdued. No doubt. I don't know if he has figured out yet that Saul had taken Bill's wrath away from himself. I know it wasn't intentional, but it sure did the trick to take the heat off of Johnny – at least for now. So Johnny and I focus on working the dredge, and Saul sits leaning against the edge of one of the sluice boxes with the M-16 across his lap, obviously putting in as little effort as possible. It is hot out, the sun not yet behind the canopy of trees. I have a brimmed hat on. Johnny has a t-shirt that he keeps wet, stuck under his ball cap, that blankets his neck and shoulders. Saul sits with his ball cap pulled low, like he is trying to hide under it. Johnny and I work the grizzly head, sometimes like mad men when more of the heavy rock - pieces of gold - come to the surface. We fill our pockets, then take turns dumping the treasures from our pockets into the reservoir boxes. Then the dredge quits pulling up material. Bill must have closed off the suction head. The dredge pump engine changes pitch when he does that.

"We might as well dump our pockets now, while we can," I say to Johnny. "I think Bill is going to be real happy with the afternoon."

"Good," is the extent of Johnny's reply.

Johnny nods his head over towards Saul, who looks like he could be sleeping.

"Don't worry about it," I reply to the question he never asks.

"These rocks are so heavy! They could pull your pants down," I say, trying to lighten up the moment.

Johnny smiles at my effort of some humour.

"Let's clean out that sluice while we have the chance," says Johnny.

With the two of us, it takes less than half the time to clean out, since it is easier to manage without so much fumbling around. We have no more than got it in place again, and the engine changes pitch, and material starts clattering on the grizzly head.

We make plans for fishing that afternoon, and have worked for probably another half hour when Saul wakes up or whatever, stands up, and pushes the M-16 at Johnny to take it. Johnny takes the M-16, Saul turns, and dives into the water. He starts swimming to camp.

Johnny watches Saul for a bit, then gives a serious scan of the pool for hazards. Saul can swim well enough, and is making good time toward the shore. Suddenly Johnny raises his arm and points over to the trees, where the snakes were earlier.

"Look!" calls Johnny, pointing.

We can see the snakes moving in Saul's direction.

Johnny raises the M-16 slowly, and with a shattering noise, fires three shots - one after the other, in just a matter of seconds.

What appears to be two snakes, roil in the water in their death throws, and we can see the blood in the water.

Saul is maybe twenty to thirty feet from shore, and swimming frantically. His feet catch the bottom and he races up as quick as he can against the resistance of the water. Making it up, he starts to run, looking back over his shoulder toward us. Suddenly he does a face-plant right into the sandy ground, all while he is still looking back at us. Saul doesn't get up.

The dredge keeps running with neither Johnny or I paying attention. The rocks spill off the grizzly head over the sides.

"Are you all right?" I holler over to Saul, cupping my hands around my mouth to act as a megaphone. "Saul! Are you all right?" I holler again.

Saul does not respond. Nothing. Just the sound of the dredge running. No motion. No reply.

"The snakes never got to him," Johnny declares "None that I could see."

"Saul! Are you all right?" I holler again.

No answer. No movement.

"I think he's passed out again," I say to Johnny, "Like I was telling you before. He just seems to pass out whenever he is under too much stress."

"Should I shut off the dredge to get Bill up?" asks Johnny.

I am uneasy about it, and it shows.

"Give me a second." I reply.

"Saul! Are you all right?" I holler again. "Answer me Saul! Let me know you're okay."

Saul rolls over onto his side, still looking back at us, and gives a faint wave.

"Thank God," I say in relief. Johnny looks relieved too.

"I can't believe Bill didn't hear all that," I declare. "That was loud." My ears are still ringing.

Saul gets up and works his way over to camp, obviously a little unsure on his feet.

Johnny sets the M-16 down on the frame of the rack where it won't fall off, and positions himself to clear the grizzly head. In all the ruckus, the grizzly head got plugged up with rocks.

"That was close," says Johnny, trying to focus on his work.

"Doesn't Bill ever take a rest?" I declare back.

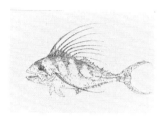

It is another half hour before the pitch of the dredge motor changes - Bill finally shuts off the intake. Johnny and I finish clearing off the sluice and emptying our pockets into the reservoir box.

"Wouldn't want to get caught with one of those in my pocket," I declare.

"Not me!" declares Johnny in agreement, pulling out the lining of his pockets to show they were empty.

Bill's air bubbles are coming up next to the rack and, in a moment, the rack becomes unstable as Bill tries to pull himself up.

"Shut off the motors," Bill calls up over the engine noise.

Bill puts his breathing apparatus up on the rack, and again tries to boost himself up, rocking around the rack pretty good in his effort. After a couple of attempts, he quits trying to climb up. He hooks the head of the dredge pickup to the rack while floating in the water, his buoyancy compensator all bloated out. It is quiet now.

"Do you want some help up?" I ask Bill.

"No. I'm pooped," answers Bill, like even that is an effort to get out.

"Can you ease the rack over to the camp? I'll just hang on here until we get to shore," Bill continues, still breathing hard from the effort to climb up onto the rack.

Johnny and I chatter back and forth, coordinating our efforts to bring the rack into shore. When we get in shallow enough, Bill finally walks out backwards until he can take his flippers off. Johnny and I tie off the rack for the night.

"What happened to Saul?" asks Bill when we get together on shore. Saul is nowhere in sight.

I relay the events of the afternoon, while Bill cracks open a beer and lights a cigarette, juggling them both while crawling out of his wet suit.

"You never heard the M-16?" I ask in amazement.

"Never heard it," answers Bill. "It's noisy down there, with the sound of your breathing apparatus and the dredge. The rocks rattle around pretty loud in the pickup head."

Saul is working his way out of their tent now, with his back to us to zipper up the netting to keep bugs and whatever out.

"Are you okay Saul?" asks Bill.

"Yeah I'm okay," answers Saul.

"So what happened on the beach?" Bill probes. "Derrick says you passed out."

"I don't know," was Saul's reply. "I got a little light-headed and needed to rest. I heard the M-16 and I knew the snakes were after me. Scared me to death!"

Bill sits in his chair, obviously fatigued, like this was too much trouble for him to think about. He butts out his cigarette, and finishes his beer, pitching his can next to several others.

"Well it seems like everything is okay," Bill declares. "So why don't you guys head off and do your fishing, and I'll see if I can get enough energy to start some supper."

Johnny and I are responsive to get at it.

"Are you going to come Saul?" I ask.

Saul seems to have as much energy as Bill.

"No. I'll stay put." answers Saul.

Johnny and I get our fishing gear and are heading out. Then Bill calls over.

"Johnny! Come over here for a second."

Johnny and I give each other a quick look, trying to hide any sign of fear, and approach Bill.

"So where did you learn to shoot like that?" demands Bill. He doesn't ask it in a friendly manner.

Johnny and I look at one another, and then back to Bill.

Johnny is clearly uncomfortable in Bill's fixed glare.

"My dad says I was good at it the very first shot I ever fired," answers Johnny in his own defence. "He said I was a natural."

Bill continued his glare at Johnny.

"A natural hey!" says Bill. It wasn't a question, and it wasn't a compliment.

CHAPTER TWENTY

It is dark. It is quiet. Except for the sporadic thrashing of clothing, of bedding.

At various moments, there is the sound of whimpering. It builds, then fades. Moments pass. Then again. And again, the thrashing.

If you were able to see what was happening, your eyes would get used to the dark. The soft glow of the digital display of the clock radio would allow you to make out the shape of a man in bed, sleeping, but in a troubled sleep. Distressed. The desperation of the whimpering is broadcasting something frantic. Fear. Again, thrashing. Again, whimpering. It is the struggle of fight or flight. A nightmare - a true nightmare. He cries out. His eyes flash open wide from the waking sound of his own struggle. He is breathing hard. He quickly pulls himself up onto his pillow, adjusting now to the reality of his surroundings. And the relief of more comfortable surroundings. It has been a dream – only a dream.

The digital display of the clock says 3:53 a.m.

Vivid. The immediate recall of the intensity of the dream.

It is Morales.

He had been on horseback. It had been dark and raining. The

wind had been blowing, and the blinding flash of lightning gave the greenish-blueish brilliance to his surroundings against the deep black background of trees and shapes. The lightning and thunder startled his mount, the horse jolted and tossed in fear, running frantically. He ducked under tree branches so he wasn't knocked from the horse. Both he and the horse surprised at the wet reflection of faces illuminated by the flashes of lightning. Shapes and faces coming from behind each tree. He and his mount frantically dodging each hazard. Shapes and faces, silver blue reflections from the edge of the clearing. The growing fear as he realized what was whizzing by his head. Darts! Blowgun darts. Hostiles. The assault of the darts, the men. Morales, desperately trying to hang onto his horse, doing all he could do to stay in the saddle. The dark. The attack was coming from the dark. It was always the dark.

Corporal Morales reaches over and turns on a bedside light. He resists acknowledging the comfort of his surroundings, the comfort of light, and the relief of knowing it was only a dream. But it gives its comfort.

Morales sits up on the edge of his bed, and slips his feet into his sandals. He recovers his balance and composure as he makes his way out to the kitchen. He pulls open the door of the fridge. He pulls out the litre carton of milk and takes five good gulps, soothing the distress that had even reached his stomach. He drinks straight from the milk carton. Living alone, he has no need for the protocol of using a glass, which he would only have to wash.

Still holding the milk carton in his hand, he steps over to look at the map of Costa Rica he has displayed on this wall, and searches out the location of San Vito. San Vito is down in the southern reaches of Costa Rica, close to the Panama border. A town of fifteen thousand, more or less. He had been there once, some six or seven years ago, and has a vague recollection of being there once as a young boy as well, with his parents. San Vito had a considerable Italian heritage. Immigration was promoted by the government of the mid-twentieth century to colonize and develop farmland in the wilderness reaches. This colony intended to secure the area, developmentally and politically.

For the past several days, Morales had been phoning out to various detachments in outlying regions to see if anyone had spotted a large white Mercedes 4x4, maybe a couple teenage passengers, stopping at a market. Maybe looked out of place - anything. On the major highways, there are thousands of non-descript white trucks, the most common color of commercial vehicles. But in outlying areas, larger new trucks are less com-mon, and may be noticed. Especially a Mercedes 4x4.

A call had come back, late yesterday afternoon from an old colleague, Corporal Mancuso, second in command at the San Vito detachment. They had trained together. Corporal Mancuso had seen a larger white Mercedes, several days prior, though he wasn't sure it was the one Morales was looking for. He could provide no greater details. It was as much a social call, returned as a courtesy; A chance to say hello and get caught up in any gossip.

But it was all he had to go on. The best lead he had.

Morales studied the map. Where the roads out to the wilder-ness areas led, and where they terminated. He knew that Bill's Mercedes could travel past where established roads ended and trails continued further into the wilderness areas. The terrain and rivers where fishing and, yes, maybe where gold could be found. East of San Vito was a range of wilderness and high mountains, where roads and trails just deteriorated to horse trails and foot paths - where only wilderness seekers probed further. Then some of the distress of his nightmare started building again. It was these outlying mountain wilderness areas where his great grandfather had last travelled and met his misfortune. Yes. His great grand father, Juan Morales, had once travelled this treacherous area in pursuit of gold. Yes. This was the country of the Bri-Bri.

Corporal Morales takes another drink from the container of milk and then sits at the kitchen table, thinking. Details of his nightmare keep coming back to memory. The faces, the blow-gun darts whizzing by his head. This wilderness area, the possible sighting of Bill's Mercedes, the awe he knew as a child of the story of his great grandfather. The legend of the Bri-Bri's. Now, his dream was beginning to make sense.

How good was the information Corporal Mancuso had provided? They were not close friends or even colleagues. How much could he trust the information?

Morales, feeling uncertain, is facing more questions than he is comfortable with.

It was one thing to chase after Bill. It was another, to put together and manage the details of how he was going to do it. How, exactly, was he to find Bill? And, if he did find him, how was he going to challenge him? He felt he was within his bounds to stop him, but clearly - more specifically – on what specific grounds? Not only to Bill, but to any others, if it became necessary. And how was he to explain why he was there in the first place? And how was he going to make a claim to any gold? He only believes this to be the purpose of Bill's trip. Clearly this is Bill's intent, is it not?

What if Bill is watching for him? What if Bill has called home and his wife, Phyllis, informs him that he had been around asking questions? What if Bill was waiting for him?

Surprise. That is his key to pulling it off. That is his ace in the hole. Surprise.

If he could manage a scenario where Bill just turns around, and there he is, caught red-handed with the gold. Difficult maybe, but possible. Then he could arrest him. Maybe he could strike a deal. Half?

If this was to work, he would have to have some time to develop some surveillance. He would have to scope things out before moving in.

What if he encountered the Bri-Bri? The Bri-Bri were not the people they were so many years ago. They knew of their resources. They knew of their rights. In their territory, they could deal with him much easier than the other way around.

But he is the police. How far could he push that? How far would it get him?

The milk carton is empty when he reaches to take another swallow.

It is the alarm that wakes Morales. His head has been more than busy through the night, and sleep did not come again easily with all the details running around in his head. The strong cup of coffee helps to bring him up to speed, and the couple hours of sleep have given him some refreshment. And it is daylight now.

It had taken him a couple of days to arrange for some time off. Details, details. Now, he feels his confidence, and a sense of purpose, returning. Many times, in his experience dealing with a criminal, they would acquiesce and fold, accepting that their gig was over. Especially when they were caught in the act. Then he would have his chance. Some of what he found Bill with - the gold - could easily fall his way. And, at the very worst, closing in on Bill could earn him some recognition.

And then again, most criminals react when caught. The fight or flight response.

But he is the police. And he is good at his job. He has confidence in his skills. He has successfully managed more desperate situations than this in the past. Many times, actually. Why should he doubt himself? The self-doubts of the night are passing.

Morales finishes up his morning clean-up and lays out his clothes for his trip. He pulls together his food supplies for a few days' travel, his wilderness kit, knife, gun, and his pack tent. Morales stops. There is another detail to take care of.

Morales picks up his telephone, then sets it down again. He tries to look up the number for the police detachment in San Vito in his local phone directory. No luck. So, he returns to calling down to his own detachment and have them look up the phone number for him. Morales scrawls the number provided on a scrap of paper, and then proceeds to put in a call to Corporal Mancuso. He is in luck. He has caught Mancuso at the detachment.

"Vinny!" greets Morales. "Glad I caught you. I am heading out your way for a few days of wilderness trekking. A bit of camping and fishing and all - you know. I need to take a break. What do you say we get together for a drink this evening? Get caught up on old times."

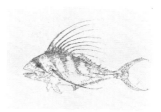

It is already dark before Morales checks into his hotel in San Vito. He will grab something to eat when he gets together with Vinny. He calls Vinny at his home at the number Vinny had given him. They agree to meet at the Sarambo Tapas Bar. Eight o'clock.

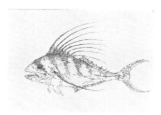

The conversation is good, and the laughs are many. They have their serious moments, discussing colleagues and bosses, and big and small crime; the successes and the screw ups. Morales speaks of his transfer to the Drug Enforcement Unit. The opportunity and advancement – the inevitable promotion. The drinks have flowed, though they were tempered somewhat by the array of fine Italian dishes. But as the drinks catch up with them both, and the fatigue of the day is settling in, most topics of conversation are exhausted, and the pretentiousness is wearing thin.

"So Eduardo," says Vinny. "Why are you really here? I have never known you to be the great outdoorsman - especially solo. A group of guys, lots of beer by the fire, lots of laughs. That I could see. But solo?"

Vinny would not remove his gaze from Morales. He expects an answer. Morales had tried to anticipate this get-together and how it would work, rehearsing it over in his mind, during the hours of his drive down. There was information he wanted also: advice on the territory, the hazards. How to get the information he needed without openly declaring his hand? He had avoided the subject to this point, hoping for some opportunity to present itself. Now it had started.

Vinny sat there with a warm grin, but his eyes were still fixed on Morales, expecting an answer.

"A cop can't fool a cop," declares Vinny.

Maybe he should come clean, thought Morales. At least, most of it. Enough to justify his activity.

Morales smiles back.

"Vinny," starts Morales. "Have you ever had a hunch you wanted to pursue? Even if it meant giving it your own time. Don't kid me - of course you have." he adds quickly.

"Yeah," Vinny says slowly, to give it emphasis. "Yeah I have. We're cops Eduardo. So, what is it you've got going down?"

CHAPTER
TWENTY-ONE

Saul has five jars standing in a line on top of a log. The log has been knocked down by the river when it flooded somewhere in past years, and the log is smooth – it has no bark left on it.

In each jar, separately, he had placed a live scorpion. He shakes each jar a little, up close to his face to see each scorpion is still alive. One is quite big - maybe as much as two inches, with a black body and brown legs - eight of them - and a brown tail. Another is yellow, not as large, and one is reddish. The two smallest ones are dark brown.

To feed his scorpions, Saul is collecting some of the dead bugs lying under the propane lantern they use in the evenings. The bugs were killed by the heat of the lamp, not poisoned, or otherwise damaged in any way. They would be safe to feed the scorpions. Collecting this feed, Saul is careful not to pick up any insects that look like they may have a stinger. He knows that the stinger of many dead bugs can still be venomous for many days afterward. It is a muscle reflex in the stinger, not needing to be wilfully used by its host. Just stimulated.

Saul puts a bug or two in each of the jars, except for the jar of one of the small brown scorpions. For that one, he continues to look around under the edges of the log till he finds a spider. The spider is close to the size of the brown scorpion. The spider retreats for cover in Saul's shadow, but Saul scratches it out into the open with a twig and directs it onto the lid of the jar from the brown scorpion. With the twig, he prods the spider into the jar of the brown scorpion, and quickly dumps out the sand left in the lid, then loosely replaces the lid on the jar.

And he watches. With delight.

The spider is quick to explore the limits of his confinement, avoiding coming in direct contact with the scorpion. Then it retreats to the farthest edge of his confines across from the scorpion and remains still, facing the scorpion. Waiting.

After a minute, the scorpion starts his approach to the spider. The spider is quick enough to avoid the assault and scurries around the scorpion in the base of the jar. This goes on for several minutes, providing Saul with the entertainment he is hoping for.

The sound of the dredge working reminds Saul of his defiant stand this morning against Bill's directives. Bill's scolding, then finally relenting, shaking his head and muttering under his breath. Bill couldn't run everybody just the way he liked.

The scorpion approaches the spider again, methodical, like some stocky boxer, more muscled and heavier on his feet than a lighter opponent. The scorpion, like the heavy-set boxer, will be able to take the punch.

But like the more agile boxer, the spider seems to know he has to fight. He can not avoid the fight. It is what has to happen. It is his only hope. And the spider makes his attack.

The tail of the scorpion whips down and hits the spider on the back once, then twice. And the stinging strikes of the scorpion are like the boxer's hay-maker - the big punch that connects, and the quicker fighter is stunned. And now, unsure on his feet, dazed, unable to gather his wits quickly enough to his surroundings, another hay-maker is delivered.

And he is down.

Saul is delighted with the performance.

Saul stands up and jumps with his fist projected up in the air.

"Yeah!" he yelps.

He can't wait to show the boys.

He'd love to find a blue scorpion. His mom had shown him one once, next to the pool, in the moonlight. They looked like they glowed in the dark. Neat!

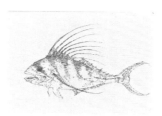

"If this is gold," I say to Johnny, holding up a piece that again looks like a piece of ginger root, "there is sure lots of it!" And again, I quickly put it in my pocket.

"I think it's gold," agrees Johnny. This is the first time we had openly acknowledged the subject.

"So, how long do you think we are going to do this?" adds Johnny after a few moments.

I give him a hopeless shrug.

"We can't keep going much longer," I finally add. "We are running out of food. If we don't catch any fish, really what do we have left to cook? Rice. Noodles. A few cans of sauce. Noodle soup."

"Fried bananas," Johnny replies in jest. "Monkey on a spit," and we both laugh.

"Water Moccasin soup," I add, and we laugh some more. I guess we are getting goofy, and our laughter tails off.

I hold up another piece of rock, what we believe is gold, and I take a few moments to empty the pieces from my pockets into the reservoir box.

A gust of wind blows up and Johnny and I both look up into the trees above as the wind swings the canopy of branches about. Some leaves float down around us and are carried with the flow of water as it swirls in the pool.

Only moments later, another gust blows up, much stronger than the first. The canopy of trees and branches above shudder again to absorb the force, and a rain of dried leaves blows down from above. Hundreds of leaves land on the water around us.

I look up at Johnny and our eyes meet. We are both wide-eyed. We both look around, taking in what is happening.

"What's this blowing in?" I remark to Johnny.

"I don't know man," Johnny answers apprehensively.

A gust of apprehension blows right through me. I can feel the hair rising on my arms with the chill of goose-bumps. I feel unsettled for more than a comfortable moment. I scan the sky and our surroundings again, then meet Johnny's eyes. He looks at me just as warily. A flood of rocks lands on the grizzly head with a racket, the rocks spilling down at our feet. We get back to work.

Bill is working deeper than before, maybe eight or ten feet deeper. He knows that every bit of depth has an impact on how long he can work under water. But this, he is sure, is good material he is pulling out. He knows it. When he breaks for lunch, he will work it out. At shallower depths, there is little concern. But now, maybe he should check it out with his dive tables. Bill focuses on his work. This material is too good to give up. Too good.

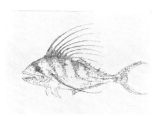

A gust of wind blows over the trees. Cigua, the horse Morales has rented, picks her head up and snorts, looking like she wants to shake the bit out of her mouth. Dry leaves are blown out of the trees and a few dry branches startle Cigua as they fall to the ground.

Morales' meeting with Vinny had proven worth the effort. Vinny knew a family who rented out horses for eco-adventures, sometimes guiding the trips for tour guides who lacked the know-how of managing wilderness trips and caring for horses. Their small ranch and farm was on the edge of the wilderness, and the dirt road up to the house was literally the end of the road.

Vinny's advice, to go horseback, was good. It was the best, and maybe the only way to traverse the wilderness areas. He planned to travel up one river valley, and if there was no sign of Bill, then to cross over a ridge and travel down another. The outfitters had all the equipment he needed, had it ready quickly, and gave him the knowledge of the terrain he needed. If he completed the round trip, he would end up back near San Vito, and the ranch. The roads Bill would have to use were too much for his own vehicle, and the rivers too much to cross with a vehicle not suited for deeper water crossings, like Bill's Mercedes was designed for.

Another gust of wind sends the trees into gyrations, and another dead branch tumbles down from above. Cigua flinches, and lurches again.

"Easy Cigua," soothes Morales.

Cigua. What a name for a horse, thinks Morales. Cigua is a supernatural character of Central American folklore. A shape changing spirit, viewed and mistaken by men as a long-haired woman, luring men into the wilderness, and into danger. Luring lone men out late on dark moonless nights, tempting such men away from their planned routes to lose them deep in canyons. It is a legend everyone knew, and, as children, everyone believed. And then, of course, there were some people who never overcame their childhood beliefs.

Morales smiles.

Morales was sure that Cigua, and the Legend of Cigua, would make for great campfire stories. Stories embellished by the various guides who led eco-adventures, for their listening entourage, eager to hear the legends and the culture of Central America.

Another gust of wind unsettles any complacent thought.

"Great!" says Morales out loud to himself.

He is tired from his late night of drinking with Vinny, and rising early to make his way. Time is running out. He has to move quickly. All the preparations to pursue Bill had taken too much time. He is several days behind. Now there is the weather to contend with. It leaves him feeling uneasy.

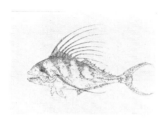

Bill and the boys had come in for lunch. Saul had not gotten anything ready for them, and it annoyed Bill. Bill checked his dive tables and decided he had better stay out of the water a couple hours before going back in. He has to give the gasses, dissolved in his body, time to escape.

But he doesn't want to give up the time. His time is running out. And he knows the gold is good - better than good. The reservoir boxes are showing results better than he ever hoped for.

Bill knows he shouldn't have a beer. It is not something that will improve his dive times. But he grabs one to wash down his lunch, lunch going to be mostly leftovers from last night's meal. And the cigarettes don't help either.

Bill finishes his beer. The boys, already their lunch are goofing around together by a log at the edge of their camp, and the sounds of their excitement draws him over.

"What are you guys up to?" queries Bill.

We are hunched down, looking into Saul's jars.

"Saul's got a bunch of scorpions. One just killed a big spider," I reply.

"Tonight we'll have a scorpion fight," adds Saul with enthusiasm.

Bill steps into the middle of us and looks over the collection of jars in disbelief.

"No, you are not!" declares Bill.

Bill picks up the first jar, looks at it for a second, takes the lid off and dumps it on the ground. Then he steps on the scorpion and grinds it into the ground.

"Come on Bill!" groans Saul.

Bill takes the next jar, and the next, and grinds each scorpion into the dirt, twisting his sport shoe to tear each scorpion to pieces.

"Jeez Bill!" protests Saul angrily.

Johnny and I step back defensively.

"What do you think you are doing?" Bill scolds Saul, raising his voice. "What if you get stung? Then what!? You're putting our whole trip in jeopardy! If we had to pull camp to get you into a doctor...." Bill leaves his words dangling.

Saul's face is flushed. He is angry. His jaw is set as he glares at Bill. Then he turns and walks off into the trees.

Neither Johnny or I say a word.

"What are you two doing, encouraging him?" demands Bill.

"We weren't encouraging him," I answer defensively. "They were in jars." I add, hoping that might aid in our defence.

Bill sets his glare on each of us. I am uncomfortable. Johnny more so.

Bill clenches his teeth together in disgust, shaking his head.

"Saul has no sense when it comes to things like this." admonishes Bill. "No sense at all. Playing with scorpions is like playing with a loaded gun. You're just looking for someone to get hurt."

A big gust of wind blows in again, and there is a clattering of dead branches in the trees. Bill looks up and scans the area, looking in disbelief. This is the first gust Bill has seen.

Bill looks annoyed, then looks around.

"Get things picked up from lunch." Bill directs, and makes his way over to the cooler, grabs another beer, and plunks himself in his chair.

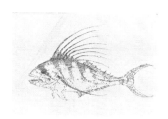

It is at least an hour later when Saul hears the dredge motors start up. At least Bill did not get on his case to go out and work on the dredge again.

His jars are still scattered next to the log where Bill had tossed them on the ground. Saul bends down and picks each one of them up and places them on the log. He looks down at the squashed scorpions. Four of them - only four of them. He looks closely for the fifth one.

A few sand particles move where the indentation is left from Bill's effort to squash the fifth one. Saul picks out a small twig and probes the sandy impression. And there is the little scorpion. Still moving, trying to unearth itself, covered in sand, but still alive. It is the little brown one. He is the tough one. He has the hardest of shells for protection. He is the most venomous. He is Saul's prize. Not all is lost.

Saul picks out the smallest jar, the easiest to conceal, and prods the little brown scorpion into it. He then makes his way over to where the lantern is hung and picks up a few dead bugs and places them in the jar.

He is feeling better now.

Bill comes in a little earlier than usual. He is getting concerned about his dive times. And fatigue. Things had just been going so good.

Johnny and I, including Saul, head downstream to go fishing. No one wants to be left alone in camp with Bill. Not today anyways.

Once we are well enough out of ear shot, I start on Saul.

"Boy, I thought you were going to get us all killed."

"Yeah, me too," adds Johnny.

"Ah!" mocks Saul. "Bill thinks he runs everything. But he doesn't scare me," declares Saul defiantly.

Johnny and I grin and laugh with each other, now mocking Saul.

"Well he scares me!" declares Johnny.

"Maybe Bill is right. Maybe you don't have any sense."

"Sense. What sense?" asks Saul defiantly.

"The sense to know what's dangerous. The sense to know you're in trouble. That sense," I retort.

"Well I am not a little Billy Boy like you are," snaps back Saul.

I grimace angrily and glare at Saul.

"Look," I say in a moment. "Go fish by yourself. Get lost."

I turn down a path that leads to the last area we had been fishing, leaving Saul behind. Johnny follows without comment.

"And don't get yourself killed," I holler back over my shoulder.

The camp fire has diminished to a few coals and the gust of wind blows a spray of sparks across the camp chairs set out around the fire pit. It is not enough to illuminate more than the outline of a couple chairs as the wind and sparks blow between them. It is pitch black - one of those nights where you can't see your hand if you hold it right in front of your face. The gust builds, as does the spray of sparks, and one of the chairs tumbles over, not heard above the roar of the wind in the trees. Small branches, bits of branches, leaves and debris from the trees is blown about. There is just the noise of the wind in the trees and the darkness.

There is a sudden flash of lightning and within a second, a crash of thunder that shakes everything. Then all there is, is darkness. Debris from the trees is blowing down and then the first heavy drops of rain pelt the tents. The frequency of the heavy drops increases rapidly and there is another brilliant flash of lightning, and again in a second, another crash of thunder. Then the next gust of wind carries the rain, coming down in a deluge like the sky had been holding it all back until it broke at the seams. Another chair blows over and is carried away in the darkness by the wind. Larger branches are blown down from the canopy of trees, some hitting our tents. The tents shudder in the wind, the force of the downpour of rain making it all worse.

A flashlight comes on in Bill's tent, the beam barely visible through the tents saturated walls.

"Saul," says Bill. "Grab your sleeping bag and head for the truck. Who knows what this could blow down on us. Take your flashlight. I'll get Derrick and Johnny. Make it quick."

Saul says nothing but rummages around for his flashlight and follows Bill's instructions. Bill unzips the mosquito netting of the tent and heads out to get Derrick and Johnny.

Bill is nearly yelling his instructions to Derrick and Johnny above the roar of the wind in the trees and the deluge of rain.

Bill comes back to gather his sleeping bag as Saul is ready to bolt for the truck, peering out in to the mayhem the storm is releasing on them.

"Hurry," directs Bill to Saul.

Saul makes a dash for the truck.

Bill bunches his sleeping bag close to him as he kneels down to secure the flaps of the tent, propping his flashlight the best he can to illuminate what he is doing. Then he makes a run for it also.

Climbing up into the cab in the driver's seat, Bill pushes his sleeping bag ahead of him, and slams the door behind him.

"We are catching hell tonight," declares Bill loudly above the noise of the downpour on the cab of the truck.

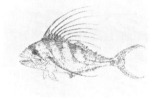

A flash of lightning acts like a brilliant strobe light as Johnny and I seem to be grotesquely running to the truck. Our actions seem broken. The passenger door opens and we stuff our sleeping bags in as quickly as we can and slam the door behind us.

"Man, it's coming down," I yell over the noise.

"I'm soaked, just from the tent to here," adds Johnny.

Saul crawled into the back of the cab. Johnny and I jockey around to get comfortable, and wrap ourselves in our sleeping bags.

"We are safer in here," says Bill. "You don't know what is going to blow down. A tent isn't much protection. We can head back to our tents when this blows over."

"If our tents are still there," declares Saul.

The lightning and thunder, and gusts of wind keep coming, like waves crashing so hard you can't make out anything through the windows.

A monkey jumps up onto the engine hood of the truck and tries to huddle away from the wind and rain. It has a box of some snack food he has stolen from the food supplies. The cover of the supplies has probably been blown loose, or blown away.

The lightning, with its brilliant flashes, lights up the monkey and all of us in the cab of the truck at the same time. Bill turns on his flashlight and shines it in the monkey's face. The monkey puts its face right up to the windshield and screams at us with his mouth wide open, showing all his fangs and bits of food and saliva in its mouth. The monkey is trying to scare us. Another staccato flash of lightning illuminates his assault. He has succeeded. Succeeded well. A chill runs up my spine. Bill bangs the side of his fist on the window and the monkey turns and runs for cover.

My heart is beating so loud I think everyone can hear it.

"I wouldn't want him in my tent," declares Bill.

We all agree.

For the next few minutes there is just the noise of the wind and rain and clatter of debris hitting the truck. Sometimes pieces are big enough to startle us all.

"I think we have stayed too long," declares Saul.

No one replies. Johnny and I know enough to keep quiet.

"No food, no Coke, probably no tent. No fun!" Saul adds again.

Though Bill sighs, no one sees it or hears it.

"Look Saul," retorts Bill. "I told you tonight, just one more day and then we will head home. My barrels are almost full of material, and yes, we are running out of supplies - food, gas, beer, and patience." Bill emphasizes the patience.

"Just do your part tomorrow," adds Bill, "and we will be out of here. And if you don't help, I am just about ready to..."

A deafening crash of thunder drowns out what Bill is saying. He does not repeat it.

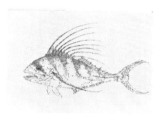

Somewhere in the night, the storm blew over and Bill prompts each of us back into our tents to try and get what sleep we can for the rest of the night. No one is sleeping well in the truck.

Getting everyone placed away, Bill can still see the sky light up from flashes of lightning as he looks around before ducking into his tent. The storm has headed up the mountain.

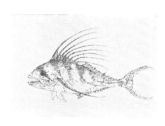

The same storm hits Morales. Every bit as intense, and every bit as disturbing. And some horses, if not most, do not do well with lightning and thunder. Many do, when somewhat sheltered and at home with feed and straw. Security, which is not here.

Cigua, wild eyed, strains on her tether, whinnying wildly with each flash of lightning. With each crash of thunder, Cigua becomes more agitated. It is almost more than Morales can do to control her, to settle her. On her tether, she strains at the stakes and loosens them in what has become saturated ground. Morales has to find and sharpen new stakes in this night, and pound them into the ground to reinforce the tether. Again, Morales is bent over, pounding a stake, re-tying Cigna's tether, and Cigua rears up and brays, hooves dog paddling above him. Killer hooves.

It was a most unsettling night. There was no sleep to be had. Cigua strained to break away from her tether. A wild eyed horse coming at you in the flashes of lightning, hooves kicking. No less than the number of times the lightning flashed was Morales reminded of the Legend of Cigua. No less than the number of times the lightning flashed, Morales had thought of his dream from only nights before. How many times had he checked over his shoulder, with each lightning flash, searching the shadows for faces?

Yes. Another sleepless night.

CHAPTER
TWENTY-TWO

$\mathbf{B}$ill is the first up. Intent on getting in a full day's work, he has wakened Saul. Coming out of the tent, there are clear blue skies, and the air is fresh and humid. The camp is showing the effects of the storm - debris everywhere, the chairs around the fire scattered, the tarp over the food supplies has mostly blown off, and several monkeys are scavenging around the food boxes for anything they can find. Bill starts to run at them, to scare them away.

Something is terribly wrong. With each step, there is a fiery pain, stabbing like a hot knife into his left foot. Bill stumbles forward, his left leg being immobilized by the intense pain. Bill falls down onto his hands and knees, and again there is the stabbing of a hot knife into his left foot. Bill rolls onto his back in pain.

"YEOW!" Bill loudly cries out.

And again, "YEOW!!" as what seems to be a hot knife stabs him again.

Bill, frantically, tries to rip his sport shoe off. It seems to take all of his effort as the pain immobilizes his coordination. The laces are tight and in the next few seconds, which seem to take forever, Bill wretches the shoe off his foot. In large motions, Bill shakes his shoe out. Onto the ground drops a scorpion. A little brown one.

Bill groans loudly, still writhing with the intensity of the pain and the multiple stings. Spotting the scorpion, Bill beats it with the sole of his shoe, again and again, as hard as he can. Then he reaches and grabs a hand-sized rock and smashes the scorpion over and over. Bill lays on his side for a few moments, looking at the smashed scorpion.

It takes all of Bill's effort to right himself and get up on his feet. He hobbles and limps in an effort to walk off the pain. Groaning and cussing to himself, Bill still grimaces from the pain.

"Saul!" Bill yells out loudly. "Derrick! Get out here."

Bill is sprawled out in one of the camp chairs, with his left leg propped up on another, his foot reaching over the edge. At Bill's feet, Johnny and I have the first aid kit out, open, rummaging through it to find something that might help. Johnny and I each examine Bill's foot. Saul stands back watching.

"It looks like you were stung four or five times. Maybe, more," declares Johnny. "You can see the little white spots where there is no blood circulating."

"It was all of that," answers Bill, his face still grimacing at times, strained by the pain.

I hand Johnny the first aid book that is part of the kit, and Johnny starts paging through it while I keep sorting through the contents of the kit.

"Insect bites is all I can find," says Johnny, after a few moments.

"What does it say?" I ask quickly.

"Wash area thoroughly and apply hydrocortisone cream. Contact a physician or seek emergency medical centre if an allergic reaction becomes apparent."

"Well, here is the hydrocortisone cream," I say, handing Johnny the package with a tube of cream inside. I set down the first aid kit.

"Don't bother with it," says Bill. "There is nothing in there that is going to help."

"It isn't going to hurt anything to try it," I protest.

Bill grunts and says, "Go ahead. Put it on."

Bill is looking over at Saul who is still standing off a fair distance. "Tell me you didn't have anything to do with this," demands Bill.

Saul is standing back, with his arms crossed, his head bent down some, peering out through the top of his eye sockets, almost like some little kids pout. He just slowly shakes his head from side to side for a moment in response to Bill's accusation.

"It's letting up some," says Bill after a few moments. "It won't kill me. So let's get at it and get to work. Saul, get some breakfast together. Johnny, gas up the tanks."

I start putting away the first aid kit.

Bill struggles to his feet, and tries putting pressure on his foot. It isn't working right for him, but he hops and hobbles over to his shoe, still lying by the dead scorpion.

"No, Derrick," Bill directs. "You get some breakfast together, and Saul, you pick up around here and clean things up."

"And you be sure to get out on the dredge this morning and help out." commands Bill to Saul, after a moment.

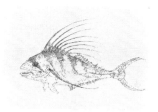

Morales is unsettled as the dim light of morning arrives. It is not a sunny morning. There is a dense, dark fog, obscuring any brightness of day. Morales has followed the trail up with no sign of Bill. His altitude is high, and a dense morning cloud has stuck to the side of the mountain, shadowed from enough direct light to burn it off. The scene is surreal. The fog is so thick; he can see it drift eerily around him. He can hardly see but a few feet into the trees around the clearing. The fog is cold, and the air is saturated with dampness from the fog and the downpour of the night before. The fog condenses on anything cold, keeping everything wet. A thousand water droplets hang from every branch, and anything Morales touches only rains down on him, making him wetter. Nothing is worse than packing up a wet camp. He can see the river level has risen during the night, voraciously fed by the water shed of the saturated ground. He knows he has to be moving. He has to cross the river before the flood surge prevents him from crossing the next valley, and following the river down to where he hopes to find Bill and his camp. The directions from the outfitter have been good. But the weather has not. Little sleep, and the pressure to move is weighing heavily on him. He has to make the crossing. Quickly.

Cigua, Morales' mount, is equally unsettled. All that has affected Morales - the lightning, the crashing thunder, the downpour, the lack of rest - has had no less impact on the disposition of the fine animal. A gentler morning, time to feed, a more patient hand, might have soothed her spirit. But it is not the case.

Morales is travelling light so it does not take him long to get packed up, even with everything so wet. Cigua is skittish, and Morales is close to losing his temper with her, saddling her up and trying to tie his pack to the saddle.

Then, trying to mount up, Cigua shies away several times. The horse and rider are not working well together.

Mounted up at the edge of the river, the water looks high. And fast. The far side of the river is barely visible with the heavy fog still hanging on. Morales peers across, the best he can, to locate where the path picks up on the other side. He is sure he can make out the path. Quite sure.

He prompts Cigua down the bank into the water. Cigua balks at the waters edge, and tries to turn around. Morales kicks her in the sides with his heels and reigns her head toward the water. Cigua steps forward, seeming unsure of her footing, and then with a plunge, they are swallowed into the water.

"Whoah!" Morales says loudly, partly from the shock of being immersed in the cold water, his own shock, and partly to calm Cigua who is panicked by the loss of footing. The water is rushing, and cold.

Morales hangs on as tightly as he can. It is almost impossible to stay in the saddle. Morales` head and shoulders, and the same for Cigua, are all that are above water. Morales tries to head Cigua in the direction of the far bank. Cigua is spooked and fearful, and tries to head back to the shore they have come from - the closest safe haven. Desperately, Morales tries to steer Cigua across to the dimly outlined bank. Cigua is not taking direction, fearful of the crossing.

Carried rapidly downstream by the current, through the dense fog, a dark shape emerges. A tree has fallen down into the river from the wind and rain. They are being swept into it. Seeing it approach, Cigua panics and tries to turn back, snorting loudly with fear.

Cigua's frantic response to turn back to shore, and the current of the river, pull Morales off the saddle. Panic ensues. Morales tries to keep an iron grip on the reigns, but he is swept out in front of Cigua in the current. He can't let go, or he is lost, swept into the branches of the fallen tree and drowned. Morales' pull on the reigns steers Cigua straight toward him. Cigua holds her head back, as high as she can, eyes wild with fear. Morales tries to pull himself back to the saddle. Cigua's hooves are thrashing frantically in the dog-paddle motion of a horse swimming. Morales has to reach Cigua's mane - something more to grab onto.

Morales is hit on his left forearm by Cigua's hooves thrashing in the water. He feels his arm snap and go limp from the injury. The pain is intense, but Morales hangs onto the reigns for dear life with his right arm. Cigua heads back to the closest shore desperately, and Morales is dragged behind through the water, holding his breath for what seems an eternity. Thinking his lungs are about to burst, Cigua finds some footing. With jarring motions, Cigua clamours for footing, tearing down chunks of the bank as she finally pulls herself up, Morales in tow. Cigua races forward up on the bank another fifty feet, trying to distance herself from danger. Morales is dragged up along the bank. Cigua stops, snorting frantically to catch her breath. Safe now for the moment but still agitated, Cigua stands still.

Like all life has drained from him, the reigns limply unwind from Morales' right hand. With desperate short breaths, Morales lays there, not moving, his left arm limp beside him.

The fog keeps drifting by.

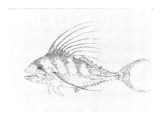

Bill works right through what is left of the morning - no breaks. Saul protests. Relationships are tense.

"What do you expect?" I say defiantly to Saul. "I am sure he is annoyed with you. Maybe annoyed doesn't come close to it."

"Well he just seems mad all the time, doesn't he?" retorts Saul. "He doesn't have to take everything out on me."

"It's not just you," adds Johnny.

"At least we have the sense not to aggravate him," I add.

"Well he isn't yelling at you," says Saul in his defence.

"Wise up Saul," I add. "All we have to do is get through the day. Tomorrow we are heading home. Just help it all happen. Try keeping your mouth shut."

The exchange has exhausted out the conversation for a few moments.

"Well this is the last trip I'm coming on," declares Saul.

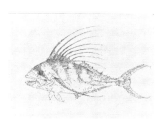

Saul seems to be standing as far away from us as he can, with what little room there is on the dredge. He is on watch with the M-16. And he has been told forcefully by Bill to keep a good watch. The water level has come up from the downpour and the water pouring into the pool is at least double of what it had been. The currents are stronger, putting more strain on everything involved with managing the sluice. It would be the same for Bill, underwater, fighting the currents.

Bill's last command to Saul, "God knows what the river will wash down - snakes, crocs. Keep a good eye. And, no more trouble. Do you hear!?" It wasn't a question.

Johnny and I work away at the grizzly head and the sluice. Bill is pulling up lots of material.

"Bill is working harder this morning than I thought he would be able to," says Johnny. "He sure pushes himself hard. His leg must be sore, and I am sure it is going to swell up on him. It has to, with that many bites."

"No kidding," I reply. "He's a crazy man right now."

"It will be good to get home," I add a few moments later.

Saul continues to ignore us, staring off into the distance. I nod my head Saul's direction.

"Still in a pout," I comment with some disgust. Nothing we are saying is out of ear reach from Saul. But he continues to ignore us.

"Well you seem to handle Bill better than anyone else can," says Johnny. "He scares me. Doesn't he scare you?"

"Yeah, he scares me," I agree reluctantly. "He is pushing everything pretty hard. I am tired of it. I'm ready to go home."

"Me too," adds Johnny.

Saul's mouth moves silently to the words unspoken. "Me too." He isn't going to give in to joining our conversation. He is angry at the world. He may be listening to us, but he isn't listening to the anger building up inside himself.

There is no breeze and the day is hot. The sun is up high in the canopy of trees, the trees providing some shade with the position of the dredge. It is very humid from the downpour the night before, and that makes it feel all the hotter. I switch over the water flow to the alternate sluice and start cleaning out the first into the reservoir box. Johnny gives up trying to keep up with the flow of rocks and material pouring over the grizzly head and takes off his t-shirt and soaks it in the water of the pool, and puts it back on. He gives a sigh of relief.

"Any chance you will take over here for a bit Saul?" Johnny calls over to Saul.

Saul just keeps staring at the water like he hasn't heard him, the M-16 still hung across his shoulders. He obviously isn't going to do any more than he is doing.

I finish cleaning out the sluice and come alongside to help Johnny clear the grizzly head. We both work quickly to get caught up. We work quietly for several minutes when I notice the air hose going down to Bill is being strained on its bungee cord.

"Bill seems to be moving to the end of his reach down there Saul," I say trying to get Saul's attention. "We need to move the rack closer to where Bill is working. Will you let out the line twenty feet?" I ask.

Saul is staring up into the trees, watching some monkeys, obviously not willing to help at all. He is not keeping a good watch of the water either.

"Come on Saul!" I say, raising my voice a little. Frustrated.

I can't wait for Saul, so I position myself to where the line is tied off on the edge of the rack. I untie the knot and start to ease out some line.

"You had better keep a good watch if that is all you are going to do." I direct at Saul, looking at him to try and make my point. The sun is flashing across Saul's face like a strobe light as the sun makes its way through the branches and leaves of the canopy above. Saul seems mesmerized by the flashing sunlight.

I pause for a moment, watching Saul, Saul looking dazed. Suddenly, showing no other sign of distress, Saul's eyes flutter and roll up into his head. All I can see is the whites of his eyes. In disbelief, I watch as Saul just keels over headfirst into the water, the M-16 still across his shoulders.

I stand wide-eyed for a moment in disbelief, watching Saul disappearing out of sight in the murky water. I drop the line and dive in after Saul. Saul has fainted again.

It has all happened so fast and unexpectedly.

Johnny only sees what is happening out of the corner of his eye. He looks up, trying to grasp what is happening. He sees the line holding the rack, which Derrick has been letting out, is untied and feeding out. Johnny makes a frantic effort to get over to it, but it is too late. The last of the bunched-up line slips over the edge, just out of reach. The rack is adrift in the current swinging on its arc, pivoting, still held by the other line, towards their camp.

Helpless. Johnny's heart is racing in fear when he spots Derrick surface with Saul in tow.

"Are you alright?" Johnny hollers to Derrick desperately.

Derrick is fighting the water in his struggle to tow Saul to shore. The rack has drifted too far, and is now out of reach. Johnny looks around frantically to find a line to throw Derrick. There is nothing to use. It is hopeless. His spirits sink more than he can believe. Johnny feels sick in his desperation.

Helpless, Johnny watches in disbelief as Derrick continues his struggle to make shore with Saul in tow. There is no M-16 in sight - no watch to keep. Only fear and desperation. The rack, drifting to shore, must be towing Bill across the bottom by his air hose, if the hose has not broken, and Bill is out of air. The dread he feels is incredible. He knows they are in trouble - big trouble. How much trouble is a big pit in his stomach, full of the worst uncertainty.

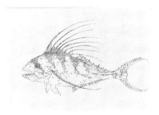

I break the surface, holding the back of Saul's t-shirt, kicking and pulling with my free arm as hard as I can. I reposition myself to hold Saul, keeping his head above the water. I hear Johnny call to me, but I am straining too hard to answer. I finally feel my feet touch bottom and I awkwardly gain my footing and drag Saul up the landing to the edge of the camp area.

I put my ear next to Saul's mouth, listening for breathing. I can't tell. I put my head on Saul's chest, to listen for his heart.

His heart is beating. Just then, Saul takes a gasp of air. He is breathing! A flood of relief comes over me. Saul starts coughing, coughing hard and long, and then vomits, coughing more, and spitting out water and vomit. Saul groans.

"Keep coughing Saul," I say loudly. "Keep coughing. Keep breathing."
I roll Saul over onto his other side, away from the vomit.

The rack has drifted into shore and Johnny has come up behind Saul and Derrick. Derrick is so focused on Saul, he hasn't noticed.

"Is he all right?" asks Johnny.

"Going to be," I answer Johnny, still focusing my attention on Saul.

Johnny stands there, uneasy, still feeling helpless.

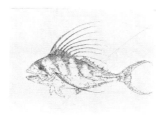

Neither of us see Bill surface behind the rack, remove his breathing apparatus, throwing it on the rack. Then his flippers.

Bill is breathing hard, his chest heaving, and his face is flushed red. He glares in the boy's direction, looking like a madman.

Hopping on his right leg with little or no support from his left leg, Bill comes up behind Johnny and, almost falling forward, reaches out and grabs the back of Johnny's t-shirt.

Johnny flashes a look behind him, sees it is Bill, and lunges forward as hard as he can to escape Bill's grip. Bill is half dragged, half hobbling on his one leg as Johnny tries to run away from his startling grip. Johnny's eyes are wide with fear. Bill trips and hobbles along, not releasing his grip on Johnny and, with a yell, he throws his other arm over Johnny's shoulder and tackles him. They tumble to the ground. Johnny frantically tries to free himself from Bills grip, but Bill has him no, around his legs and is pulling himself up to pin Johnny. Johnny groans and squeals in desperate sounds, terrified by what is happening.

Bill throws a fist at Johnny, hitting him in the upper shoulder and neck. Then Bill hits him again. Johnny struggles with all his might, but he is pinned.

"Bill! Quit!" Johnny yells out.

Bill hits Johnny again on the side of his face, as he pulls himself more on top of Johnny.

"Derrick!" cries out Johnny as loud as he can.

Bill is manoeuvring to get a better hold of Johnny, and he raises his fist again.

I grab Bill's forearm, just as he is throwing his punch. I am pulled to the ground by the force of the punch, but the force of the punch is broken.

Hitting the ground face first, I cannot recover my balance. Bill has grabbed my shirt, and I am pinned to the ground next to Johnny. With his free hand, Bill delivers a good punch to my back shoulder.

"Bill! Bill! Quit!" I holler. "It was an accident!"

Bill is not on top of me, so I am able to manoeuvre some, and I try to squirm out of Bill's grip. But Bill pulls me back in close.

Bill hits me again.

I let out a yell. "Bill!" yelling as loud and long as I can.

Bill manoeuvers to take another swing at Johnny. My yell had just stopped.

Then *thunk*. A sound so distinctive. A sound so distinctive, I know I will never forget it.

Bill groans and limply rolls off of Johnny, releasing his grip on me, and rolls over on his back.

Saul stands there like holding a smoking gun in his hand. Saul holds a three-foot branch, like a club. It now hangs down from his hand, down to the ground. He has clobbered Bill on the head with it.

Saul stands there dazed, half scowling at Bill, but shocked also by what he has just done. His jaw is set hard, staring down at Bill. It is all too much to comprehend.

I am the first to get up on my feet, and Johnny moans as he struggles to get his legs untangled from Bill.

The three of us stand there, speechless, looking down at Bill.

Bill's head is bleeding. I get down on my knees, next to Bill, to look at the wound.

Bill is breathing.

"Get the first aid kit," I direct Johnny.

Johnny starts, but is to struggling to move, trying to recover from the weight of Bill's assault and the blows to his head.

"Saul, you get the first aid kit," I re-direct.

Saul barely looks up at me, and then tosses the branch aside. With no more response, he walks casually toward the Mercedes.

Johnny gives up trying to move around and gets down on one knee next to me.

"I thought he was going to kill me," Johnny says as a matter of fact.

"How bad does it look to you?" I ask.

I work my hands in Bill's hair to show Johnny the extent of the wound. Bill's head is cut open, the cut about one and a half to two inches long. The way the blood clumps in Bill's hair, it is difficult to see clearly. The wound is to the top back corner of the left side of Bill's head.

"It's a hard part of the head," says Johnny, referring to the strength of the human skull.

"Well if Bill doesn't have a hard head, nobody does," I say as a matter of fact. There is no humour to the statement.

"But look at his leg," says Johnny.

Bill is still in his wet suit, but it is a shorty, the legs no longer than mid-thigh. His leg is obviously quite swollen, and much more flushed with colour than the other leg.

For a few moments, Johnny and I look down on Bill, taking in the situation.

"So, what do we do now?" I ask Johnny.

And that is a serious question.

I did my best to fit compresses, several layers thick, over Bill's head wound and secured them in place with wraps of gauze around Bill's head.

Bill moans as we try to reposition him to make him more comfortable. That is a good sign.

"Get Bill's pillow and sleeping bag from the tent," I direct Saul. "We should keep him warm," I add.

Repositioning the pillow under Bill's head, Bill groans again, and his eyes flutter open. Bill makes an effort to right himself, but he is unable to do so. With a groan, he settles back into the pillow. We cover him with his sleeping bag, trying to make him more comfortable.

"Can you hear me Bill?" I ask a little loudly, trying to get through to Bill.

"Yeah," Bill draws out, somehow resigned to his situation.

"I think we should pull out," I declare again, speaking up for Bill to hear.

Bill tries to adjust his position, but does not try to get up.

"Yeah," Bill says slowly. "Pull out. Can you do it?" he asks.

"Yeah. We can do it," I reply.

"Don't leave anything behind," adds Bill. "Throw it all..." and Bill fades off. "Throw it all in the back of the truck." Bill adds with his next breath.

I stand and look around the camp for a few moments, figuring out how to proceed. And then, I start giving directions to Johnny and Saul.

I tell Saul to just pull the stakes and roll up each tent, leaving everything in the tents if he can. Put wallets and whatever into the cab of the Mercedes. Set each of their kit bags out. I tell Johnny how we are going to winch the sluice up into the back of the truck, using the loading ramps. I've helped Bill do it several times. Then, I tell them, we will throw in all the odds and ends, the cooking stove and supplies, into the food boxes. Fold-up chairs and tents can go in after.

I climb down from the cab of the Mercedes, having backed it up to within ten feet or so from the waters edge. Johnny and I pull out the two loading ramps and position them to winch up the sluice into the box.

"The water level has gone down by a foot," remarks Johnny.

We can see the water has retreated back from the fine debris left, outlining the high-water mark.

"That's good," I reply. "We still need to cross the river."

We load the dredge up in the back of the truck and Johnny and I secure it to tie-down points in the truck with ratcheting tie-down straps. It has loaded smoothly enough, but that is the way Bill had designed the equipment.

We work quickly, and Johnny is coming up to speed, having shaken off most of the effects of Bill's assault. I get back in the cab of the Mercedes and pull it up to the centre of the camp. I give directions to Saul and Johnny as to what to pack in to the truck next, and I go back to check on Bill. Bill seems to be resting peacefully, sleeping. Bill is breathing well and seems in no greater distress than the situation might suggest. He must be exhausted.

We load the food boxes up into the back of the truck and fix them in place with tie-downs. The tents go in next. Water jugs, coolers, folding chairs, and tarps, loosely folded, are put wherever they will fit. It isn't pretty, but it is done. Johnny and I slide the two loading ramps up into the box and then put the tall tailgate sections in place up in the back of the truck box, and secure them with their latches. Saul is loading their kit bags into the back of the cab. I stand back and look around. That seems to be all of it.

It has taken us about an hour to pull up camp.

This all done, we gather at the back of the truck.

"I guess now we have to try and get Bill in," I say.

"How are we going to do that?" asks Saul.

"I don't know," I answer. "I'll back the truck up closer to him for a start."

I reposition the truck and the three of us gather around Bill.

Down on one knee, next to Bill, I shake Bill while calling him.

"Bill wake up. Wake up," I repeat.

Bill groans a bit and opens his eyes.

"Bill. We have to get you up in to the truck," I instruct.

Bill looks around, trying to get a bearing on his surroundings, but remains laying down.

I get Saul to help me prop Bill up into a sitting position.

Bill is awake but seems stunned.

Saul and I try to help Bill stand up, one of us supporting him under each arm, but it isn't working.

"Johnny, help him up from behind," I direct.

"Can you help Bill?" I encourage.

We get Bill standing, and we help Bill hobble the few feet to the passenger door of the cab. Bill is weak, not at all steady on his feet, his left leg hardly supporting him at all.

"Can you climb up Bill?" I ask.

"I'm trying," says Bill, resigned to us trying to boost him up.

"It isn't working," says Bill.

Bill is puffing, trying to catch his breath from the exertion to climb up.

"Put me in the back," says Bill. "In the box."

"How?" I ask.

"Make me a cot on a loading ramp, and slide me in," says Bill. "Use the winch if you have to."

"Bill, let's try this again," I insist.

The height of the cab is the problem. I roll the window down on the passenger door to give Bill a place to grab onto. I direct Johnny to get in the cab and help pull Bill up. And with what looks as awkward as anything can, I push Bill up, squatting under Bill's bad leg, pushing up with my body. Saul is pushing up from under Bill's shoulder, and Johnny is pulling from above, pulling with a grip on Bill's wet suit. Bill uses what strength he has left in his arms, and somehow, we manage. Bill is up in the seat. I close the door to the cab with a push.

"Saul, grab Bill's pillow and sleeping bag," I say. "Fit them in around Bill to make him comfortable."

With that, Saul climbs in the driver's door, and crowds into the back with Johnny. The three of us all work at stuffing the sleeping bag between Bill and the passenger side door, and we place the pillow for Bill to rest his head on. Bill, exhausted from the effort, leans into the padding, lets his head lean over onto the pillow against the window, and closes his eyes. We all take a few moments to catch our breath.

I reposition the driver's seat, and put the truck in gear. We have done it. This far anyways.

The road seems rougher than I remember, but maybe it is that I am pushing the Mercedes faster than when we had come in. There are pools of water on the trail out, and several times, we have to pile out of the truck to move a tree off the road that the wind of the storm has blown down. One tree took all the effort we had to move it. Debris, blown down from the storm, is everywhere, cluttering the road. Runoff creeks have scarred the road, but the Mercedes is big enough to handle it. But the ride is rough. I am pushing the Mercedes as fast as we can handle.

I don't know how long we had been travelling, but I can see the sun is getting low in the sky. Finally, we come to the river crossing. This is going to be the most treacherous part of the trip out - to cross the river and make it to the main roads. Johnny, Saul, and I get out of the Mercedes and stand at the bank of the river. The bank of the river has been cut back some from the flooding waters, but it is clear the flood waters have subsided some. This is the crossing. The river is shallower here, but also wider than to this point. The water looks high and fast. Certainly higher and faster than when we had first crossed over. But it is the only crossing. The sun has not set yet, but it is low in the sky. We don't know how bad Bill is. We have to keep going.

I climb back into the cab. Bill has been sleeping, even through all the tossing of the Mercedes on the trail. I shake Bill and call out to him.

"Bill. Bill. Wake up."

"Bill, we are at the river," I add. "Do you think we can cross?"

Bill stirs and, with considerable effort, he raises his head to look out, bracing himself up against the door of the cab with a hold on the dash of the Mercedes. It is obviously painful. Bill holds his head up for a few moments.

"It'll cross," says Bill. "Just don't stop. Head up wherever it feels it is getting shallower."

Bill lays his head back down.

"It'll cross," says Bill again.

I climb back out to where Johnny and Saul are standing on the bank of the river.

"Bill says it will cross," I declare.

Yeah. Johnny and Saul aren't so sure.

Neither am I.

We agree that we have no choice but to try. But I am sure that we all have visions of us all being swept away down the river. But Bill has always said that the Mercedes could handle anything. It was some encouragement, some assurance. But this looks crazy. But we agree. This is something we have to do. I make sure Johnny and Saul see where we have to pull out on the other side.

We all climb back into the Mercedes. We each look at one another, only seeing the uncertainty of the other.

"If you see something I should be doing, tell me," I blurt out.

I shift the Mercedes into its low range, and put it in gear.

Part of the bank collapses as I head the Mercedes in, but the truck takes it in stride. In the low range of the Mercedes transmission, the engine is revving fairly high, but the Mercedes is only moving at a walking speed. In this range, the Mercedes has tons of power. And as the Mercedes ploughs in to the water, as the water level rises around us, it looks worse yet.

Bill manages to prop up his head again, and is watching, somehow, reading the surface of the water.

"Over here," Bill says, over the noise of the engine, pointing more to the right.

I steer over. The Mercedes lurches as it spins over boulders and finds new footing on the river bottom. The cab rocks and shakes. The Mercedes loses footing and at times I am unsure we are making headway. But each time, we regain traction and the Mercedes continues to plough through what has to be four feet of water sometimes dropping even lower. The disturbance of such a large vehicle in the water creates a scary turbulence in our wake downstream. I cannot see the water piling up on the passenger side of the Mercedes, the upstream side. That is probably a good thing.

Bill's feet are in water, the water seeping into the cab, but he does not react or say anything. That is also probably a good thing.

The engine is loud enough that you have to speak loudly over it, the rev's going up and down as it strains but never misses a beat. Johnny, Saul, and I are wide eyed. I am tensed up in my driving position, and Bill is putting in all he has to hold his head up and look forward.

The Mercedes starts heaving up in the front end, and the rear end seems to drift downstream a few feet. Bill points to go a bit to the left. I adjust, and the Mercedes picks itself up as it regains its footing, and then we are up on a much shallower bank. The water runs slower, and now I steer straight for where the trail picks up on the other side. The Mercedes crawls up the eroded bank, pulling down pieces of the bank, and, with a final forceful lift, we are up on dry ground. The crossing has been made.

Johnny, Saul, and I cheer. Johnny gives me big pats on the back. Saul and Johnny do a high five, and Bill lays his head back into the pillow and says, "I told you, you could drive this up a palm tree." Bill closes his eyes.

I only now realize that I had been mostly holding my breath, and with some relief, I start to fill my lungs with clearing breaths.

The crossing has been made.

I have made the crossing.

CHAPTER TWENTY-THREE

It was like his own breathing and his own heartbeat were all he could hear, but each of them were resonating so loud in his head that nothing else could be heard.

But the noise was settling now, and gradually, the sound of his own breathing and heartbeat quiet to where he is starting to hear other sounds. As the other sounds become louder, his mind plays with them in his dream state.

Morales hears the crackling of what sounds like a distant fire. Struggling to regain consciousness, the sound of the crackling fire grows louder as it snaps and pops. There is the smell of smoke, and the smell of something else that smells good. In his dreamy state, he imagines a pot of soup cooking on the stove. The smell of food is good.

He wants his head to clear. He wants to be part of this. He keeps pushing to be part of this.

Morales tries to will his eyes to open, but his eyes seem to be sticking shut. Focussing with what seems to be all his effort, finally, his eyelids flutter open. His vision is murky, but he blinks, and his vision begins to clear as his eyes come into focus. A face appears over him. A big smiling face. Not a pretty face, but a rough face - a mans face with crooked white teeth, a scrawny moustache, and dark blotches – no, facial tattoos - and as big as ever, a big grin.

"Buenos Dias," says the mans face in Spanish. "Hello," he says in English again in a moment.

His voice seems unnaturally loud and clear.

Morales knows somehow that he is feeling too dreamy, that he must be drugged. But it does not bother him. A faint logic tells him that he is being treated well, and this is part of the action of whatever the drugs may be.

"Are you Bri-Bri?" asks the man in Spanish.

Morales tries to focus his attention, gather his wits. As he emerges into the present moment, he forms an answer.

"No. I'm not Bri-Bri," he replies.

"Then where did you get this necklace?" the man asks, holding up the butterfly pendant that is hanging around Morales' neck.

Morales, with his good arm, picks up the butterfly pendant from the mans hand and turns it over, examining it. His vision is clearing and his eyes are focusing.

"This was handed down to me from my great grandfather." Morales replies. "I think I am the first one to ever wear it."

"Was your great grandfather Bri-Bri?" the man asks.

"No. But he traded with the Bri-Bri," Morales replies again.

The man just nods.

Thoughts start racing through Morales' mind. This man must be Bri-Bri. He has not ever encountered a Bri-Bri, but he has seen pictures in brochures of the eco adventure groups. Facial tattoos were prominent.

"Are you Bri-Bri?" asks Morales

The man settles back, kneeling a few feet from Morales.

"Yes. I'm Bri-Bri," he answers calmly.

Morales knows that he feels calmer than the situation might otherwise call for. He is not alarmed. It must be the drugs they have given him.

"So how did you find me?" asks Morales.

The man gives a faint smile.

"Coming down from the mountain," the man starts. "We come down to buy goods. I learned Spanish well, so I am good for these trips. I can negotiate," he says proudly.

"We found you yesterday," the man continues, "on the bank of the river. You were not awake. You were injured. I think it is good you were not awake. Your arm - it was not in place in the shoulder. We had to put it back in."

The man holds his two hands in a tight grip, one above the other, like he is holding Morales' upper arm, and makes a hard jerking motion up towards Morales shoulder, gesturing re-setting a dislocated shoulder.

"Very painful," the man adds. "And your arm was broken. We had to straighten it and put it in a splint. Very painful." He again adds. "My wife is very good at this. She has trained well with our village doctor. And she has given you medicine. For fever, and for pain."

The man calls out to his wife and she enters, squatting down to enter the lean-to they had made from branches and banana plant leaves. Morales did not catch her name.

"See, he is awake," the man says to his wife.

"And she made you this soup, to make you strong," he adds.

His wife scoops some soup from the pot into a bowl, and brings it over to Morales. She feeds him a spoonful. Morales can't believe how good it tastes. She gives him a second spoonful which Morales takes with delight. He smiles and thanks to her by nodding his head.

"So what happens now?" asks Morales.

The man looks at his wife, and they share a look of understanding.

"We will care for you for a day, or two, or three, until you are strong enough to travel," the man answers. "Until your pain is less. Then we will help you down to the outfitter. You have his horse. I have seen the mare before."

"Is the horse still here?" asks Morales, seeming surprised.

"Yes. On the tether."

The man's wife feeds Morales several more spoons of soup.

"And you are a policeman?" asks the man, pointing at Morales' police badge that is set next to him.

Morales takes note that his gun is no where in sight.

"Yes, I am a policeman," answers Morales. "Corporal Morales."

"Are you here for criminals?" asks the man, the expression of his eyes showing it to be a serious question.

"No," Morales answers. "Just looking to get away for a few days."

The gentle conversation continues.

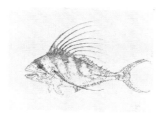

Saul opens the passenger side door to the Mercedes. The Mercedes is in the parking lot of Hospital San Vito, under the shade of a huge ash tree. It is past early morning, now mid-morning.

"Mom and Grandma have just pulled in," announces Saul.

Johnny and I both look dishevelled, having tried to catch what sleep we could in the morning heat. I climb down from the Mercedes, out into the parking lot and start to walk toward Mom and Grandma. Saul is getting a big hug from Mom as I approach, and then Saul turns and gets another hug from Grandma.

"Oh I'm so glad you are safe," says Mom as I approach, and she gives me a big hug.

"Yes, so glad," adds Grandma as she also gives me a hug. "How is Bill?" she asks.

"He's okay," I answer. "But I think they are going to want to keep him for a day or two. He is going to be all right," I add.

"Tell me more of what happened." begs Grandma, her face showing serious concern.

"Well it's a long story," I declare. "Let's get up to see Bill. I'll tell you about it when we get a chance."

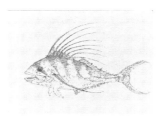

"And Bill says he was hit on the head with a rock by Johnny," says the Doctor. "Are you still thinking you might want to talk to the police about that?" directing the question at Bill.

"Yeah." Bill says insistently.

"That is not what happened!" I declare forcefully. "That is not what happened at all. I'm not going to let you do this Bill. It is wrong! And you are wrong."

"You were beating the crap out of Johnny," I say emphatically, "and I tried to stop you, and you started pounding on me too. It was Saul that hit you Bill. Saul! Not Johnny! And it wasn't a rock, it was a good-sized branch of wood."

I am standing at the foot of Bill's bed, facing him, not being hostile but deliberate. Confrontational, yes. But not hostile. Emotional, yes. But not angry. Saul stands back next to Mom. The room goes quiet. And Johnny, the side of his face evidently bruised and swollen, stands back behind us all, closest to the door of Bill's room.

I turn to face Mom.

"I don't get it Mom," I protest. "Bill always accuses Johnny of everything. It's not right. And I, I can't put up with it any more," I say emphatically. "Johnny only helped save his life, worked his tail off for him, didn't do anything wrong, and Bill takes it all out on him."

"Okay, okay," says the doctor, patting his hands down in the air in a gesture to quiet things down. The doctor looks at Saul, standing next to Mom.

"And this is all true?" the doctor says directing his attention to Saul.

Saul stands, looking uncomfortable, being put on the spot, and nods three or four times.

"But I thought Bill was going to kill them," Saul finally blurts out, in his own defence.

"Okay, okay," the doctor says again, making the same gesture to quiet down.

"So this is your grandson?" the Doctor asks, directing the question at Bill.

Bill nods his recognition, but so does everyone else.

"So I take it there will be no need for the police." the doctor declares.

Everyone is focused on Bill. Bill reluctantly gestures his acceptance of this version of events.

"Maybe it is you, Johnny, who would like to contact the police," says the doctor, everyone now turning to Johnny at the edge of the room.

Johnny looks surprised, then shocked, and his complexion seems to pale. Johnny shakes his head from side to side in denial of the doctor's suggestion.

There is a pause, and all is quiet in the room.

"Look, what I suggest we do is take this conversation downstairs to a meeting room. We are only disturbing other patients here," says the doctor. "Jessica, I would like you to come, with the boys, so I can hear more about these fainting spells. Mrs. Platten," he says to Grandma, "Maybe you would like to spend some time alone with your husband."

Grandma nods, seeming bewildered by all she has heard.

The doctor huddles the rest of us out through the door of the room and down the hallway.

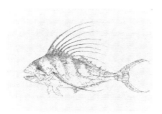

Phyllis stands next to Bill and takes his hand. Bill responds. And with the utmost care, concern, and sadness, written all over her face, Phyllis looks down at Bill, with his I.V.'s, his stitches protruding from a shaved white patch of scalp, his swollen leg propped up, and his troubled look.

"Bill. What have you done?" she laments with a sigh.

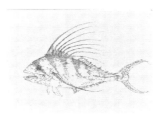

Sitting all five of us at the table, the doctor directs his questions.

"And is Saul breathing when you have found him like this?" the doctor asks, directing his question to me. I look questioningly toward Johnny.

"I'm not sure" I answer. "He might not be, but he is breathing when he wakes up."

"And when these fainting spells happen, they don't last for more than about thirty seconds, give-or-take, that you have seen?"

Johnny and I agree with the doctor's statement. We had been providing as much detail as we could. We each take a sip of the drinks the doctor had given us from a small kitchen on the way down.

"And Saul," the doctor directs his question. "Do you feel tired, really tired, and out of sorts after one of these episodes?"

Saul nods, still chewing on a bite of breakfast pastry.

"Well," the doctor says, looking up from his note pad and clip board, "Jessica. I believe your son is experiencing epileptic seizures. Not the most serious ones, but serious enough. They can be very dangerous if left untreated. I guess you have already witnessed that, with all that has happened."

Mom's face becomes very distressed, and though she seems to be trying desperately to hold on, she begins to cry. Putting her head down, she begins sobbing heavily. This is just all too much for her, with everything else that is happening.

The doctor gets up and pulls a chair up right beside Mom and takes her hand, compassionately, in both of his.

"Jessica, listen to me," the Doctor starts softly. "It is not that bad. With medication, Saul may never have another seizure for the rest of his life. And about half of children, with seizures like this, will grow out of them on their own by adulthood, and not need ongoing medication. Saul will have a perfectly normal life. But all this needs to be monitored. And the seizures need to be controlled for the time being."

Mom looks up, her eyes still full of tears. She reaches through her pockets to find something to clear her tears away. The doctor points to a box of tissues at the far end of the table, and Johnny gets up and brings them over to Mom. The doctor pulls out several and hands them to Mom and places the tissue box on the table.

"I will write you a prescription for the medication today, and refer you to a specialist to monitor the situation with your local doctor. You may have to make a few trips to San Jose, but all will be well. Do you hear me?"

A big lump forms in my throat, and I fight back the welling up of emotions I feel. The compassion of the doctor, and Mom, struggling with the news, has gotten to me.

But relief, a huge wave of relief sweeps over me. Saul's issues are finally going to be addressed.

"And this son of yours, Derrick," starts the doctor, "is a fine young man. I am impressed! He has been dealing with a lot, from all I hear, and standing up for what he truly believes is right. That makes him a good man in my books."

The doctor stands up and reaches across the table with his hand stretched out to shake my hand. I awkwardly try to stand, my chair getting in the way, and reach over to shake the doctor's hand. I can see the doctor sees I am blinking hard, trying to hold back my emotions. The doctor gives me a strong affirming handshake, and he does not release it for a considerable moment. He gives me a quick nod, almost like a salute.

"And you, sir," the doctor says, directing his attention to Johnny. "I see you as a fine young man also."

The doctor walks closer to Johnny and reaches his hand across to give Johnny the same strong, affirming handshake.

"It sounds like you have been putting up with a lot also," the doctor adds.

"And Saul," the doctor directs his attention. "You sound like quite the character," he says, tossing his head over toward Johnny and I. "Stick close to these guys and you are sure to do well. And take good care of your mother. Try not to add to her worries," the doctor adds while shaking Saul's hand. "And I want you to take it easy for a few weeks, until the medication has its effect. Okay Saul? Will you agree to that?"

Saul nods.

The doctor, still standing, picks up his clipboard.

"I'll leave you alone here for a bit," he says. "I'll come back in ten or fifteen minutes and answer any questions you might have. You will have questions by then," he adds assuredly.

"And I'll bring you back that prescription, and a referral to a specialist," he adds.

The doctor pauses, with a compassionate look towards Mom, and nods his head several times as though acknowledging all the issues Mom is facing.

"Jessica, everything will be all right," he assures, and he quietly walks out of the room, closing the door behind him.

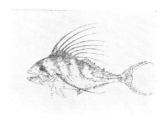

Mom agrees to driving the Mercedes home with us, and Grandma will stay on with Bill and drive the Jeep home when Bill is released. Someone has to oversee the hotel, guests, and work schedules, and we are all eager to get home. And it seems that everyone needs time to let the tensions ease from the events of the last number of days. I know I do. The drive home will give us time to bring Mom up to date with all that has happened.

In the parking lot, Mom spots all of the University of Panama decals on the Mercedes and asks us to remove them. And I remember to change the licence plates back. We are in Costa Rica now, and Mom says the last thing she needs is trouble with the police if we are stopped.

Corporal Vinny Mancuso, Morales' associate in San Vito, sits at a table in a truck stop by the highway with two other constables for a coffee break. They are teasing the waitress serving them, part of the fine details of good police work. Neither Vinny, nor the others, even come close to noticing the big white Mercedes pass by on the highway, travelling North.

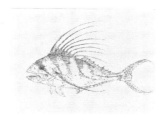

Jessica pulls the Mercedes up to the compound gate and turns off the engine. The boys have had hours to tell her the stories of the last week - some adventures - and each of their troubles. A lot of questions were asked, and a lot answered. Jessica had moments where she felt overwhelmed by the stories the boys were relating, and moments where she thought fondly of the compliments the doctor shared with the boys. Her emotions still well up inside of her. She is certainly going to relay these events, at the right moment, to her mom and especially her dad. Over and over again, she asks herself: how did she let this all happen?

Derrick fetches the keys for the compound from the office, and unlocks the gate, and he and Johnny slide it open. The boys are glad to be home. Derrick backs the Mercedes up close to the workshop door with Johnny directing him, and they begin to unload equipment, the dredge, and the two forty-five gallon drums into safety. The drums are really heavy to unload. But they are safe now.

Saul runs out on the beach with the latest of his stray dogs, and starts to run his fastest. He remembers the words of the doctor. He remembers, and slows down a little.

It is dark now, and Derrick and Johnny lock up the shop. Supper is on, Johnny having been invited, and Derrick resolves to wash the truck down first thing in the morning. Everything, then, would look just like usual.

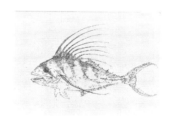

The next morning, the sound of the phone ringing downstairs prompts Derrick to get himself out of bed. He and Johnny had made plans to go fishing for an hour or so, first thing, before getting at any chores for the day. Jessica is not the task master that Bill is, and she encourages the boys to go. Things are pleasant here right now, Derrick thinks to himself. They had been for the last couple of days.

Jessica pours Derrick a coffee at the breakfast table set out on the veranda. A jug of orange juice, a plate of breakfast pastries, and a colourful platter of cut fruit laid before them. Jessica tops up her own cup and sets the coffee pot down on the table as Saul joins them, and pulls his chair up to the table. Jessica opens the pill bottle and hands Saul a pill, which he takes, and pours himself a glass of orange juice to wash it down. Jessica sits with the boys.

"You are feeling good?" she asks Saul.

"Yeah," is the extent of his reply, accompanied with quick little nods.

Mom lets out a sigh.

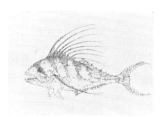

"Grandma and Grandpa are coming home today," she says, shifting her glance to look at each of us looking for our reaction.

Nothing is said for a few moments.

"Can I still go fishing?" I ask.

"Yes, of course," replies Mom. Mom takes a big breath. "I'm not going to let things go back to the way they were," she says, again looking back and forth at Saul and myself.

We continue eating while looking up at Mom, but neither Saul or I reply.

Mom is fighting back a welling up of tears, and she shows it.

"I'm not going to let things go back to the way they were again," Mom repeats. "I'm sorry if I have let you down," she adds emotionally.

"You didn't let us down Mom." I start. "How did you let us down?"

Mom regains her composure with a few breaths and looks up.

"I feel I have let you down by...," Mom pauses looking for words, "...by letting Dad push everything so hard." Again, Mom pauses.

"I will stand up to him more and try to make things better for you – make sure that you are treated better. And I'll make sure you are asked, rather than told, what to do all the time." Mom continues. "And no more of Grandpa's crazy schemes. And I'm asking that you boys tell me, let me know, if things are not going right, if you think you are not being treated properly. Talk to me. Let me know."

"Mom, we have to stand up for ourselves, don't we." I declare. "I don't think you have done anything wrong. I think we should be standing up for ourselves."

"Derrick." Mom says softly. "I'm just asking that you will talk to me. I'll do my part and pay more attention to what is going on. I'll be more critical of what is going on."

I give a shrug, a kind of general acknowledgement that I generally agree, and generally consent.

"I know that some things have been difficult here, at times," Mom says, "But your grandparents have taken us in, during what were very difficult times after your father died. I know it is not perfect, but they have done a lot for us." Mom pauses. "And there have been a lot of good times. So I'm asking for you both, for all of us, to understand this. I am certainly not laying on any kind of a guilt trip here. There is no justification for things to have gotten out of hand like they have. Yet we do have an obligation to contribute what we can, and be thankful. But that should probably be more of my doing than yours."

"Bill's not all bad," I say. "He is good most of the time."

"He got crazy on our trip," throws in Saul quickly.

"I don't mind helping out," I add. "I want to. But I am not going to let him keep bullying Johnny and not stand up to him."

We all pause for a few moments.

"I'll go see Johnny's mother today, and try to explain what has happened," Mom says. "And we have to be careful about how we approach Bill on issues with Johnny."

"How's that?" I gently challenge.

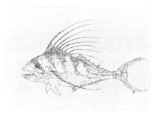

"Well I guess these are things I should be talking to you about," Mom pauses. "I think we all realize that Bill is prejudiced, that he doesn't think well of..."

And Mom continues for some time.

Mom has cooked a big dinner, anticipating Bill and Grandma's arrival. But as they had not arrived yet by dinner time, Mom has us eat on our own so we can get on with our plans for the rest of the evening. Just as we are finishing, we all hear the Jeep pull up in the parking lot. Mom stops what she is doing and walks over to Saul and I, and gives us each a hug where we sit. Nothing is said. Then she starts toward the veranda.

Bill is taking the steps one at a time, on his crutches, somewhat unsure of himself. He seems to be able to put some weight on his left foot.

Bill and Mom now face each other, each with an expression revealing the uncertainty they must both feel as to how they will be received by the other.

Mom crosses the distance and gives Bill a hug.

"Welcome home Dad," she says.

"It's good to be home," replies Bill.

Grandma is bringing up her overnight bag onto the veranda. Mom gives her a big hug and they all head inside.

I am the first to greet Bill inside, walking towards him.

"Good to see you home Bill," I welcome. "How are you feeling?"

"I'm doing okay," answers Bill. "I'm sure glad to get home."

"Yeah, so was I," I reply. "How is your leg?"

"Doing better," replies Bill. "The swelling is going down and I can put some weight on it now. Shouldn't need these things in a day or two," he adds, referring to the crutches.

"Good!" I answer.

"Bill," I continue, "Johnny and I unloaded everything in to the workshop as soon as we got home, and I washed the truck down first thing the next morning. It all looks good."

"Thanks Derrick," Bill says sincerely. "Thanks for all you did to get me out too," he adds.

Bill extends his right arm, still resting on the top of the crutch, extending a handshake.

I take a step closer and shake Bill's hand.

I let out a breath I didn't realize I was holding as I shake Bill's hand.

"Yeah, thanks Bill," I acknowledge.

After a moment, I start for the door, then stop and turn towards Bill.

"Johnny and Saul helped as much as I did," I declare to Bill.

Bill sets his jaw, and his lips parted, not in a smile, and not in a grimace either.

"Yeah. I'll be thanking each of them," says Bill. "But I know, you carried it." he adds.

Still looking at Bill, I give a small shrug.

"Well. Thanks Bill."

I turn and proceed on out the door. Pausing, I look back over my shoulder and call back to Bill.

"See you later," and I carry on my way to meet Johnny.

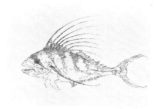

During dinner, the conversation is cautious, and Bill is cautious. Jessica presents her regrets as to how she has allowed things to deteriorate, having maybe taken too much for granted. She needs to take a greater initiative in her own life, and her boys. Phyllis is apologetic and overwhelmed at times, as Jessica discloses many events that the boys had relayed to her on the drive back from the hospital.

Bill is like the accused in a court room, Phyllis his lawyer by his side. Bill remains quiet through the proceedings, uncomfortable whenever Phyllis would turn and give him "that look." Jessica and Phyllis, two mothers, shed a few tears, here in each others company.

"I can do better," Bill declares, either in his defence, or as a promise for the future.

However, the conversation has strained them all, and with all the turmoil, both physical and emotional, that they had all been through, they all look for relief, some hope, and maybe a promise.

It was then that Jessica says, "I'm planning on taking the boys up to Seattle to visit Jim's parents for a few weeks."

EPILOGUE

So, that's how I ended back up in Seattle.

At that time, it seemed that everyone needed a break from one another - at least for a while. Grandma, I believe, was feeling like she and Bill could use some time together to sort things out on their own, without any interference from us. Interference doesn't sound like the right word, but you know what I mean.

Mom was wanting a break, time to maybe "break the mold" so to speak, so that the nature of our relationships did not slip right back into the same patterns that had been established over the last years. Mom was clear that there were things that were going to have to change for us to go back, but probably less clear on what the specifics of any change would have to be.

And I think there was a certain apprehension that, if we stayed, things might get worse.

Dad's parents were so glad to have us all up. They were more than hospitable in their welcoming us into their home.

Seattle was such a change from Samara. For all of us.

And with all the changes, things just seemed to carry on, on their own course.

Mom certainly called back to Bill and Grandma, had many

lengthy talks with her mom, and many talks leading to tears. But it wasn't that they were fighting.

Dad's parents had just recently had a senior couple move out of a house they rented out, the couple moving into a senior's facility. My grandfather had been doing simple renovations and painting to get it ready to rent out again.

They offered the house to Mom.

Their encouragement to get me into a Seattle High School was based on the premise that it would provide me far greater opportunities after graduation, universities and all.

And I don't know if it was the most important or not, but an old friend of Mom's started dropping by, his parents being longterm friends of my Dad's parents. I guess they had mentioned she had returned.

And life is just like that sometimes, isn't it? It just goes along, and when nothing seems like it is ever going to change, things start to happen.

Mom talked to Saul and I about the possible changes and choices. But, in the end, I guess I realize now that Mom just wasn't that happy with things in Costa Rica. She wanted more. She had had a career once, before Dad died. She had an opportunity to pursue that again here. She wanted more opportunity for each of us.

I missed my friend Johnny, and all the things we did together, mostly at first. I reflected often, especially in quiet moments, of our life in Samara. But Seattle had its own beauty. And there was so much to do! New friends calling, and a greater sense of independence.

My grandfather, here in Seattle, was an avid fisherman. Mom always said that was where I had got it from. Salmon fishing in Puget Sound. He even took me with him and his friends on a

Salmon Charter up to Alaska that fall, which he has done again, several times since.

Mom seemed happy. Things were working out.

Mom went down to visit her parents, the first time just before she started work as a legal aide at a prominent law firm. Saul accompanied her for a week, on her next trip.

I had a part-time job during the school year, and worked full-time during the summer months. I couldn't easily get away.

And Mom went back to visit her parents when she could.

We got to where we laughed about our times and shared stories of Costa Rica, and life with Bill and Grandma.

Things are different now. Time seems to be flying by.

It was after I had graduated from high school, and had just gotten my acceptance letter to the University of Washington, Marine Biology program, when Mom got a phone call from Grandma.

Bill had had a heart attack.

For anyone who has experienced a similar event, you know the realization of the love you feel, the fear of loss, the strength of family ties, all awakens within you, and it takes on a new urgency.

And Grandma asked to talk to me, and relayed that Bill was

asking to see me.

Mom made arrangements for Saul and I to fly down with her.

Bill was going to be alright, but apparently it was going to take a while for him to get back on his feet again. They were recommending heart bypass surgery. I guess his lifetime of smoking had caught up with him.

Landing in the airport in Liberia, a direct flight from Seattle, I was shocked by the heat and humidity. I had become unfamiliar with it. Johnny had taken the time to drive out to meet us also, and I drove back to Samara with him, which was great. A time to get caught up. So much had changed, yet we were close, just the same as always.

Bill's hospital was close to Samara, in Nicoya. The next morning, I borrowed Bill and Grandma's Jeep to drive up on my own. Grandma was insistent that I do, so that Bill and I could have some time together that he was asking for. Walking into the room, I saw that Bill was hooked to an array of electronic monitors, an I.V., and it shocked me that he looked so unimposing lying in the bed, from what I had been remembering. And, he looked older.

Bill stirred, facing me as I entered the room. He stretched out his hand to greet me. Shaking his hand, Bill pulled me closer, carefully managing his many attachments, and gave me a big hug.

"I'm so glad to see you." he said. "I'm so glad you came."

I returned his hug.

Bill was fighting back some tears, which the next moment had me doing the same.

"Pull up a chair," said Bill.

Bill manoeuvred himself around in the bed to face me as best he could.

"This is just about how I last saw you," I said. "In a hospital bed."

Bill smiled, and seemed to reflect back in his thoughts.

"You're looking good," said Bill. "You've grown up so much. A man now." And after a pause, "And I guess I'm an old man."

"Everyone says you are going to be all right Bill." I answered.

"Well, all right for what has happened, but..." Bill did not finish the thought.

"But I have been needing to talk to you Derrick." Bill started. "I...", Bill paused, "I need to tell you how sorry I am for how I treated you. I guess I lost my balance. I don't know why. Some people say I got Gold Fever." Bill coughed for a few seconds. "I guess I got a little wild in the head. I guess to be honest, it's a mental health issue. It's not the first time in my life I got a little manic. I'd rather think of it as Gold Fever, but...." Again, Bill paused. "I have been on a medication for it for the last couple of years."

"And I treated you badly," Bill continued, "and I'm sorry for any abuse. I am sorry Derrick. I am asking that you will forgive me."

"You weren't that bad Bill." I said. "You probably treated me better than anyone else. I'm all right."

"But I am asking that you will forgive me Derrick." started Bill. "And I know, that forgiveness is a process, not an event. I know it takes time to forgive. I am asking that you will give it that time. I know that I haven't been able to forgive myself."

"Sure Bill. I forgive you." I said.

I felt awkward. Bill just looked at me, blinking a few times as if lost in thought.

"I am serious Bill," I reassured. Bill attempted a brave smile, nodding.

"And what you did for me, I want to thank you." Bill started. "You probably saved my life. I was behaving so recklessly. You worked so hard to help me."

"I wasn't the only one." I said.

"No," Bill answered. "I will get to that. I don't know if you ever figured it out, but I made a lot of money from what we did. And you boys helped me, and I guess I was taking advantage of you. I guess I got greedy."

Bill paused and reflected for a few moments, then continued.

"Derrick, there are times I feel like such a fool. And it was your loyalty that I was depending on. I guess I was even taking advantage of that. So I want to make things right. Do at least what I can do."

I left the hospital feeling pretty good about things, and after thinking on it, proud of the fact that my relationship with Bill had matured. We had even laughed about some of Saul's antics, and Bill even brought up the scorpions. We tossed around questions as to whether Saul had any involvement in that or not, but agreed that it was best to take it up with Saul.

So that is how this latest chapters of our lives evolved.

Bill's surgery went well, though it took him many months to build his strength back up. But he did.

Bill arranged a joint bank account with me in Seattle, and paid my university costs - tuition, books, spending allowance, the works. It had a huge impact on my situation in life.

Bill had finally brought up Johnny in our visit that day, and I brought him up to date with Johnny's situation. Johnny had married, and they were expecting a child. Johnny was happy. He was working for a refrigeration company, one that installed and maintained commercial coolers and air conditioning systems. Johnny was saving to take the Refrigeration Technician course, which would take him many years to save for. It would triple Johnny's earning capacity. Bill took it on, paid the full course fees, and replaced Johnny's lost income for the six-month duration of the course.

Even I was amazed.

Bill and Grandma eventually helped Mom with a down payment to buy a house in Seattle. Dad's parents contributed also. Mom's work was going well. Her suitor continues, and they are making plans for the future. Mom is happy.

Saul chose not to continue schooling after graduating from high school. He is a character. He went on some adventure, a road trip with some buddies, the first winter after high school, skiing up in Canada. He never came back. Saul lives with a group of guys and girls up in the mountain resort town of Lake Louise, and works as a Lift Operator, sometimes Ski Instructor, at one of the local ski resorts.

I am planning to fly up to visit him for the Christmas break this winter.

I later learned that some of the seizures Saul was experiencing were triggered by something called Photosensitive Epilepsy. With his medication, to the best of my knowledge, Saul has never had another seizure since.

And, to the best of my knowledge, Saul hasn't killed anybody yet either. Just kidding!

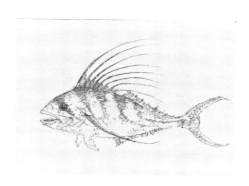

ACKNOWLEDGE-MENTS

The first person to read my work, a chapter at a time, was my wife Gloria. Her acknowledgement of its basic goodness was gratifying.

My daughter Alyssen has constantly been my most enthusiastic supporter. Alyssen also created the artwork for the Roosterfish used for the page breaks. If you get to examine the artwork closely, you can find that Alyssen embedded "I love you Dad" in the drawing.

And my daughter Angela has been a resounding supporter.

Their encouragement helped me believe my efforts were worthwhile and continued throughout to be a significant motivation.

The greatest effort, contributions, through feedback, encouragement, editing, and coaching my project to completion, was my friend, Phil Lancaster (Dr. Phillip Lancaster PhD.). His manuscript evaluation and editing skills contributed most significantly to the finished product. His constant encouragement helped me believe there was worth to my efforts.

Supporters, whom I shared the writing with as it progressed, sharing near completed drafts, I would also like to acknowledge. Each provided encouragement and valuable feedback.

Jennifer Kightly
Wynna Jorgensen
Douglas Foss
Lisa Jane Watson
Patricia Thornton
Marion Schaeffer
Lisa McCormick
Marilee Stebner
Dan Walker

Preparation for publishing included several more individuals.

Anna Kouwenberg – ARK Squared Productions – Cover Art - (https://arksquared.com)
Alyssen Foss – The Rooster Fish - Artwork
Caralee Hitchcox – Print Editor and publishing assistance.
Joanne Wellham - Republishing edits

Each of you contributed something that I valued, that had an impact on the product to date. To each, a special acknowledgement, and thank you.

Ron Foss

Made in the USA
Middletown, DE
17 October 2021